LAIDLAW

Other Laidlaw mysteries by
William McIlvanney

The Papers of Tony Veitch

Strange Loyalties

WILLIAM McILVANNEY

LAIDLAW

A HARVEST BOOK
HARCOURT BRACE & COMPANY
SAN DIEGO NEW YORK LONDON

Requests for permission to make copies of any
part of the work should be mailed to:
Permissions Department, Harcourt Brace & Company,
8th Floor, Orlando, Florida 32887.

Library of Congress Cataloging in Publication Data
McIlvanney, William, 1936–
Laidlaw.
I. Title.
PZ4.M1498Lai3   [PR6063.A237]   823′.9′14   76-62708
ISBN 0-15-648109-X

Printed in the United States of America

First Harvest edition 1993
A B C D E

1

RUNNING WAS A strange thing. The sound was your feet slapping the pavement. The lights of passing cars batted your eyeballs. Your arms came up unevenly in front of you, reaching from nowhere, separate from you and from each other. It was like the hands of a lot of people drowning. And it was useless to notice these things. It was as if a car had crashed, the driver was dead, and this was the radio still playing to him.

A voice with a cap on said, 'Where's the fire, son?'

Running was a dangerous thing. It was a billboard advertising panic, a neon sign spelling guilt. Walking was safe. You could wear strolling like a mask. Stroll. Strollers are normal.

The strangest thing was no warning. You wore the same suit, you chose your tie carefully, there was a mistake about your change on the bus. Half-an-hour before it, you had laughed. Then your hands were an ambush. They betrayed you. It happened so quickly. Your hands, that lifted cups and held coins and waved, were suddenly a riot, a brief raging. The consequence was forever.

And the meaning of everything was changed. It had no meaning or too many meanings, all of them mysterious. Your body was a strange place. Hands were ugly. Inside, you were all hiding-places, dark corners. Out of what burrows in you had the creatures come that used you? They came from nowhere that you knew about.

But there *was* nowhere that you knew about, not even this

place where you came and stood among people, as if you were a person. You could see who people thought was you in the mottled glass. His hair was black, his eyes were brown, his mouth wasn't screaming. You hated his ugliness. There was a green bottle with what looked like a fern inside it. There was a nose with enormous nostrils. On the black surface there were cloudy streaks where the wipings of a cloth had dried. A man was talking.

'See ma wife, son.' He was speaking towards where you should be standing. 'See when Ah go in here the night? Be like "The Sands of Iwo Jima". Ah've been away since yesterday mornin'. Met an old mate yesterday after ma work. Christ, we had a night at his place. One half borrowed another, ye know? Ah wis helpin' him to get over his wife. Died ten year ago.' He was drinking. 'Ah think Ah'll go out an' get knocked down. Give me an excuse.'

You used to think things like that could be a problem, too. You cried when you broke a vase your mother liked. You hid the pieces in a cupboard. You worried about being late, offending somebody, things you shouldn't have said. That time wouldn't come again.

Everything had changed. You could walk for as long as you liked in this city. It wouldn't know you. You could call every part of it by name. But it wouldn't answer. St. George's Cross was only cars, inventing destinations for the people in them. The cars controlled the people. Sauchiehall Street was a graveyard of illuminated tombstones. Buchanan Street was an escalator bearing strangers.

George Square. You should have known it. How many times had you waited for one of the buses that ran all through the night? The Square rejected you. Your past meant nothing. Even the black man on the black horse was from another country, a different time. Sir John Moore. 'They buried him darkly at dead of night.' Who told you his name? An English teacher who was always tired. Yawner Johnson. He told you interesting things between yawns. But he hadn't told you the truth. Nobody had. This was the truth.

You were a monster. How had you managed to hide from

6

yourself for so long? Some conjuring trick—to juggle smiles and nods and knives and forks and walks for the bus and turning the pages of a paper, for twenty years to make your life a blur behind which what was really you could hide. Until it came to introduce itself. I am you.

George Square was nothing to do with you. It belonged to the three boys walking tightrope on the back of a bench, to the people waiting in the bus-queues to go home. You could never go home again.

You could only walk and be rejected by the places where you walked, except the derelict tenements. They were big darknesses housing old griefs, terrible angers. They were prisons for the past. They welcomed ghosts.

The entry was dank. The darkness was soothing. You groped through smells. The soft hurryings must be rats. There was a stairway that would have been dangerous for someone who had anything to lose. At the top a door was broken. It could be pushed closed. Some light came in very dimly from the street. The room was very empty, some plaster from the ceiling on the floor.

It was strange how little blood there was, just some dark flecks on the trousers. so that you could imagine it had never happened. But it had happened. You were here. The body had been like leprosy. You were the leper, a contamination crouched and rocking on its haunches.

The loneliness was what you had made of yourself. The coldness was right. You would be alone from now on. It was what you deserved. Outside, the city hated you. Perhaps it had always excluded you. It had always been so sure of itself, so full of people who didn't open doors tentatively, who had a cocky walk. It was a hard city. Now all its hardness was against you. It was a mob of bitter faces turned towards you, it was a crowd of angers all directed against you. You had no chance.

Nothing to do. Sit becoming what you are. Admit yourself, the just hatred of every other person. Nowhere in all the city could there be anyone to understand what you had done, to share it with you. No one, no one.

2

LAIDLAW SAT AT his desk, feeling a bleakness that wasn't unfamiliar to him. Intermittently, he found himself doing penance
for being him. When the mood seeped into him, nothing
mattered. He could think of no imaginable success, no way of
life, no dream of wishes fulfilled that would satisfy.

Last night and this morning hadn't helped. He had finally
left Bob Lilley and the rest still on the surveillance in Dumfries.
On the strength of solid information, they had followed the car
from Glasgow. By a very devious route it had taken them to
Dumfries. As far as he knew, that was where it was still parked—
in the waste lot beside the pub. Nothing had happened. Instead
of catching them in the act of breaking in, three hours of picking
your nose. He had left them to it and come back to the office,
gloom sweet gloom.

It was strange how this recurring feeling had always been a
part of him. Even when he was a child, it had been present in its
own childish form. He remembered nights when the terror of
darkness had driven him through to his parents' room. He
must have run for miles on that bed. It wouldn't have surprised
him if his mother had had to get the sheets re-soled. Then it had
been bats and bears, wolves running round the wallpaper. The
spiders were the worst, big, hairy swines, with more legs than a
chorus-line.

Now the monsters were simultaneously less exotic and less
avoidable. He was drinking too much—not for pleasure, just

8

sipping it systematically, like low proof hemlock. His marriage was a maze nobody had ever mapped, an infinity of habit and hurt and betrayal down which Ena and he wandered separately, meeting occasionally in the children. He was a policeman, a Detective Inspector, and more and more he wondered how that had happened. And he was nearly forty.

He looked at the clutter on his desk. It was as if on the desert island of his feeling this was all that chance had left him to work with: the two black-bound books of *Scottish Criminal Law* and *Road Traffic Law*, the red MacDonald's, establishing precedents, and the blue book on stated cases, the telex-file on British crime, the folder of case-reports. He wondered how you were supposed to improvise fulfilment out of that lot.

He was aware of the neatness of Bob Lilley's desk across from him. Did neatness mean contentment? He glanced over to the pin-board on the wall facing the door: shifts, departmental memoranda, a photograph of 'The Undertaker'—a con-man Laidlaw liked—overtime payments, a list of names for a Crime-Squad Dinner Dance. 'These fragments I have shored against my ruin.'

Guilt was the heart of this kind of mood, he reflected, and it surprised him again to realise it. The need to be constantly sifting the ashes of his past certainly hadn't been inculcated in him by his parents. They had done what they could to give him himself as a present. Perhaps it was just that, born in Scotland, you were hanselled with remorse, set up with shares in Calvin against your coming of age, so that much of the energy you expended came back guilt. His surely did.

He felt his nature anew as a wrack of paradox. He was potentially a violent man who hated violence, a believer in fidelity who was unfaithful, an active man who longed for understanding. He was tempted to unlock the drawer in his desk where he kept Kierkegaard, Camus and Unamuno, like caches of alcohol. Instead, he breathed out loudly and tidied the papers on his desk. He knew nothing to do but inhabit the paradoxes.

He was looking through the Collator's Report when the phone rang. He looked at it for a moment as if he could stare it down. Then his hand picked it up before he wanted it to.

9

'Yes. Laidlaw.' The hardness and firmness of the voice was a wonder to the person crouched behind it—a talking foetus!

'Jack. Bert Malleson. You did say anything of interest that came up, you wanted to know. Well, I've got Bud Lawson here.'

'Bud Lawson?'

'Remember a case of severe assault? It's a while ago now. But it was in the city-centre. It was a Central Division case. But the Squad was in on it. In the lane between Buchanan Street and Queen Street Station. The victim almost died. Bud Lawson was suspected. But nothing was proved. There was a connection. Some kind of grudge.'

'Yes.'

'Well, he's here now. Seems a bit strange to me, He's reporting his daughter missing. Because she didn't come back from the dancing last night. But it's only a few hours. I'm wondering about that. I thought you might want to speak to him.'

Laidlaw waited. He was tired, would soon be home. This was Sunday. He just wanted to lie in it like a sauna-bath, scratch his ego where it itched. But he understood what Sergeant Malleson was wondering. Policemen tended not to see what was there in their anxiety to see what was behind it. Zowie, my X-ray vision. But perhaps there was something in it.

'Yes. I'll see him.'

'I'll have him brought up.'

Laidlaw put down the phone and waited. Hearing the noise of the lift, he brought Bob Lilley's chair across in front of his own desk and sat back down. He heard the voices approaching, one frantic, the other calm, like ravaged penitent and weary priest. He couldn't hear what they were saying. He wasn't impatient to find out. There was a knocking. He waited for the inevitable pause to pass. What was he supposed to be doing, hiding the dirty pictures? The door opened and Roberts showed the man in.

Laidlaw stood up. He remembered Bud Lawson. His wasn't a face for forgetting. Angry, it belonged on a medieval church. Laidlaw had seen him angry in outrage, demanding that they bring out their proof, as if he was going to have a fist-fight with it. But he wasn't angry now, or at least he was as near to not

10

being angry as was possible for him—which meant his anger was displaced. It was in transit, like a lorry-load of iron, and he was looking for someone to dump it on. His jacket had been thrown on over an open-necked shirt. A Rangers football-scarf was spilling out from the lapels.

Looking at him, Laidlaw saw one of life's vigilantes, a retribution-monger. For everything that happened there was somebody else to blame, and he was the very man to deal with them. Laidlaw was sure his anger didn't stop at people. He could imagine him shredding ties that wouldn't knot properly, stamping burst tubes of toothpaste into the floor. His face looked like an argument you couldn't win.

'Sit down, Mr. Lawson,' Laidlaw said.

He didn't sit, he subsided. His hands were clenched on his knees, a couple of smaller megaliths. But the eyes were jumpy. They were trying, Laidlaw decided, to keep track of all the possibilities that were swarming through his head. In that moment Laidlaw was sure Bud Lawson's concern was genuine. For the first time, he admitted Sergeant Malleson's suspicion explicitly to his mind, in order to reject it.

With that realisation, Laidlaw felt a twinge of compassion for Bud Lawson. He remembered the pressure they had put on him before, and he regretted it. So Bud Lawson was a mobile quarrel with the world. Who knew the grounds he had? And doubtless there were worse things to be. Whatever else was true, he seemed to care about his daughter.

Laidlaw sat down at his desk. He brought the scribbling-pad nearer to him.

'Tell me about it, Mr. Lawson,' Laidlaw said.

'It might be nothin', like.'

Laidlaw watched him.

'Ah mean Ah jist don't know. Ye know? But Sadie the wife's goin' off her head wi' worry. It's never happened before. Never as late as this.'

Laidlaw checked his watch. It was half-past five in the morning.

'Your daughter hasn't come home?'

'That's right.' The man looked as if he was realising it for the first time. 'At least when Ah left home she hadn't.'

Laidlaw saw a new fear jostle the others in the man's eyes—
the fear that he was making a fool of himself here while his
daughter was home in bed.

'How long ago was that?'

'Maybe a couple of hours.'

'It took you a while to get here.'

'Ah've been lookin'. Ah've got the auld motor, ye see. Ah
cruised around a bit.'

'Where?'

'Places. Jist anywhere. Around the city. Ah've been demented.
Then when I was in the centre anyway Ah remembered this place.'
He said it like a challenge. 'An' Ah came in.'

Laidlaw reflected that something like a stolen bicycle would
have been more concrete. Bud Lawson had got away ahead of
the probabilities. What he needed wasn't a policeman, it was a
sedative. The main purpose of what Laidlaw was going to say
next would be lay therapy.

'You'd better tell me it from the beginning.'

The man's confusion funnelled through a filter onto Laidlaw's
pad.

Jennifer Lawson (age 18). 24 Ardmore Crescent, Drumchapel.
Left the house 7.00 p.m., Saturday 19th. Wearing denim
trouser-suit, yellow platform shoes, red tee-shirt with a yellow
sun on the chest, carrying brown shoulder-bag. Height five
feet eight inches, slim build, shoulder-length black hair. Mole
on left temple. ('Ah mind that because when she wis wee, she
worried aboot it. Thocht it wid spoil her chances with the
boys. Ye know whit lassies are like.') Occupation: shop-girl
(Treron's). Stated destination: 'Poppies' Disco.

It looked neat on paper. On Bud Lawson's face it was a mess.
But Laidlaw had done all he could. He had been a pair of professional ears.

'Well, Mr. Lawson. There's nothing we can do at present.
I've got a description. We'll see if anything turns up.'

'Ye mean that's it?'

'It's a bit early to declare a national emergency, Mr. Lawson.'

'Ma lassie's missin'.'

'We don't know that, Mr. Lawson. Are you on the phone?'

'Naw.'

'She could've missed a bus. She wouldn't be able to inform you. She could be staying with a friend.'

'Whit freen'? Ah'd like tae see her try it?'

'She *is* an adult person, Mr. Lawson.'

'Is she hell! She's eighteen. Ah'll tell her when she's an adult. That's the trouble nooadays. Auld men before their feythers. Ah stand for nothin' like that in ma hoose. Noo whit the hell are yese goin' to do aboot this?'

Laidlaw said nothing.

'Oh aye. Ah might've known. It's because it's me, isn't it? Ye wid jump soon enough if it wis somebody else.'

Laidlaw was shaking his head. His compassion was getting exhausted.

'Ah refuse tae be victimised. Ah want some action. D'ye hear me? Ah want something done.' His voice was rising. 'That's the trouble wi' the whole bloody world. Naebody bothers.'

'Here!' Laidlaw said. His hand was up. The traffic stopped. Laidlaw was leaning across the desk towards him. 'I'm a policeman, Mr. Lawson. Not a greaseproof poke. You put your philosophy of life on a postcard and post it anywhere you like. But don't give it to me.'

Laidlaw's silence was a confrontation.

'Look,' Laidlaw said. 'I can understand your worry. But you'll have to live with it for the moment. She may well be back home this morning. I think you should go home and wait.'

Bud Lawson stood up. He turned the wrong way in his attempt to find the door. For a second he looked oddly vulnerable and Laidlaw thought he saw through the cleft of his indecision another person flicker behind his toughness. He remembered his own foetal fragility of some minutes ago. A tortoise needs its shell because its flesh is so soft. And he felt sorry for him.

'Come on,' he said. 'I'll show you out of this place.' He had torn the page off his pad, still had it in his hand. 'It's like doing a crossword just getting out of here.'

13

At the door Laidlaw remembered that Bob had a Production on his desk—a labelled cassette to be produced soon as evidence in a case. He locked the office and put the key above the door.

Bud Lawson let himself be led. They went down the three flights of stairs. As they passed the desk, Laidlaw was aware of the sergeant looking at him, but he didn't look back. In the street, the morning was fresh. It should be a nice day.

'Look, Mr. Lawson.' Laidlaw touched his arm. 'Don't rush to any conclusions. Let's wait and see. Maybe you should concentrate on helping your wife just now. She must be out of her mind with worry.'

'Huh!' Bud Lawson said and walked across to his 70 Triumph, a mastodon in a football-scarf.

Laidlaw was tempted to shout him back and put it another way, say with his hands on his lapels. But he let it pass. He thought of what he had seen inside Bud Lawson's armour-plating. It was as if he had met him for the first time. He shouldn't spoil the acquaintance. He breathed the absence of exhausts and factory-smoke, and went back in.

At the desk the sergeant said, 'Nothing, Jack? Well, you asked for it. I could have dealt with it. I hope you don't mind me asking. But why do you sometimes want to deal with whatever comes up?'

'When you lose touch with the front line, Bert, you're dead,' Laidlaw said.

'You think you have?"

Laidlaw said nothing. He was leaning on the desk writing on his slip of paper when Milligan came in, a barn door on legs. He was affecting a hairy look these days, to show he was liberal. It made his greying head look larger than life, like a public monument. Laidlaw remembered not to like him. Lately, he had been a focus for much of Laidlaw's doubt about what he was doing. Being forcibly associated with Milligan, Laidlaw had been wondering if it was possible to be a policeman and not be a fascist. He contracted carefully, putting a railing round himself and hoping Milligan would just pass. But Milligan was not to be avoided. His mood was a crowd.

'What A Morning!' Milligan was saying. 'What! A! Morning!

Makes me feel like Saint George. I could give that dragon a terrible laying-on. Lead me to the neds, God. I'll do the rest. Did I see Bud Lawson on the road there? What's he been up to?'

'His daughter didn't come home last night.'

'With him for a father, who can blame her? If she's anything like him, she's probably been beating up her boyfriend. And how are things in the North, former colleague? I just popped in from Central in case you need advice.'

Laidlaw went on writing. Milligan put his hand on his shoulder.

'What's the matter, Jack? You look as if you're suffering.'

'I've just had an acute attack of you.'

'Ah-ha!' Milligan laughed loftily, astride a bulldozer of wit. 'I hear an ulcer talking. Look. I'm happy. Any objections?'

'No. But would you mind taking your maypole somewhere else?'

Milligan was laughing again.

'Jack! My middle-aged teenager. Sometimes I get a very strong urge to rearrange your face.'

'You should fight that,' Laidlaw said, not looking up. 'It's called a death-wish.'

He put the piece of paper folded in his inside pocket.

'Listen. Anything you get on a young girl, let me know.'

'Personal service, Jack? You feel involved?'

The sergeant was smiling. Laidlaw wasn't.

'Yes,' he said. 'I know her father.'

3

His hands, illumined in the lights he passed, rose and fell helplessly on the steering. They were enormous hands that had driven rivets on Clydeside for thirty years. They weren't used to being helpless. Just now they signalled an anger that, lacking a focus, took in everything. Bud Lawson was angry with Laidlaw, the police, his daughter, his wife, the city itself.

He resented the route by which he was having to go home: along the motorway to the Clyde Tunnel Junction, right into Anniesland, left out Great Western Road. The first part of it reminded him too strongly of what they had done to the city he used to know. Great loops of motorway displaced his past. It was like a man having his guts replaced with plastic tubing. He thought again of Gorbals, the crowded tenements, the noise, the feeling that if you stretched too far in bed you could scratch your neighbour's head. To him it felt like a lost happiness. He wished himself back there as if that would put right Jennifer's absence.

He knew it was serious simply because she wouldn't have dared to do this to him if she could help it. She knew the rules. Only once before had she tried to break them: the time she was going out with the Catholic. But he had put a stop to that. He hadn't forgotten and he never forgave. His nature ran on tramlines. It only had one route. If you weren't on it, you were no part of his life.

It was that inflexibility which trapped him now. In a sense,

16

Jennifer was already lost to him. Even if she came back later today, she had done enough in his terms to destroy her relationship with him. With a kind of brutal sentimentality, he was thinking over past moments when she had still been what he wanted her to be. He remembered her first time at the shore when she was three. She hadn't liked the sand. She curled her feet away from it and cried. He remembered the Christmas he had bought her a bike. She fell over it getting to a rag-doll Sadie had made for her. He remembered her starting work. He thought of the times he had waited for her to come in at nights.

He had passed the Goodyear Tyre Factory and was among the three-storey grey-stone tenements of Drumchapel. They didn't feel like home. He stopped, got out and locked the car.

He came in to Sadie at the fire. She was wearing the house-coat out of his sister Maggie's club catalogue. On her its flowers looked withered. She looked up at him the way she always did, slightly askance, as if he were so big he only left her the edges of any room to sidle in. Her very presence was an apology that irritated him.

'Is there ony word, Bud?' she said.

He stared at the tray-cloth he had pinned above the mantelpiece, where King Billy sat on his prancing charger.

'Ah went tae the polis.'

'Oh, ye didny, Bud.'

'Whit the hell wid Ah dae? Ma lassie's missin'.'

'What did they say?'

He sat down and stared at the fire.

'By Christ, there better be somethin' wrang wi' 'er efter this.' He looked at the clock. It was a quarter to seven. 'If there's no somethin' wrang wi' her the noo, there'll be somethin' wrang wi' her when Ah get ma haunds oan 'er.'

'Don't say that, Bud.'

'Shut yer mooth, wumman.'

His silence filled the shabby room. He took off his scarf and dropped it on the chair behind him. Sadie sat rocking very gently, making a cradle of her worry. He looked across at her. She looked so gormless that a suspicion formed in him slowly.

'Ye widny know anythin' that Ah don't, wid ye?'

'Whit d'ye mean?'

'Ye know whit Ah mean. She's never done anythin' like this in her life afore. She's no up tae something that Ah don't know aboot, is she?'

'Bud. Hoo can ye think that? Ah widny hide anythin' from you.'

'Ye tried it before. The time she wis goin' aboot with the Catholic. Till Ah put a stoap tae it.'

'Ah never knew aboot that till you found oot.'

'Aye, that's your story. An' ye're stickin' tae it. It'll no be tellin' any the two o' ye if ye're in cahoots aboot somethin'. Ah'm warnin' ye.'

He stared at her and her skinny obsequiousness offended him. One child. That was all she had been able to produce. And four miscarriages, small parcels of blood and bones that hadn't got enough from her to make a human being. There wasn't enough room in her to hold another child.

Seeing him watching her, she talked a smokescreen.

'Wid ye like a cup o' tea while we're waitin', Bud? Will Ah make ye wan?'

Since he didn't say no, she went through to make it.

A baffled rage fermented in him. Normally, he went head-first through whatever threatened him. But this was different. This was squaring up to fog. The difference pumped up the pressure of his anger into something awesome.

Sadie had kept the fire going. It was dying down. He lifted the poker and halted with it in his hand. Jennifer had wanted them to have a gas-fire put in. But he liked coal. On that irrelevant thought he blacked out into a lonely fury.

When he came out of it, he stared at the poker twisted to a staple in his hands. It was an I.O.U. made out to someone.

4

THE BOY HAD slept. That amazing fact alone put him back inside his own body. It was a terrifying place to be. He woke lying awkwardly against the wall where exhaustion had left him. Consciousness had burned out suddenly like a bulb. Now just as suddenly it had renewed itself. He was still himself.

The scabby wall against which his head was leaning seemed to be pressing against him, as if about to topple. He felt pinned against it by the impossibility of ever getting up and doing something. The enormity of what he had done had hardened into fact during the night. He knew it was there and inescapable.

Yet strangely it was still not a part of him. The feeling wasn't so much that of having done something as of having been part of an event outside himself, like an explosion. He saw her body, the odd splay of her legs, the head cocked in an absurdly human way, the position into which the blast had thrown her. He felt pity for her.

But he was left wondering what she was doing there. Something had happened of which he was only a part. What was it that had happened? He didn't know. He knew that he was in a strange room, that he was dirty, that he was very cold. To get from where he was to what had happened seemed impossible. But it was what he had to do.

It didn't help to close his eyes again and try to hide. The terrible fever was finished. The luxury of being overwhelmed by

19

guilt was gone. He had thought he was drowning in it but instead it had beached him here. He was left to go on living, to find out how he could inhabit what had happened.

He tried to stand up and found that he could. The ache of his legs was things becoming possible again. He watched his hands automatically dusting his trousers. He started to walk. The stairs which were completely strange to him gave him the sensation of leaving a place without ever having been in it. He had to be careful of the broken bannister. Light showed through the corrugated iron sheeting across the outside door, where he had forced it to get in. The metal bent before his hand and he ooked out.

The street was empty. He stepped outside. The sunlight dispelled his purpose for a moment. He stood baffled in the empty street, just a part of the dust and silence. It was very difficult to know whether to go right or left. He walked to the right. Within yards, he came out onto a road junction. It was then he recognised where he was.

Across from him was Glasgow Green. The Clyde was over a hundred yards away on his right. Being in a real place was being where people could find you. The knowledge frightened him and the fear gave him an arbitrary purpose. He crossed the road.

Outside the Green was a phone-box. He went into it. The door swung shut behind him, nudging him into the booth. He lifted the receiver and held it to his ear. The phone was working. He put it back down. The word 'Cumbie' was written with black paint on the metal fixture where you put in the money. Above it was written 'Blackie'. Was 'Blackie' the name of another gang? Was it somebody's nickname? He took change out of his pocket and laid it on the small black ledge. He lifted the receiver and put it to his ear again.

He dialled a number without having to remember it. When he heard it ringing, he was surprised that he had made something happen. He stood with patient dread, trapped inside the silence of the city while the phone drilled in the distance, trying to break his isolation.

5

THE ROOM WAS a permanent hangover. Waking up in it, Harry Rayburn was always faced with coming to terms with himself all over again. It was the room in the house where he spent most time and it was furnished with the debris of past attitudes. Those attitudes were an unresolvable argument in which he was a very tired chairman. The two Beardsley prints looked uncomfortable beside the framed photographs of boxers. The largest one was Marcel Cerdan. The huge, elaborately patterned lampshade clashed with the ascetic whiteness of the walls, making the room look like a Calvinist brothel. The round bed appalled him, obliged him to sink nightly into his own embarrassment. His dressing-gown was a kimono.

More than once he had lain here and laughed at his pretentiousness. The room was such a wardrobe of psychological drag. But this morning he had no time to achieve that distance from his attempts to come to terms with his own nature. The phone pulled him out of bed and he put on the kimono without thinking. He bumped towards the phone in a confusion that was part hangover, part way of life. He felt momentarily bad about answering the phone in such a mess. As he lifted the receiver, he ran his hand through his hair.

'Hello?'

'Harry? It's Tommy. Tommy Bryson.'

The name went through him like a spear.

'Tommy! Where are you? Do you want to come up?'

It struck him that the last word was strange, unless it meant upstairs, to the bedroom. He was fussing with his hair again.

'I can't. Harry.'

The way he said the name made a crossroads of feeling in Harry. It was a plea and that was what Harry had longed to hear but it was so fraught with pain that he dreaded what it was going to lead to. He waited to find out what he would have to feel.

'Something's happened. Something terrible.'

'What is it, Tommy?'

'I need your help. I've killed a girl.'

The statement spread between them like a steppe.

'Tommy,' Harry said.

They listened to each other's silence hopelessly.

'Tommy.'

The name died out between them. Harry was amazed to find that his voice knew what to say.

'What is it you want me to do?'

'You bring me paper and a pen. I need to write things down. I need to know what's happened.'

It was pathetic, as if somebody dying of throat-cancer should ask for pastilles.

'But first. Would you go and see my mother, please? Do you remember the address?'

'I remember.'

'Tell her something. Make up something. I don't want her to go to the police. I don't want that.'

'You could come here, Tommy. They'll not look for you here.'

'No, I can't,' Tommy said, 'no, I can't.'

'Where are you, then?'

The pause was self-deception, a choosing whether to trust, but the choice had already been made.

'I'm in the Bridgegate. Off Jocelyn Square. It's condemned. Above. "Alice's Restaurant". There's corrugated iron across the door of the entry. But I forced it. Don't come till later on. When things are quiet. But see my mother just now. See her right away.'

'Tommy,' Harry said.

22

'Will you do all that?'

'I'll do it.'

'All right.'

'I love you, Tommy. Don't forget that.'

But the phone was already down. It wasn't until he had said it that Harry realised how true it was. As he laid down the receiver, he knew he had just had a terminal conversation. This was a kind of arrival. The pretence that he wasn't really bothered by not having seen Tommy for the past couple of weeks was over. All the pretences with which he had furnished his house were over, or at least their compulsiveness was over. If he used any of those rôles again, it would only be to help Tommy.

He remembered what he had said to Tommy the last time they spoke. 'You're terrified that you're gay. I *know* I'm a homosexual.' But although he had admitted his homosexuality to himself for a long time, he had admitted it only to contrive more effectively ways of protecting himself from other people. His life had been spent acquiring compensatory qualities that weren't natural to him but which enabled him to survive. The hardness of his own experience made him forgive Tommy at once, whatever he had done. As far as Rayburn was concerned, everybody else deserved to be Tommy's scapegoat.

The toughness he had learned would have an honest purpose now. He would use it to help Tommy to get away. It was his revenge on his own experience.

6

SUNDAY IN THE park—it was a nice day. A Glasgow sun was out, dully luminous, an eye with cataract. Some people were in the park pretending it was warm, exercising that necessary Scottish thrift with weather which hoards every good day in the hope of some year amassing a summer.

The scene was a kind of Method School of Weather—a lot of people trying to achieve a subjective belief in the heat in the hope of convincing one another. So the father who lay on the grass, railing in his children with his eyes, wore an open-necked shirt, letting the sun get at his goose-pimples. Two girls who were being chatted up by three boys managed to look romantically breeze-blown rather than cold. An old man sitting on a bench had undone the top two buttons of his overcoat, heralding heatwave. A transistor played somewhere, evocative of beaches. People walking through the park moved unhurriedly, as if through the an air muggy with warmth.

But it was the children who were most convincing. Running, exploring bushes, they had that preoccupation which is at any time a private climate. It was one of them who found the reality hidden in the park's charade of warmth.

A boy of about eleven, chrysanthemum-haired, he was on his own. For some time he had been stalking the park mysteriously, ignoring everybody else, with that cut-off look children achieve when following corridors of private fantasy. He parted bushes, he skirted trees. Exploring a dense clump of bushes, he suddenly

24

stopped. His head came up, his mouth gagged open. He looked as if the day had stuck in his throat.

Then, 'Mister!' he was screaming. 'Hey, mister, mister. Mister!'

The man in the open-necked shirt came at a run. Others came. The voices clustered and scattered like gulls. The park became a vortex with those bushes as its centre, pulling some towards it, pushing others away as they shooed their children.

The hubbub rose and travelled beyond the park. The screams of panic and horror were translated into even, professional voices.

7

'THERE WAS THIS girl. Called Margaret. She was twelve. No brothers or sisters. She lived alone. With just her Mammy and her Daddy. Aw! One night her father wanted to go to the pictures. Her mother agreed. But it was an X-film, so Margaret couldn't go. They decided they'd need a baby-sitter. But Margaret got all huffy. "I'm twelve now," she said. "I'm not a baby. I can look after myself." But her mother said she must have a baby-sitter. And there was Anne, just down the road, who was nineteen and liked baby-sitting with Margaret. And Margaret's mother happened to know that Anne wasn't doing anything special tonight. And Margaret's father said anyway it was illegal to leave somebody of Margaret's age alone in the house. But Margaret insisted. She took a tantrum. Just like our Jack when he starts to chew the legs of tables and things. So at last her parents went out. There was Margaret, sitting by the fire, watching the telly. The house to herself. And thinking: "This is great! I'm just like a grown-up." When suddenly —' He snapped his fingers. 'The lights went out. The electric fire went cold. The telly blacked out. Total darkness. It was like going blind. Margaret was very frightened.'

Laidlaw savoured the pause. It was the moment they all liked. It was why they called the game 'What happened next?' He had started the story deliberately to provide an air-raid shelter against Ena's attacks. The morality of her raids on him had lost definition lately. It used to be she that exempted the children

26

from them. Now she was bombing Dresden. She liked to bounce her ammunition off the children to get to him, saying things like, 'No wonder you had a nightmare last night, Jack. Your daddy wasn't here to protect you, son.' The anger Laidlaw felt against that abuse of children frightened himself.

Now that anger was defused in watching their faces. Moya, the oldest at ten, was being slightly cynical about the involvement of the other two. But behind the aloofness she was working out the possible dénouements. Sandra, a year younger, was blatantly desperate to get to the answer before her older sister. Jack, six years old, was too busy just identifying with the horror of Margaret's situation.

'What happened next?' Jack asked.

'Margaret sat. Too frightened to move. Then she heard the handle of the back door being turned. Someone—something?—trying it. Back and forward. And she couldn't remember whether the back door was locked or not. She wanted to scream. But then they might hear her. She stood and walked into a chair. It was so sore. But she didn't call out. She felt her way through to the front room of the house. But it was just as dark. Even the lights outside were in darkness. Pitch black. Then, as she stood there, she heard the letter-box of the front door being lifted very quietly. She could imagine two eyes staring in. Two eyes? Maybe three eyes. Would you believe nine? She screamed.'

The telephone rang. Ena answered. Laidlaw hoped it wasn't for him, but it was.

'What happened next?' he said to the children as he went through.

It was the Commander of the Crime Squad telling him there had been a girl's body found in Kelvingrove Park. Milligan of Central Division would be the D.I. for the main investigation. But Laidlaw was to help. What it meant to him first of all was the reaction Ena would inevitably have. He wasn't disappointed. She was in the kitchen. He closed the door so that the children wouldn't hear, passing off their pleas for a solution with 'Later'.

'There's been a murder,' he said.

Ena paused over the vegetables she was chopping for Monday's soup. She was staring straight ahead at the striated glass of the cabinet.

'All I want is a nice, uninterrupted Sunday,' she said.

'I know.'

'No you don't. You don't know at all. What the hell do I care who's been murdered? My children need a father.'

'Oh, come on,' Laidlaw said. 'Don't try to attack me on that front. My relationship with them's made of steel. It's not at hazard, and you know it.'

'Do I? Do they? You say you know. Do you know what this kind of thing does to me? To the whole family? I mean, how often does this happen? What's happening to us is a crime, too. But then you know.'

Ena was waving the knife about distractedly.

'Yes, I know. I also know the difference between *Hedda Gabler* and *East Lynne*. And you are 'East Lynne', missus. You want to live as if the rest of the world was just a necessary evil. Somebody is fucking dead. That may be a nuisance to you. But it's a fucking sight worse for them.'

He realised he had been shouting.

'Don't swear. The children can hear you.'

'Fuck-off! Swear-words they'll survive. What they might not survive is your indifference to everybody else but them.'

He gave the children hurried kisses like bruises on the way out. They didn't speak. In the car he was still as tight as a fist. It was getting worse. They quarrelled in short-hand now. Their tolerance of each other had almost completely eroded. Alone in the car, he could admit the injustice of what both of them had said. Over the years they had developed a savage directness, because each had come to understand that the other stood for what couldn't be agreed to. It only took one remark to appear on the horizon and the other knew the waiting mass of un-acceptable attitudes to which it was acting as scout.

Laidlaw could acknowledge to himself how disproportionate to the surface of what had happened his anger had been. But he knew the depth of the threat he had really been answering. It

28

was why he felt uncomfortable among the friends they visited. Beyond the small areas they cultivated conversationally, the arbours of friendship, the ornamental clichés, the well laid out preoccupations, lay a desert-tract of silence where the garbage of what didn't concern them rotted. Occasionally in the street they might catch a glimpse of one of the strange shapes that flitted across that silence or in a newspaper headline hear an echo of the unearthly sounds that haunted its emptiness. But the door that led from them to it was firmly shut. Laidlaw couldn't keep that door shut. Reality kept kicking it open.

Like today. The drive from Simshill in Cathcart to the Kelvin-grove Park was the distance between pretence and fact. He parked the car above the park and walked downhill into it, so that he saw the scene in a oner. It wasn't too attractive.

They might have been shooting a film. The cordon formed a semi-circle along the river, the furthest stanchion being maybe seventy yards from the river's edge. Within that area the police were moving around fulfilling their odd purpose, maggots on the carcase of a murder. A couple had the dogs out. Someone was taking photographs. A man and a boy seemed to be giving statements. People were moving about like bizarre technicians, as if they were tracing a gas-leak.

But they weren't the most bizarre thing about the scene. That was the crowd beyond the cordon. Laidlaw didn't like looking at them. They had the strange unity he had noticed in such groups, craning and communing with one another, a hydra talking to itself. A father carried a girl on his shoulders, her feet stirruped in his armpits. A small boy sucked a lollipop. Laidlaw never understood them. It wasn't as if they could help. They were just voyeurs of disaster.

Not liking being a part of them, he elbowed his way through to the policeman at the rope. Then he turned and shouted, 'Ticket-holders only!'

'What's wrong, sir?' the policeman asked.

'Look at them,' Laidlaw said. 'What's that all about? And they probably think this dead lassie is the mystery. They probably think whoever did this is pretty weird.'

'They're just curious, sir.'

'Very.'

'They're not so bad.'

'What Band of Hope do you attend? Don't leave her alone with them anyway. They'll be taking a toenail home for the kiddies.'

'That's a bit cynical, sir.'

'Don't tell me. Tell her.'

He walked towards where she was. She lay blued with what looked like cold. She was partly covered by foliage, like an obscene and inverted parody of what we tell to children. Death found under the gooseberry bush. Her legs were a terrible abandon. Her bruises had congealed on her and blackened thighs and face and belly, and her left breast was charred with them, ash from a bad fire. Against his will, Laidlaw thought of Moya. He remembered the first time of seeing her, battered with her own birth. Hard to come, hard to go. A policeman covered her again with the coat.

'Oho, it's Interpol.'

As he looked up, Laidlaw's eyes went past Milligan to some scene of his own.

'We're guaranteed a solution now,' Milligan persisted.

'We've found the brassière, sir.'

The young policeman held it out towards Milligan. It was yellow with white lace.

'Christ, it's a regular paper-chase he's left us,' Milligan said. 'I just hope he keeps it up. Could lead us right to him.'

'That's everything except the panties,' the policeman said.

Laidlaw watched the young policeman put the brassière down beside the other things, the brown shoulder-bag, the yellow platform shoes, the red tee-shirt, the denim trouser-suit. Yes. There was only one other thing to check. He didn't want to check it because he knew it would be there. He crouched down over the girl, moved back the coat. Her head was skewed at a funny angle on her neck, as if she was listening for something. Gently, he moved the hair back from her forehead. The hair was stiff—surely not with lacquer, Laidlaw thought. It was probably frozen sweat and dust. On her left temple he saw a beauty spot, the one she had thought would spoil her chances. He straightened up.

'Look,' he said to Milligan. 'I think I know who this is. She lives in the Drum. Ardmore Crescent.'

The young policeman was looking at him in awe. Out of such innocent moments legends grow.

'Bud Lawson's lassie!' Milligan said at once. 'Of course. She hadn't come home.'

'That's right,' Laidlaw said. 'I've got my car here. I'll go and fetch him.'

'McKendrick. You go with him,' Milligan said. Then turning to Laidlaw, 'Just in case you forget to tell us something.'

'I don't mind telling you anything,' Laidlaw said. 'You never understand it anyway. And do you think we could hurry it up? And move her out of the glare.'

'What glare?' Milligan asked.

'Just move her.'

'Detective Inspector Laidlaw. You know better than that.'

The voice was sonorous with authority. Laidlaw turned and saw the Procurator Fiscal behind the customary barrier of cigar-smoke. It kept out the smell of the world. Today he was giving the park an audience.

'The doctor will be here any minute. She will not be moved until then. I thought your wide experience would have taught you that.' Milligan was enjoying the reprimand. 'She cannot be moved until she is certified dead. Meanwhile, I don't think she's suffering too much discomfort.'

'That's because she's dead,' Laidlaw said. He looked towards the crowd. 'It's just that I wouldn't want her father to have to buy a ticket to view the corpse. I'll bring him to the mortuary.'

McKendrick had liked the exchange. Because he had felt sick when he saw the girl, he felt as if Laidlaw had been speaking for him. He had heard Milligan dismiss Laidlaw as an amateur and he was glad to find it was a slander. In the car he would have liked to talk to Laidlaw but he respected the silence until Laidlaw broke it.

'What's your name, then?' Laidlaw asked.

'McKendrick.'

'Your first name.'

'Ian.'

'Well, Ian. You can wait in the car when we get here if you want. It's up to you.'

McKendrick thought about Milligan.

'I think I'd better come in. If you don't mind.'

'Suit yourself. I was just thinking how nice it is delivering grief to folk. I thought we might spare you this once.'

'I suppose I have to get used to it,' McKendrick said. 'It's not that I don't appreciate your idea. It's just . . . well. I have to get used to it.'

'You're probably right, Ian. Just don't get too used to it. I know folk who don't even notice any more. They deliver dead bodies as if they were butcher-meat.'

Drumchapel engulfed them like a quicksand.

'Some place,' Laidlaw said.

'Aye, there must be some terrible people here.'

'No,' Laidlaw said. 'That's not what I mean. I find the people very impressive. It's the place that's terrible. You think of Glasgow. At each of its four corners, this kind of housing-scheme. There's the Drum and Easterhouse and Pollok and Castlemilk. You've got the biggest housing-scheme in Europe here. And what's there? Hardly anything but houses. Just architectural dumps where they unloaded the people like slurry. Penal architecture. Glasgow folk have to be nice people. Otherwise, they would have burned the place to the ground years ago.'

Laidlaw recognised Bud Lawson's car. They parked behind it and went up the outside stairs to the entry. The Lawsons lived downstairs, right-hand door. Laidlaw pushed the bell but they couldn't hear any sound. He glanced at McKendrick, pressed again and had his hand raised to knock when the door opened.

'Ah'm awfu' sorry. Have ye been ringin'? Bell's broken. Jist makes a wee kinna buzzin' noise. Ah've been at ma man tae get it—'

She had seen McKendrick's uniform. She was a small woman, her face looking older than the rest of her. Her body seemed somehow to hang on her, like somebody else's clothes. Talking about the bell, her apology had found a surprisingly intense focus and then her concentration had moved just as wilfully to

32

McKendrick. Laidlaw had seen that quality of arbitrarily shifting perspective before, always in people whose environment was putting them under pressure. It was as if they had been overtaken by the hardness of their experience and mugged by it, so that they lived the rest of their lives concussed.

Now you could see the truth of why they were here arrive in her eyes. They didn't have to say anything. She knew the worst because she always expected it.

'Oh my God,' she was saying. 'Ah knew it, Ah knew it, Ah knew it. Oh my God! Whit's happened to 'er?'

'Mrs. Lawson?' Laidlaw was saying.

'Oh my God! Something terrible has happened.'

'Wumman. Come oot the road.'

Bud Lawson stood between her and them. Behind him they could still hear her mouthings, but as if a door had closed on her.

'Whit is it?'

'Could we come in, Mr. Lawson?' Laidlaw asked.

McKendrick closed the door and they all moved awkwardly into the living-room. Mrs. Lawson seemed almost blown before them, like paper in the wind. She ended up aimlessly by the old-fashioned, scarred sideboard, shaking her head at a china figurine, an old woman seated on a bench. Bud Lawson was standing in the middle of the floor.

'I'm sorry, Mr. Lawson,' Laidlaw said. 'I'm very sorry. I think Mrs. Lawson should sit down.'

'Jist tell us whit ye came tae tell us.'

'It's about Jennifer, I'm afraid. We think we may have found her. I'm sorry. But if it's her . . . then she's dead.'

Mrs. Lawson's voice rose and fell in a sound McKendrick couldn't bear. All that happened in Bud Lawson's face was that a knot formed in his right cheek where the jaw was clenching. He turned his head slightly away from where his wife was standing.

'How did this happen?' he asked.

Laidlaw shook his head and walked towards Mrs. Lawson. She let herself be led and put in a chair, crying. Laidlaw left his hand on her shoulder.

'How did this happen?'

'No, Mr. Lawson,' Laidlaw said. 'The first thing is for you to identify her. If it's Jennifer. You can give your wife the details then. I'll tell you in the car.'

Bud Lawson got his jacket from a chair and put it on. He was ready to go.

'Mr. Lawson,' Laidlaw said. 'What about getting a neighbour in? For your wife.'

Bud Lawson looked at him as if he didn't understand. Laidlaw nodded to McKendrick. McKendrick went across the entry and told the woman there. She explained to her family and came across at once, sitting on the arm of Mrs. Lawson's chair with her arm round her. They left her saying, 'Sadie, Sadie, oh Sadie.'

McKendrick went into the back seat of the car. He sat staring at the cratered back of Bud Lawson's neck, as if it was the surface of a strange planet.

8

THE HIGH COURT of Glasgow is at Jocelyn Square. It is an imposing building. its main entrance pillared and approached by wide steps, its side doors having carved above them 'South Court' and 'North Court'. The suggestion is vaguely Grecian, implying the long and formidable genealogy of justice. On its right the Clyde that made the city flows tamely under bridges.

The Court confronts Glasgow Green like a warning. The Green itself is gated and railinged now, the city's commemorative window-box of a once wilder place. From that green root the miles of stone have spread, north to Drumchapel, Maryhill, Springburn, Balornock and Easterhouse, south across the river to Pollok, Castlemilk, Rutherglen and Cambuslang, still part of the same confrontation between nature and law, the Green and the Court.

Adjoining the Court is a small, single-storey building, standing unobtrusively on a corner like a casual bystander. The lower parts of its walls are old weathered stone. The upper parts are red brick. It's as if a workman were wearing spats. Above the doorway is the word 'Mortuary', discreet as a wink.

This is the police mortuary, the tradesmen's entrance to the Court, as it were. Here are delivered the raw materials of justice, corpses that are precipitates of strange experience, alloys of fear and hate and anger and love and viciousness and bewilderment, that the Court will take and refine into comprehension. Through the double glass doors come those with a grief to collect. They take away the offal of a death, its privateness, the irrelevant uniqueness of the person, the parts that no one else has any further use for. The Court will keep only what matters, the way in which the person became an event.

To come in here is to be reminded that the first law is real estate, and people are its property. It was a reminder that always sickened Laidlaw. They stood in the entrance hall with its polished floor. A man was here to look at his dead daughter and they must ring a bell, request an audience. Laidlaw's finger on the brass button jarred himself. It summoned him to make a fruitless choice: indulge in grief by proxy or imitate a stone. The shirt-sleeved, waistcoated man who came recognised him, unlocked the second set of glass doors and ushered Bud Lawson into calamity and Laidlaw into his own small dilemma.

Laidlaw left Bud Lawson with McKendrick in the waiting-room and went to check. In the long room the mortuary attendant was working against the background of the rectangular doors, like refrigerators in which three bodies could be stored. He nodded pleasantly as Laidlaw came up.

The girl's naked body lay on a metal table with raised edges. The man was washing it. Water sluiced down the runnels at the edge of the table. Laidlaw stood beside him, noted again the mole, as if it might have been make-up that would wash off. He was thinking of Mrs. Lawson. The man was very deft, had an obvious expertise in washing dead bodies. Laidlaw remembered that his name was Alec and he liked bowling.

'Been an attractive lassie,' Alec said.

'I have who I think is the father with me.'

Alec waited for a moment longer.

'Nearly there,' he said. 'Give me a coupla minutes to get her dressed. She had a bad time, eh? Any ideas?'

'Somebody who was in Glasgow on Saturday night.'

'I was visiting relatives in Edinburgh,' Alec said. 'Score me off your list.'

Neither of them had smiled. The sounds remained completely separate from their expressions, a ritual form of words where there was no conversation.

'Tell me when you want us,' Laidlaw said.

In the waiting-room Bud Lawson was still following the relentless parade of his own thoughts, like an Orange March nobody dare cut across. In the car he had briefly expressed anger at Laidlaw's attitude of this morning, his insistence that it was too early to jump to conclusions. But now even Laidlaw had become irrelevant to whatever reactions were massing in Bud Lawson. He was going somewhere alone.

When Alec came in, Laidlaw took Bud Lawson through to where the body was. It lay on a white metal trolley, neutered by wrappings that were like cheese-cloth and familiar to Laidlaw. No part of the person it had been was visible. It was already a parcel for the law courts.

Laidlaw positioned Bud Lawson at its head. Alec was at the other side of the trolley. Even the head itself was tightly wrapped, a standard practice because the head had frequently to be opened in post mortem. The only loose part of the mummy-cloth was a triangular flap over the face. It was this that Alec lifted, like a window into death.

The face was completely composed, the mouth held gently shut by the cloth beneath the chin. Her youthfulness was blinding. Framed in white, she was like an involuntary nun.

Bud Lawson groaned and buckled. Laidlaw gripped him and was immediately shaken off. Bud Lawson straightened up. He stared down at his daughter. Nothing happened in his eyes. To Laidlaw watching, having seen so many reactions to the same fact in this same cold place, this was the strangest, because it was no reaction. It was like corpse confronting corpse. Bud Lawson stared at his dead daughter, looked steadily across at Alec and nodded once. And that was that.

Laidlaw was glad when the formalities were finished and they stood in the street outside.

'We'll want a photograph,' Laidlaw said.

'Whit?'

'Of Jennifer.'

'See ma wife.'

Bud Lawson was watching traffic pass in the street.

'Well, would you come down to the Station with us now?'

'Whit fur?'

'There may be questions.'

'Ah'm in nae mood fur questions. Ye can come tae the hoose if there's anything tae ask.'

'Well, let us run you home then.'

'Ah don't want yer bloody run.'

Bud Lawson walked away. Laidlaw and McKendrick were left to report to the Central Division. Laidlaw, having checked that he wasn't wanted for anything else today, gave Milligan the notes he had taken this morning and agreed to meet him at nine o'clock the next morning for the post mortem. He phoned the Commander and explained. The Commander was agreeable to Laidlaw's going off. 'It's been a long weekend for you. Anyway, I'm calling the new D.C.—Harkness—in today. I'll get him started. He'll be working with you.'

Driving home, Laidlaw put the day's events in the left-luggage department of his mind. Tomorrow would be soon enough to collect them. He needed rest, a good sleep. Only one image wouldn't be shelved, persisted: Bud Lawson's reactionless face as he walked away, following his own compulsive thoughts like inaudible flutes. Laidlaw wondered where they would lead him.

9

BUD LAWSON STOOD at the window, looking out on Duke Street. How often had Jennifer come towards this window from Fraoli's café? She had always liked visiting Bud's sister Maggie Grierson and her husband Wullie. In moving back and forward across this street she had grown up, lost the fairness of her hair and become dark, abandoned what Wullie called her 'schoolboard specs', changed her mind about what was her favourite pop-group ('Mair often than Ah chinge ma semmet,' Wullie said), developed breasts and secrecy. She had always said that this was where she would like to stay. 'This is the real Glesca,' Maggie had told her. Her absence from it now was not believable.

In the room behind, Maggie Grierson sat looking at her brother through her tears. She knew exactly what he was seeing. Duke Street's drab width had been her home for nearly forty years, and there was nowhere else she wanted to go. For her it had kept the quality of the old Glasgow, a sense of the street, a realisation that streets were places for living in, not just passing through. She knew a lot of the people in its three-up tenements. She knew who was never out the bookie's, who drank in the Ballochmyle Bar, who ran up a lot of tick in Mulholland's Dairy. The places in the street had become as familiar to her as her own furniture.

But now it was all memories. It seemed to her it would always be closed, as it was today. From now on it would always be Sunday.

She saw Bud looking down towards Gateside Street. Behind those tenements was the swing-park where Jennifer had often played. One summer evening she had come from there herself and knocked at the door of the Bristol Bar, where Wullie was having a pint. 'It's time to go home, Uncle Wullie,' she had told him. Nine she would be at that time. The men had kept it up on Wullie for weeks.

This house had been full of her. Their weeks revolved around her coming, and she always came. Growing up hadn't distanced her from them at all. Remembering her worth and the hopes they had had for who she would be, Maggie found nothing outside herself that measured her feeling. Outside, there were only the shuttered fronts of the fruit shop where she had waited in the queue and the bakehouse opposite, where she liked to go for hot rolls on the mornings when she had stayed. There was only the walk up Cumbernauld Road to Alexandra Parade and the park where they'd often walked. There were only the few things of hers that Maggie had kept, like the smelling-salts she'd bought as a present for Maggie when she was seven, thinking it was perfume.

Beyond that, there was only Maggie's faith in Jennifer. Her inability to make anybody else but Wullie and herself see how much had been lost was a fiercesome bitterness. She cried again. Not even Jennifer's own father had appreciated her. Looking at her younger brother, Maggie found no forgiveness for him. Bud was a mean-spirited man. He wouldn't give you the kiss of life without counting the breaths you owed him. He had never fully accepted Wullie as a person because he had been baptised a Catholic, although Wullie hadn't been in a church since he left school. When Bud had come looking for Jennifer this morning, he had been like the Gestapo checking a suspect. Ever since he had found out about that Catholic boy called Tommy, he hadn't allowed her to stay the night with them, in case they were shielding her. They would have done, too. Telling them this afternoon, he had acted as if Jennifer had affronted him in getting murdered. He still looked more angry than sad.

Wullie came in. Bud turned from the window. Maggie saw how Wullie didn't look at her because he didn't want to add to his pain by sharing hers. She thought what a decent man he had been all his life and how little was left for him. She regretted again that she had never given him children.

'Did ye see Alec then?' she asked.

'Aye. He's a nice man, Alec. Ah mean, he disny know you fae Adam, Bud. But says he'll run ye hame an' pick up ither people on the road. Ah said we would get the bus. He's waitin' for ye.'

Bud went out without saying a word. It took Maggie and Wullie more than half-an-hour to get ready. They hung about helplessly in an irrevocably empty room.

'Well,' she said. 'We better get the bus.'

They walked along to George Square. While Wullie was paying the driver, she noticed that the only empty seats were at the back. But a man near the front got up and said, 'Here, missus. You an' yer man sit there.' He went to the back. He must have noticed that she had been crying. It was his way of showing sympathy.

The house absorbed them into its gloom with a murmuring of hellos in the hall and a soft shutting of doors. Others were there already. Since they could find no form for what they were feeling, things that happened accidentally had become rituals. Because Bud Lawson had been in the kitchen when the first man arrived, that was where Wullie found himself, among the men.

Maggie was shown into the living-room where Sadie sat among the women. Around her their sighs and headshakes were gentle, subversive, a comfort they must give in spite of her inability to receive it. Their clichés went on tiptoe. 'Oh my Goad, is this no' a terrible thing.' 'Ye canny believe it.' 'Ah don't know whit the world's comin' tae.' 'Ah'll make a cuppa tea.' Sadie sat motionless, leaking tears, and whenever anyone crossed her vision she offered a placative smile. It was a strange event in the ruins of her face, that smile, given without discrimination, like someone in a road accident apologising to the traffic that has hit her. Maggie saw it as partly a condemnation of her brother.

In the kitchen, interrupted only occasionally by the passing back and forth of a woman, the men were different. While the women were hunkered down with a fact, learning to live with it, the men were chafing against it. Their room was restless. One of them would always be looking out of the window or tightening one of the taps on the sink or footering with his cup. Wullie felt uncomfortable. He felt that this had nothing to do with Jennifer. It had only to do with Bud, and beside him Airchie Stanley, sitting and feeding off Bud's silence.

Someone had produced a bottle of whisky. Wullie thought it might have seemed inappropriate except that nothing was appropriate. Only a couple of glasses had been found. The rest used cups. Slowly the whisky had played upon their grouped moods until their anger found expression. It happened at first in isolated moments.

Somebody said, 'Folk like that shouldny be allowed tae live.'

There were noddings. The silence was a fearsome unanimity.

'Whit harm did that wee lassie ever dae anybody?'

No harm at all, the silence said.

'Even if they get 'im, some doactor'll likely see tae it he jist gets jiled.'

Their righteousness was total. These were rough men. Several of them lived with violence as part of their way of life. One of them might like to talk of the time he'd met a safe-blower or had a drink with a well-known criminal. But there were crimes and crimes. And if you committed certain of them—like interfering with a child or raping a girl—they emasculated you in their minds. They made you a thing.

The kitchen became a place sterile of pity. Gradually they talked themselves out of being men. They were all vigilantes.

'Ah only ask fur wan thing,' Bud Lawson said. It was the first time he had spoken for over an hour. His eyes had no tears near them. They were clear and blank. 'Jist let me hiv 'im fur five minutes.' The cup he turned in his hands looked like a thimble. 'Ah jist want tae hiv 'im in ma haunds. That's all Ah want. An' Ah'll never ask fur anythin' again.'

All of them deeply wanted to grant his wish. Airchie Stanley thought to himself there might be a way.

In the living-room the women still sat protectively round Sadie. For her there was nothing to do.

10

HARKNESS WAS GLAD of the interruption to his Sunday. It had been worrying him. Because he was on call this weekend, Mary had suggested they spend the day at her house, where he could be reached. She hadn't mentioned it would be like paying a visit to a Christmas card.

Lunch had been trying to converse with Christmas crackers. Her parents talked in mottoes. 'Too many people worship money nowadays.' 'What you never had, you never miss.' And Harkness's favourite: 'God helps those who help themselves.' It was a while since he had heard that one and when Mary's mother said it, he felt a brief shock of pleasure, as if he'd pulled a sturgeon out of the Clyde.

Perhaps because they had a guest, they seemed determined to range far and wide among the problems of the world, obliterating each with a scattergun of prejudice. Vandalism was 'spoiled children'. Africans had been 'given too much power for their own good'. The unions were killing our society. Throughout the meal they passed clichés back and forth like condiments. Harkness gagged himself with food.

After lunch, Mary's mother was in the kitchen, cleaning up and putting clothes to steep in water. Because it was Sunday, she couldn't wash them but steeping was all right. She had apparently read the small print from Mount Sinai. Mary's father was reading the papers. Harkness was being shown the house.

It was a nice place but it bothered him the way houses that have been made self-consciously attractive always did. The whole experience, the talk that had lost all awareness of its own arbitrariness, the carefully arrived at prettiness of the rooms, was like being trapped inside somebody else's hallucination. And Mary's coy retreats from his groping hands denied him something real to hold on to. He wasn't far from jumping out of a window when the phone rang.

Mary's mother took it at once. Harkness wondered if that meant she had been lurking downstairs in the hall, waiting for Mary to call for help. It was his father phoning from Fenwick.

Nothing was more likely to bring Harkness back to reality than that rough voice talking guardedly into the mouthpiece. His father was usually a very open man but on the phone he came over like MI5. He didn't trust phones and it was only under protest that he'd allowed Harkness to have one installed. When you added to that his disapproval of Harkness's being in the police, you could understand the reluctance with which he gave the message: Harkness was wanted at the office.

Suppressing a cheer, Harkness expressed thanks and regret to Mary's parents. He said he would try to look in afterwards. At least Mary's mother didn't come to the door with them.

His car was conveniently parked on the Kilmarnock Road, facing into Glasgow. He wondered what was happening at the office. He hoped it was something important. This was his first weekend on the Crime Squad and he hadn't wanted it to pass without his being called out. His year as a D.C. under Milligan in the Central Division had been interesting but Harkness wanted more. He wasn't sure exactly what the more he wanted was, but he had applied for the job on the Crime Squad to see if it was there.

His father hadn't been pleased because it meant his son was all the more set on staying a policeman. His father had left school during the Thirties. He hadn't found a permanent job till after the war. He remembered the way the police had treated strikers and hunger-marchers in the West of Scotland. He hated them simply and sincerely, and he couldn't forgive his son for

44

becoming one of them. With just the two of them in the house, they argued incessantly.

But working, as now, he felt no doubts. He was twenty-six and physically strong and confident. He was effectively in use, like an engine firing on all cylinders. It wasn't till he reached the Commander's office that the engine stalled.

'Harkness,' the Commander said, and left it at that. It was offered like a classification, as if he was the first person ever to have called Harkness that and he was giving him time to get used to it. The Commander was looking through some papers. From where Harkness stood, he could see the woman and the two boys smiling their reassurance to the Commander from the photograph on his desk. The Commander put down his papers.

'There's been a murder. In Kelvingrove Park. The body of a girl was found there today. Sexually assaulted and then murdered.'

He spoke in spasms, like a teleprinter, and he seemed to be checking each statement as it came out of his mouth.

'You're a young man, Harkness.'

That was true. He paused over the remark, seemed to find it unchallengeable.

'A young man, but already an experienced one.'

'Thank you, sir.'

Harkness's comment felt fatuous to himself but it was a way of saying 'present'. The Commander gave the impression of talking to himself.

'You'll be working with Detective Inspector Laidlaw on this case. He's one of our less conventional men. You may have heard.'

'I know he's said to be very good, sir.'

'He can be very good. Not as good as he thinks he is, of course. But then nobody could be. You'll begin working with him tomorrow.'

'Yes, sir. Thank you.'

Harkness waited. The chief got up and walked up and down a bit. It was Napoleon-addresses-his-troops time.

'There are one or two things I want to say to you. You will be

45

working with Detective Inspector Laidlaw. Let me explain what that means. At least what it might mean, unless he's changed his methods since last week. Which is possible.'

Harkness began to be interested.

'He'll be going his own way. "Free-lancing", he calls it. Which is a fancy word for a very simple thing. You'll find Detective Inspector Laidlaw rather likes fancy words. See that you don't get the habit from him. All that's involved is that he—and, in this case, you along with him—will be separate from the main body of the investigation.'

The chief stopped and looked out the window, as if making sure the city was behaving.

'This is a bad crime. The murderer and the victim may have been unconnected up to the time of the crime. And that could make it very hard to solve. But time is pushing. This is a sensational crime. The press will make a lot of it. People will be frightened. A man as unbalanced as that may do it again at any time. We're under pressure. For these reasons I've agreed to let Laidlaw go his own way for a few days. Up to a point, that is. And that's where you come in. You will be the liaison between Detective Inspector Laidlaw and the main investigation, which will be controlled by Detective Inspector Milligan of Central Division. You'll find that Laidlaw likes to lose himself in the city at times like these. What is it he calls it? 'Becoming a traveller,' I think. You can ask him what that means. I certainly don't know. Anyway, that's all very well. But he tends to lose touch with us. You will prevent that. You will be in daily touch with Detective Inspector Milligan. You will carry information to him and from him. Unless the two investigations cross-fertilise, there is no point, You're the fertilising agent. Understood?'

'Yes, sir,' Harkness said, the talking fertiliser.

'You'll meet Laidlaw at half-past nine tomorrow morning at Central Division. He'll come straight from the p.m. to get you there. I also want you to report to D.I. Milligan there just now. That should be like old times for you. See if there's anything he wants you to do.'

'Very good, sir.'

'Good luck. Don't be put off by Laidlaw's ma[nner]
to be an abrasive man. That's all.'

'Thank you, sir.'

'Harkness,' the Commander said.

Harkness felt as if he was being filed. There was someth[ing]
about the way the Commander spoke that made Harknes[s]
uncomfortable. But he couldn't understand it. He came out
into the corridor smiling with expectation, until it occurred to
him bizarrely that somebody's murder was his opportunity.
He stopped smiling.

11

THE BRIDGEGATE WAS empty. Harry Rayburn had parked the car well away and he was walking. He passed the second-hand furniture shop and 'Alice's Restaurant', an old café whose only pretension was its name. The corrugated entrance was Number Seventeen. He paused, looking back along the street and then towards the corner with Jocelyn Square, where 'The Old Ship Bank' was closed like everything else.

The metal across the door was sprung as Tommy had said. But having been weathered so long in one position, it wasn't easy to force open. He had trouble easing the travelling-bag through the opening.

The entry was dark. He wondered whether to call Tommy's name. But, thinking about it, he knew he must be upstairs. At the top of the stairs, he negotiated the last steps very carefully because they were corroded. The bannister wasn't safe. Of the two doors, one was heavily cobwebbed in the dim light. It had to be the other.

He pushed it open. The small hallway had three doors, one facing him that was presumably a cupboard. and two others opposite each other. He hesitated, and opened the door on his left, into an empty room. He closed it, stepped across the hall and opened the other door.

He saw Tommy at once, saw him not in isolation but as part of a larger scene that gave him its significance and which he simultaneously interpreted. He was pressed against a corner,

48

looking over his shoulder. Rayburn was aware of the scabby wall he stood against, different layers of paper showing against it like a record of failure to cover its bleakness; he was aware of the empty fireplace, the remnant of chintzy curtain on the window, flag of defeated respectability. At the centre of this small ruin of domesticity was Tommy, seeming to Rayburn at once its destroyer and its victim. He was what it denied and so he had been obliged to deny it in order to happen. He had arrived where, within himself, he had probably always been.

They watched each other. Rayburn made to move towards him and Tommy held up his hand.

'Don't touch me, Harry. That's the first thing. Don't try to touch me.'

Rayburn left the travelling-bag in the middle of the floor like bait and moved back to the doorway. Tommy looked at the bag.

'Did you bring the things for writing?'

'They're there. And there's food there and some blankets. And candles and matches. But why won't you come back with me? We could go now.'

'Did you see my mother?'

'I saw her.'

'What did you tell her?'

'I told her you were in trouble with the police and couldn't come home. I didn't say why. I had to tell her that much. Because I asked her to say you had gone to London two weeks back, if they asked. It was all right.'

Rayburn thought of the small, grey-haired woman he had talked to that morning, as clean and about as yielding as stainless steel. She had wanted to know only one thing really, that Tommy was all right. She knew, Rayburn was sure, that whatever Tommy had done was very serious, but she hadn't hesitated to accept the part he had given her.

'Who was it, Tommy?'

Tommy shook his head.

'Was it that girl you told me about?'

Tommy nodded. His right hand had been in his pocket all the time. As he brought it out now, kneading it, Rayburn realised that what he held in it was a pair of panties. There was blood on them.

'Tommy. I can help you. I can get you away from here.' He started to move nearer to him again. 'Let me—'

Tommy cringed.

'I don't want anybody to touch me!' he shouted. 'I don't want to talk. I don't want anybody else here.'

Rayburn stared at him. In Tommy's utter isolation Rayburn had found a complete commitment. Tommy stood like an admission of what Rayburn had managed to avoid.

'I'll come back, Tommy. I can get help. You've heard me talking about Matt Mason. He can help. Matt Mason'll help.'

He turned towards the door.

'Come back tomorrow, Harry. Please.'

Rayburn nodded and went out. He knew that if he didn't get Tommy safely out of there, there would be nothing else he wanted to do again.

12

THE MAN JUMPED back onto the pavement as the car swerved to avoid him. He looked after it indignantly.

'You missed him,' Milligan said. 'You'll never get promotion that way, Boy Robin. That was Barney Aird. You should've knocked him down. Crime Prevention, they call it.'

'I'm going to miss the compassion you bring to the job.' Harkness said.

Milligan was looking out at the passing scene with a kind of sunny malice.

'No,' he said. 'Where you're going you'll get plenty of that. Laidlaw? You'll have to wear wellies when you work with him. To wade through the tears. He thinks criminals are under-privileged. He's not a detective. He's a shop-steward for neds. It'll be a great experience for you. Boy Robin meets Batman.'

Milligan started to hum 'Robin Hood, Robin Hood, riding through the glen.' Harkness understood that Milligan hadn't forgiven him for leaving to join the Crime Squad.

'He's supposed to be a good man,' Harkness said.

'He's maybe a good man. Even kind to animals, probably. But he's not a good *polis*-man.'

Harkness changed down at the lights.

'How not?'

'He doesn't know which side he's on. He's pig in the middle. Not clever.'

'You think it's always Them and Us?'

51

'Well, *they* think that, don't they? I'd be a bit simple not to agree. Turn the other cheek in this caper and they'll have to knit you a new face at the Western. I don't suit Fair Isle. Doesn't go with my eyes.'

He turned their blueness innocently on Harkness. Harkness laughed. He had always found Milligan funny.

'Laidlaw seems to survive.'

'Time enough yet. He's a slow developer. His ideas haven't shaved yet. Wait and see. He'll either grow up or pack up. No third way. Happens to us all. You come into this job wanting to give everybody a chance and what they take is a liberty. But you learn. It's just taking Laidlaw longer than usual. That's all.'

'There's crooks and crooks.'

'All right. But I'm talking about *crooks*. It takes a professional to deal with *them*. And Laidlaw's an amateur.'

'So what's a professional?'

'Boy Robin. You've worked with me for more than a year. Are you a slow learner? A professional *knows* what he is. I've got nothing in common with thieves and con-men and pimps and murderers. Nothing! They're another species. And we're at war with them. It's about survival. What would happen in a war if we didn't wear different uniforms? We wouldn't know who was fighting who. That's Laidlaw. He's running about no man's land with a German helmet and a Black Watch jacket.'

They had turned into Ardmore Crescent.

'He's never faced up to what this job's about. It's about catching the baddies. And doing whatever you have to do to catch them. You have to batter down whatever's in your road. Doors or faces makes no odds. There's seventeen over there. You watch how it's done, son. You can take wee notes if you like. Where you're going, you might need them.'

By the time Harkness had pulled into the kerb, Milligan was getting out. Harkness followed him into the entry. The door was opened by an elderly man. Milligan flapped open his wallet, showing his identity card.

It was a ticket to an enclave of the Gothic in Drumchapel: ˈmit two to the House of Gloom. Outside, the drab modernity of bleak streets, an imposed assumption about the meanness of our lives; inside this door, a dark subversion of that rationale, a sense of the inner distances grief imparts, the manic architecture of the heart that can make eerie castellated turrets and gloomy secret chambers in a council house.

The hall was enriched by shadows, seeming bigger than itself. Through the half-open door of the living-room, a single wall-light glowed. The muttered voices were a coven. The kitchen door was closed. From behind it came uncertain sounds, the men imprisoned in their helplessness.

'I'd like to see the parents of the deceased,' Milligan said.

To Harkness speech seemed like a foreign language here.

'Oh, they're in an awfy state, sir,' the old man said. 'Sadie especially. Ye couldny get sense oot o' her. They've had an awfy time, ye know. Ah'm jist a neighbour, like.'

'I still want to see them,' Milligan said.

His voice was like an act of vandalism. He was looking at the old man as if he was about to arrest him.

'Whit's this, Charlie? Whit's this?'

It was a younger woman. She was gesturing them all to be quiet.

'It's the polis, Meg. They want tae talk tae Bud and Sadie,' the man whispered.

'My Goad. The wumman's oot o' her wits. Could ye no' leave them alone the noo?'

Out of deference to her feelings, Milligan lowered his voice to a boom.

'Missus,' he said, 'there's been a murder. Investigations have to be made. Where's Mr. Lawson?'

'The men are a' in the kitchen,' the woman said.

'Eh, Bud's oot for some air,' the old man was saying.

But Milligan had already opened the door. The room was heavy with cigarette-smoke like stage mist. Among its whorlings three men sat.

'Mr. Lawson?' Milligan asked them.

There was a silence.

'One of us took Bud oot for a walk.'

'Airchie Stanley.'

'When will he be back?'

'No sayin'.'

Milligan closed the door.

'It'll have to be Mrs. Lawson,' Milligan said.

'Oh my,' the woman said. 'Wait here a minute.'

As she went in, the living-room door swung open. The doorway, separating them from a quality of grief they could never share, was a burnous lifted. It was a roomful of women busy at their sorrow. Harkness watched the younger woman break the circle and go over to the small woman by the fire. The hurt face came up, a blur of incomprehension. Then she began to cry again, as if it was the only answer she had to everything. Some of the women moved to her, closing ranks against the men. Harkness felt responsible.

But Milligan simply waited for them to come and meet his purpose. They did. What followed was harrowing for Harkness. They were shown into a bedroom that had obviously been the girl's, a shrine to David Essex. The younger woman came to sit with Mrs. Lawson.

Milligan moved meticulously back and forward across an already dead past like someone ploughing a cemetery, while Mrs. Lawson kept being side-tracked by the incidental bones that he turned up. The only thing she could tell him about last night that Laidlaw hadn't given him was the name of Sarah Stanley, the girl who had gone to the disco with Jennifer. The girl was in the house and came through with her mother. Jennifer had left with a man she didn't see, Sarah said. He had been waiting outside when Jennifer said cheerio. Milligan went on with patient questions, but that was all they learned.

They left the house with two photographs. In the car, Milligan handed Harkness one of the photographs.

'That's for Laidlaw,' Milligan said. 'In payment for the information he gave me.'

Harkness looked at it. She was standing in the street. She was pretty and she was laughing.

'That wasn't too pleasant in there,' Harkness said.

'We got the photos,' Milligan said. 'The rest has nothing to do with us. We'll check in at the caravan on the road back. And that's us for the night. There'll be nothing else happening the night. Even murderers have to go to their beds.'

Milligan laughed. Harkness started up the car.

'I wonder where Bud Lawson is,' he said.

'In the pub.' Milligan spoke with certainty. 'Getting fou.'

13

THE MAN STANDING at the bar had become drunk slowly. But his declaration of the fact was sudden and spectacular. He pushed himself off from the counter as if it was a jetty. He seemed to be treading water. His eyes were seeing far horizons. The downstairs lounge of the Lorne Hotel was his oyster. He was ready to serve notice on the world.

The place was busy. He started to approach various tables by indirections. Now he seemed to be heading off in a vaguely westerly direction, now he wasn't. His shuffling footwork was a cunning illusion. He was, as it were, surrounding everybody. His arms had begun to move with a kind of amorphous menace and he was talking.

'Ho-ho! Yese fancy yerselves, do ye? Ah didny come a' through the war fur this. In an' oot, in an' oot. Quick as a flash. Houf, houf! Houf, houf!'

It was a nasal sound, the noise amateur boxers make when hitting the heavy bag to time their punches. But then it wasn't amateur night at the Lorne.

'Nya-hah! How about that then? The more ye know the less the better. Houf, houf!'

He was circulating haphazardly, trying different tables. In Hollywood films it's gipsy fiddlers. In Glasgow pubs it isn't. With that instinct for catastrophe some drunk men have, he settled for a table where three men were sitting. Two of them, Bud Lawson and Airchie Stanley, looked like trouble. The third one looked like much worse trouble. He had thinning hair and eyes that seemed as impressionable as pebbles. A thick scar ran down his left cheek and vanished under his chin. It was him the drunk man chose.

'Ho-ho! A big guy. Ah've never been known to lose. Ah'm doom on two legs. Get up, ya midden!'

The man with the scar stood up. The barman materialised beside the drunk man and took his arm.

'Is this man causing a disturbance, sir?' he asked the man with the scar.

'Unless he's yer cabaret, Ah'd say he is.'

'Come on, sir. You'll have to behave.'

The drunk man was offering resistance.

'On ye go, sur,' the man with the scar said. 'It's past yer bed-time.'

The drunk man focussed for one clear second on the man with the scar. Then he became wisely drunk again and was led out, content to challenge a table and apostrophise the carpet on his way. He hit the end of Sauchiehall Street as if it was the edge of the world, and he might fall off.

'The thing is,' the man with the scar said, sitting back down, 'he probably thinks he wis unlucky getting flung oot.'

'Anyway,' Airchie Stanley said. 'How about it?'

'Behave yerself,' the man with the scar said. 'Ye've seen too many gangster pictures.'

'But you know people, like. Ah *know* you know them.'

'Whit dae ye mean by that?'

'Now, now. Don't take offence. Ah mean, Ah know you've got contacts.'

'You know nothin' about me,' the man with the scar said. 'Except that Ah mairrit yer cousin. An' the way you're talking, Ah'm beginnin' tae think it wis a bad marriage.'

The man seemed to be feeling a disproportionate amount of anger. His scar had been gettin whiter as he talked, becoming as livid as a lightning-flash. Bud Lawson sat between the two of them saying nothing. It had been Airchie Stanley's idea. He left him with it.

'Ye divert me,' the man said. 'Ye get me along here so that ye can talk like an American coamic. Dick Tracey or somethin'. Whit's the gemme?'

'Look,' Airchie said. 'Ah've explained the thing to ye. Fair an' square. Ye know whit's happened tae Bud's lassie.'

The man sipped his whisky.

'Well. You've got an ear tae the ground. All Ah'm sayin' is if ye heard a whisper, we'd appreciate it. Ah'd raither Bud got 'im than the polis. Fair enough?'

The man stroked his scar.

'Fair enough for therty year in the jile.'

'Who needs tae know?'

'Look behind ye,' the man said quietly.

Airchie looked round quickly. All he could see were the customers drinking and chatting. He looked back at the man.

'All you dae,' the man said, 'is you pick a packed lounge tae set somebody up to get murdert. That's how clever you are. Yer mooth's that loose Ah'm surprised yer teeth stey in. Why no' hire the tannoy in Central Station?'

'Naebody can hear us.'

'How many other people have ye telt?'

'Not a wan. That's the God's truth. Ah telt the boays at Bud's Ah wis jist takin' 'im oot tae get some air.'

'Anyway, that's the least o' it. How am Ah supposed tae find oot who did it an' where he is? The polis'll have a big enough job doin' that.'

'Yer connections.'

'Listen! You know me. Ye've seen whit Ah can dae.'

'You can handle yerself,' Airchie said instantly and placatively.

'Correct. But you know who Ah work for. An' Ah'm no feart. But Ah know catchweights when Ah see it. A thing like this wid need his say-so. He could put the three o' us in a bag an' droon us like kittens. Ye don't offend that big man.'

'Fair enough. Ah jist thought Ah wid ask.'

'Ye've asked then. An' Ah've telt ye.'

Airchie finished his drink. The man with the scar watched Bud Lawson. He hadn't spoken, even when they were introduced. He impressed the man. He had sat staring at the table,

58

very powerful-looking and utterly still—a stick of gelignite just waiting for a match.

'Look, sur,' the man said. 'Ah can appreciate whit you must be feelin' like. But this is a wild idea. Ah'll tell ye whit. If Ah get any word—an' it's hundreds against—Ah'll see aboot passin' it on. That's all Ah can say. Noo Ah think we should separate before this man gets the T.V. cameras in.'

'Right, Bud.' His friend was on his feet, signalling farewell. 'That's good enough fur us. Much appreciated. Be seein' ye. Cheerio.'

'Cheerio,' the man said. 'Watch ye don't fa' ower yer mooth goin' oot the door.'

Bud Lawson hadn't touched his drink. The man lifted it. He might as well get something out of the conversation.

14

'ALL OF US at some time or other,' the minister was saying, 'have been to the seaside.' It wasn't exactly a riveting start. 'The sea attracts us. Yet we hardly stop to think of it as the source of all life. For us it's hardly more than a social amenity. Weather permitting—and that's all too rare, I can hear you say, in Scotland—we fill the car with food and children and go down to the sea on trips. We play. We laugh. We splash water on one another. We eat our sandwiches. And it's not until Wee Johnny finds himself in difficulties—or Wee Mary is caught in the current—or perhaps a stranger drowns—that we remember the awe-inspiring power of the sea. In some ways, the presence of God is like that.'

Harkness was finding it hard to focus on who he was. He found it impossible to connect himself as he was with Mary's mother offering him 'a wee cup of tea' and home-made ginger biscuits. He sat eating biscuits while the photograph of Jennifer Lawson weighed on him like the corpse, while Mary's father sat watching 'Late Call' on the telly as if it was news of Armageddon.

The room seemed as unreal as a stage-set. They all seemed to know their parts. He watched Mary's father, trying to catch a glimmer of dismissal of what he was hearing. There was nothing. Mary's father stared solemnly at the set as if the minister was telling him something. Harkness began to worry about Mary's father. He also began to worry about ministers who clasp their hands across their knees and talk about God as if they were His uncle, who seem to suggest that He's not such a bad lad when you get to know Him and that whatever His past, He means well in the future. He also began to worry about Mary's mother making ginger biscuits and about Mary. Harkness began to worry about everything.

He felt bruised with contradictions. Where he had been was being mocked by where he was. Yet both were Glasgow. He had always liked the place, but he had never been more aware of it than tonight. Its force came to him in contradictions. Glasgow was home-made ginger biscuits and Jennifer Lawson dead in the park. It was the sententious niceness of the Commander and the threatened abrasiveness of Laidlaw. It was Milligan, insensitive as a mobile slab of cement, and Mrs. Lawson, witless with hurt. It was the right hand knocking you down and the left hand picking you up, while the mouth alternated apology and threat.

Tomorrow with Laidlaw he would no doubt see some of it he had never seen before. Jealous of his own affection for the place, he reminded himself that what he would see would only be a very small part of the whole.

'Tonight let us reflect for a moment on this great mystery which surrounds us,' the minister was saying.

Harkness's thoughts were a secular gloss on the minister's words. He watched Mary's father complacently watching television, her mother reading the *Sunday Post*, Mary herself putting papers in her briefcase for tomorrow's teaching—each with a finger in the dyke of their own illusions. He decided, to his surprise, that he didn't want to share their illusions. He wasn't sure, as he had thought he was, that he and Mary would be getting engaged. The things which were happening outside, and which he didn't know about, seemed more real to him than this room.

15

In another room, Matt Mason was enjoying the end of a nice Sunday. He had slept away the morning and in the afternoon had taken Billy Tate out from Helensburgh on the boat for a couple of hours. Now he was listening to two of his visitors insult each other familiarly and pleasantly.

'You know,' Roddy Stewart said. 'I find it hard to recognise your father in the way you talk about him. Your picture doesn't square with the fourteen stones of vibrant apathy I used to know and hate so well.'

'At least he was coherent,' Alice said. 'Your father spoke English like a native. Bantu, I'd say.'

The phone rang. As Matt Mason got up, he winked at Billy Tate.

'End of the round, you two. You do the inter-round summaries till I get back, Billy.'

The phone was in the hall. He closed the lounge door.

'Matt Mason here.'

'Hullo, Matt. This is Harry.'

The name affected Mason like a spasm.

'I've told you not to phone here,' he said. 'What is it?'

'My God, Matt. I'm in terrible trouble. Have you got a minute?'

'About one. I've got people here.'

Mason let the silence stand, the way he might stare down a wino who begged for money in the street.

'Listen. You know that girl who was found murdered today?'

'Not personally, no.'

'For God's sake, Matt, listen to me. This is serious. There was a girl found murdered today. In Kelvingrove Park. The boy who did it is a—friend of mine. I know him well.'

Mason made a face as if he was going to be sick into the mouthpiece.

'How well? You mean, *very* well?'

There was a pause.

'Very well.'

'I think I know what that means in your case,' Mason said.

Memories bothered him like the foul breath of a drunk man. He looked round the hall, noticed the expensive coats on the table where the housekeeper had left them. The memories threatened this place. They didn't belong here.

'He's holed up in a place. I need your help. I need it very badly.'

In the lounge somebody was laughing. Mason decided to be cautious.

'I'll phone you tomorrow,' he said.

'You will, will you? Make sure you do. I'm desperate.'

'I'll phone you tomorrow.' Mason blocked the line very gently with his finger and said into the dead phone, 'Fine then. And thanks for phoning.'

He put down the phone and walked through a blizzard of implications, hoping none of them showed on his face when he opened the door.

'Aye,' he said. 'Sorry about that.' Then he added in a mock English accent, 'The pressures of big business, you know.'

There was hardly any reaction from the others. Only Roddy's eyes contracted for a second, looking at Matt to check if the call might involve his services, before returning his attention to Alice.

'Anyway,' she was saying. 'He would have been even more successful if he hadn't caught pleurisy when he did.'

'Come on, Alice,' Roddy said. 'Your father didn't just catch pleurisy. He *seized* it. With both lungs. Before it got away.'

Billy laughed. Mason looked round the group. He was impressed with himself. Roddy was one of the sharpest lawyers in Scotland. Billy Tate had been one of the best inside-forwards in the history of Scottish football before he retired and bought his pub. It wasn't a bad sign that they were the kind of people you could have dropping in on a Sunday for a drink. Their wives were no problem to have to look at, but Margaret was easily the best-looking woman in the room. She usually was. Mason looked and saw that it was good, too cosy to be spoiled by the kind of draught that had blown down the phone just now. That was one hole in his security that would have to be blocked up. He stood.

'See when you two come,' he said to Roddy and Alice. 'I don't feel like a host. I feel like a promoter. You fan them with a towel, Billy. I'll get more drink.'

Everybody smiled.

16

ENA LAY IN bed upstairs and listened to Laidlaw packing. His movements were so positive. He walked back and forth pacing out his purpose. In the silence of the house it was like someone doing sentry duty. It was a familiar event and she knew the ritual that he made of it, as if he was doing more than pack a suitcase. He was constructing a solution-kit—a tooth-brush missing and a crime might go unsolved. She hoped he was remembering to pack his migraine pills.

She wondered how often he had filled that suitcase. At first she had hated when it happened. Now, although she might use it as an official ground of complaint, she wasn't sure that she didn't feel relief. They were, she had decided, probably what incompatible meant.

He was so hard to live with. It was the demands he put on people that she found most difficult. Moral aggression, she called it to herself. It was as if his career as an amateur boxer had extended itself into his social life, though not on a physical basis. Seeing him walk into a room, she always thought: 'Introducing in the red corner . . .'

She heard Jackie whimper. Before she could rise, his father was coming up the stairs. She didn't move. Jackie needed the lavatory. Jack took him and brought him back up to the small bedroom next to their own. As Jackie got back into bed, she heard him speak.

'Was it a monster, Daddy?'

65

'What are you talking about, son?'

'The thing at the door when Margaret was in herself. Was it a monster?'

Jack answered very seriously.

'No chance. It was the girl from down the road. Coming to baby-sit. Margaret let her in and the electricity came on. And they had a very good night.'

'Sandra said it would likely be a monster.'

'That's how clever she is. There *are* no monsters, Jackie. No monsters, son.'

'None at all?'

'None at all.'

'That's good. I'm glad. I don't like monsters, Daddy.'

'You're a sound judge, son. I wouldn't fancy them myself if they were here. But there's only people.'

Ena knew that for Jackie the certainty in his father's voice had burned the monsters out of his room for the night like a blow-torch.

'Good night, Daddy.'

'Good night, Jackie.'

She heard Jack go back downstairs. She felt a brief longing for the way they had once been. But the questing intensity in him that had first attracted her was also what had separated them, because it had never stopped. She had thought it was looking for a destination of which she might be part. Now she felt convinced that the nearest he would get to a destination would be when they pulled his eyelids down. He worried everything into bone and then moved on.

She heard him coming back upstairs, coming to bed. Knight errant of the Crime Squad, she reflected bitterly. The trouble was, it occurred to her, that with him you never knew whether you were the maiden or the dragon.

17

St. Andrew's Parish Church looked bleak, a big, dark oblong locked and shuttered, like a warehouse for a commodity gone out of fashion. Harkness wondered if it was still in use. Even the trees along both sides of it seemed at first dead. But staring at their branches shaking gently, he could see the first buds of spring, small fists of green.

He was standing opposite the church in the green doorway of the police station—a red-brick building at the corner of St. Andrew's Street and Turnbull Street, housing Central Division and the Administrative H.Q. He had come outside to wait for Laidlaw because it was so pleasant, the kind of morning that made you want to take a holiday from who you were. It wasn't a day for being a policeman, he decided. The air was a permit to do anything and it was valid for everybody.

He crossed the street and walked round the church in the sunshine. Coming back to the front of it, he saw two men crossing the street towards him. One was tall and wearing glasses. The other was short and stocky, going grey. He wore a reefer jacket.

'Excuse me. Ye got a match, Jimmy?' the smaller one asked.

Harkness noticed the unlit cigarettes in their mouths.

'Sorry,' he said. 'I don't smoke.'

'Sensible fella,' the tall man said.

The small man took the cigarette from his mouth. Harkness could see that his hand was shaking.

'We jist got oot o' that nick there,' he said. 'Dyin' for a drag.'

'There's a café round the corner in the Saltmarket,' Harkness said. 'Get matches there.'

'Aye. We should just about wrestle the price o' one between us.'

Harkness was wondering about offering them the price of a cup of tea but they had already walked away. They weren't begging, just indulging in the Glaswegian pastime of giving strangers bulletins on your progress. Harkness was pleased with the small exchange because they hadn't recognised him as a policeman. He must mention that, the next time his father got on to the subject of how he was getting to look more like a policeman every day.

Turning away from them, he suddenly noticed something on the first small tree on the right-hand side of the church. It was a single red berry. His feeling of the moment took it as its coat of arms: secret growth to come. He was twenty-six. That wasn't ninety. He rejected his father's sense of him as somebody who had made a final choice. He thought of the atmosphere of assumptiveness that had oppressed him in Mary's house yesterday. He wasn't ready to be defined. He remembered the months he had spent in Spain and France when he was twenty, especially the long, lazy journey from Sitges to Paris.

It had been a good time, a seemingly endless ante-room to an infinite future. Standing in St. Andrew's Square, he got back the feeling he had had then. Everything was still possible for him. Meanwhile, he would hold his commitment to what he was doing lightly. And then he saw Laidlaw.

Laidlaw was walking up Turnbull Street towards the Station. Harkness had had Laidlaw pointed out to him, although they had never met. He recognised the deceptively tall figure, deceptive because the width of the shoulders acted against the height, making him seem smaller than he was, and the very positive features that gave the face clear definition even at a distance. The most striking thing about him was something Harkness had noticed every time he had seen him—preoccupation. You never came on him empty. You imagined that if a launch arrived to rescue him from a desert island, he would have something he had to finish before being taken off. It was hard to think of him walking casually, always towards definite destinations. Harkness remembered that he was one of them. Infinite possibilities would have to wait.

He crossed the street and stopped in front of Laidlaw. They were outside the door of the station.

'Detective Inspector Laidlaw, sir? D.C. Harkness. Reporting.'

'Hullo,' Laidlaw said. 'It's bad for your back standing like that. What's your first name?'

'Brian.'

They shook hands.

'Jack. Don't call me 'sir'. If I get *your* respect, that'll be fine. But I don't need your mouth's. Have you had breakfast?'

'Yes.'

'I haven't. We'll go and get me some.'

They walked past the police station along St. Andrew's Street, turned up the Saltmarket and then walked along the Trongate towards Argyle Street. To break the silence, Harkness told Laidlaw about the two men who had asked him for a light.

'No wonder *they* were in the nick,' Laidlaw said. 'If they didn't know *you* were polis. I was just thinking it might be more discreet working with the Police Pipe Band. Where do you get your gear anyway? The Plainclothes Policeman's Stores?'

It took Harkness a moment to absorb the remark. It seemed such a wanton intrusion of insult into a nice moment. Argyle Street was pleasant with sunshine and shoppers. Perhaps it was the contrast between the man who suggested they use first names and the man whose first remark was an insult. Perhaps it was the effect of the expansiveness he had been feeling before meeting Laidlaw. But something made Harkness respond not as a policeman, just as himself.

'The jacket may not be too fancy. But it comes off fast enough.'

'It might be a harder job getting it back on. Over the plaster casts.'

'Any time you want to test your theory.'

They both stopped in the street and looked at each other. Laidlaw started to laugh and Harkness found himself joining in.

'Jesus Christ,' Laidlaw said. 'That didn't take long. Threatening G.B.H. to your superior within five minutes. I'll say one thing. I hate promotion-seekers. And you have just passed ze initiation test.'

They turned into the Buchanan Street Pedestrian Precinct. It was getting busy already. They walked among the flowers and the benches, a couple of which were occupied even this early. In Gordon Street they went into the 'Grill 'n' Griddle'. It was empty except for them. Laidlaw had eggs, toast and coffee. Harkness took coffee.

'I'm sorry,' Laidlaw said. 'Maybe I was just trying to pass some of that post mortem off on you.'

'Bad?'

'There's never been a good one. Especially when Milligan's there. Peeing verbally on the corpse.'

'What does Milligan have against you?'

'Not half as much as I've got against him.'

The waitress brought the food. She was a handsome woman with glasses. She was complaining that their rolls hadn't been delivered yet.

While he was eating, Laidlaw asked, 'So what've you got?'

Harkness passed the photograph of Jennifer Lawson across to him, and then a slip of paper with Sarah Stanley's name, address and place of work.

'That's in return for the information you gave Milligan,' he said. 'And I found out in the office this morning who owns "Poppies". A man called Harry Rayburn.'

'Any form?'

'Nothing we know about.'

'You saw Bud Lawson last night?'

'No, he was out. Mrs. Lawson. But that was all we got.'

Laidlaw went on eating. He was looking at the photograph on the table.

'No pants,' he said. 'What does that mean to you?'

'She didn't wear any? Or he panicked. Didn't even know he had them with him. Or a fetishist?'

Laidlaw was nodding, still chewing.

'The pathologist's report'll show that the vagina was brutally torn. No trace of sperm. But there were traces of sperm in the anus.'

'That's not such a wild variation.'

'No. But you could see it as making her neuter in a way, couldn't you? Also. The anal tissue suggests she was dead by the time he got there. It was his second assault.'

Harkness felt sickened. He had been aware, while they talked, that the waitress had gone out to the front part of the place, where a small grey-haired woman took the cash and sold cigarettes and sweets. They were telling each other about their families. How John had got engaged and Kay was enjoying school and Michael wanted a dog. Their platitudes seemed to him so wholesome he could almost smell them, like home-baked bread. Beyond them, in the Gordon Street part of the precinct, people were walking past the window in the brittle morning air as if they were advertising ordinariness. This morning's sense of the future was being polluted already, by what they were saying.

'Hell,' Harkness said. 'It's hopeless. How are we supposed to connect with something like this? How do we begin to relate to *him*?'

'Because he relates to us.'

'Speak for yourself.'

'What do you mean?' Laidlaw said. 'You resign from the species?'

'No. He did.'

'Not as easy as that.'

'It is for me.'

'Then you're a mug. You'll be telling me next you believe in monsters. I've got a wee boy of six with the same problem.'

'Don't you?'

'If I did, I'd have to believe in fairies as well. And I'm not quite prepared for that.'

'How do you mean?'

Laidlaw had finished eating. He sipped at his coffee.

'Look,' he said. 'What I mean is, monstrosity's made by false gentility. You don't get one without the other. No fairies, no monsters. Just people. You know what the horror of this kind

71

of crime is? It's the tax we pay for the unreality we choose to live in. It's a fear of ourselves.'

Harkness thought about it.

'So where does that leave us?'

'As stand-ins,' Laidlaw said. 'Other people can afford to write "monster" across this and consign it to limbo. I suppose society can't afford to do anything else, or it wouldn't work. They've got to pretend that things like this aren't really done by people. We can't afford to do that. We're the shitty urban machine humanised. That's policemen.'

Harkness was cultivating the demerara gently with the spoon.

'Come on,' he said. 'Step outside that door. It's a nice spring morning. Those people walking about out there. What they're doing is different from this character's way of living.'

'They're using a language!' Laidlaw said. 'Your way of life is taught to you like a language. It's how you express yourself. But any language conceals as much as it reveals. And there's a lot of languages. All of them human. This murder is a very human message. But it's in code. We have to try and crack the code. But what we're looking for is a part of us. You don't know that, you can't begin.'

'Forgive me if I feel a bit sick with a part of us.'

'All right,' Laidlaw said. 'You can even cry if you want. It clears the eyes.'

Laidlaw lit a cigarette. He put the photograph and the piece of paper inside the small wallet that held his identification card. Harkness was watching him.

'I don't see how all that helps us much,' Harkness said.

Laidlaw smiled.

'Not a lot, right enough,' he said. 'But there's one important thing that follows from it. It keeps us from making the commonest mistake people make when they think about a murder like this.'

'What's that?'

'They see it as the culmination of an abnormal sequence of events. But it's only that for the victim. For everybody else—the murderer, the people connected with him, the people connected with the victim—it's the *beginning* of the sequence.'

'So?'

'So here endeth the first lesson. You were asking how we can connect. That's how. Milligan and his mob can reconstruct the crime if they want. We do something very simple. We just look for whoever did it. In the lives round him, what he's done must make ripples. That's what we're looking for. We do it by talking to some people. Harry Rayburn for starters.'

'We can begin by asking him if he's seen a man carrying a pair of knickers and a placard saying "I am sexually insecure".'

Laidlaw looked at him.

'That can be your question,' he said.

18

The body of an eighteen-year-old girl was found yesterday among bushes in Kelvingrove Park. Police said the girl, Jennifer Lawson, had been sexually assaulted.

'It was a particularly brutal murder,' Detective Inspector Ernest Milligan said.

Almost a hundred policemen carried out inquiries in the area and a murder H.Q. in a caravan was set set up near where the body was found.

Detective Inspector Milligan warned people in the area that it was unsafe for women to be out alone after dark while the murderer was still at large.

The dead girl was the only daughter of Mr. and Mrs. William Lawson of 17 Ardmore Crescent, Drumchapel.

The cause of death is believed to have been strangulation.

MATT MASON PUT *The Glasgow Herald* very gently on the table. It and the other two papers were like stains on the polished darkness of the wood, blemishes on his way of life. 'TEENAGER BRUTALLY MURDERED—The Dance That Led to Death.' 'THE BEAST OF KELVINGROVE PARK.' He forked a piece of bacon into his mouth and it couldn't have tasted worse if he'd been a Rabbi.

He rose and crossed towards the window. This was the only uncarpeted room in the house, because in a colour supplement he had seen a dining-room with a wooden floor, but walking on it he made very little sound. Though small and going heavy, he moved lightly. Roddy Stewart had sometimes joked about it,

74

saying he could walk on snow without leaving footprints. 'I came out the womb on tiptoe,' Mason said.

He stood at the window, a small, squat man, his hair thinning, it might have seemed from the worries of suburbia, staring out at an acre of garden. His eyes dismissed the pleasant morning, had a grudge against it. A day like this he could do without. Nobody sent for it.

He watched a blackbird land on his big lawn, balance its beak like a nugget of gold and then take off, as if it didn't care for his company. It must have been born and bred in this area, he thought, a Bearsden blackie. Everybody here was born with their nose in the air. It was only an overgrown village on the north-west edge of Glasgow, but getting from there to here had been a hard road—the North-West Frontier. Here he could believe that when the doctor held them up by the ankles and skelped their arses, they didn't cry, they just coughed politely. The children probably played at tig with gloves on. He wasn't one of them but he was here, in as big a house as any of them. And he was staying.

He listened to Mrs. McGarrity doing the housework. It occurred to him bitterly that this should have been the best time of the day. He liked coming in here to find the breakfast-things set on the sideboard, the hot-plate, the coffee, the dishes, like something out of a Ronald Colman film. It was his greatest vanity to sit here in the morning alone, as he had essentially always been, and confirm the size and solidity of what he had built, as surely as if he had laid each brick himself, from the half-baked dreams of a wee boy in the Gallowgate. Ragged, snottery nosed and hungry, he had never believed that was how he should be, and he had found his only available blueprint for a different kind of life in Hollywood films. From them, he had constructed this part of his life as deliberately as a set.

He didn't delude himself about how much credibility his performance in it had for his neighbours. He knew that a lot of the people around him found him vulgar and unacceptable. That didn't bother him too much. He was anaesthetised from their attitudes by the possession of a very calm certainty. Like a secret withheld from those who were born to this kind of living, he knew precisely what it cost. The cost was lives. He knew

75

because he had been obliged to take a couple. He hadn't taken more because it hadn't been necessary. The fact that if it were he was ready rendered him not very susceptible to other people's sense of superiority.

Moving back across the room, he sat down again at the large mahogany table, like a board-meeting of one. There were decisions he had to make. He took a clean cup and poured himself more coffee. Harry Rayburn was the past. Mason had only ever used him because he was Margaret's cousin. He had been fairly dealt with, squarely paid. Now he was claiming more, involving Mason in something that could threaten his security. That was double-charging. That was foolish. It was as if he had forgotten who Matt Mason was. Fools tended to be foolish more than once, so he was dangerous.

Like someone checking his notes, Mason inventoried briefly what he had, as if this were a normal morning. The house had to be worth more than forty thousand pounds. There was a housekeeper living in with them, doing everything except answering the phone. Margaret was still upstairs in bed, probably preparing to have a headache. Her hardest work was sitting under a hair-dryer. At one time her uselessness had bothered him, especially when he thought of Anne, who had died just when he was really beginning to make it. But now he took a certain pride in her. Not everybody could afford a wife whose only talent was bed. When he was angry, he could still call her a migraine with tits. But they were good tits. Then there were the businesses and Matt and Eric at the private school.

He added it all up like a sum. The answer was a long way from the Gallowgate, too far ever to go back.

He sipped at his coffee again and it was cold. He looked at the papers and to him they were like threatening letters. Threats weren't to be yielded to but they were to be taken seriously. If Harry Rayburn had any sense, he would have handled this himself. But he had insisted Mason come into the game. Some game; it would be like playing tennis with a hand-grenade. Mason still wasn't sure what he was going to do. But he knew whose court the thing would be in when it went off.

Mason measured the problem calmly. The only connection

he had now with Rayburn was that he had invested money in 'Poppies'. But he hadn't exactly advertised that in the *Financial Times*. The police wouldn't be able to connect him with Rayburn. If Harry blew it and got himself sucked in as an accessory, what problem was that for Mason? That was Harry's problem.

He went out of the dining-room. Although he was using the phone in the room he called the study, he made sure Mrs. McGarrity was upstairs before he closed the door. There were no phones upstairs. It was taken at the second ring.

'Hullo.'

'Harry? Matt Mason.'

'God, am I glad you rang. I'm sweating blood here. I nearly phoned you. I'm sweating blood.'

'All right. I'm not buying a ticket for the opera. Just tell me what you want.'

Mason was intently trying to interpret Rayburn's silence. He knew that in the right mood Harry could be dominated the way some women could. The quietness in Rayburn's voice when he did speak made Mason think this might be one of those times.

'I was trying to tell you last night. The person who killed that girl Lawson is somebody I know.'

'Who?'

'It's not somebody you know. There's no point in telling you that.'

'Fine. I'm delighted to keep it that way. Cheerio.'

'Matt!'

Mason had no intention of putting the phone down.

'Matt. I know where he is. And I want to get him out of the city.

'So there's plenty of buses.'

'Come on. If you didn't buy a ticket for the opera, I didn't fucking buy one for the Pavilion.'

Now that both had decided where they weren't, they met across a silence. Mason felt the force of suppressed hysteria in Rayburn's voice. If he pushed too hard, the shrapnel might go anywhere.

'What is it you want?' he asked.

'I want your help.'

'Just like that.'

77

'Matt. I worked with you for a long time.'

'You got a nice pension. A pub to be exact.'

'I thought it was more than money.'

'Nothing's more than money.'

'I mean I thought we were friends.'

'And I thought you had brains. Harry, you're talking like a Valentine again. You're out of season.'

Mason waited to see what adjustment of attitude he might have to make.

'Matt. I need your help.'

'It's not my help you need. If you want your mate out of Glasgow, it's Houdini and the Holy Ghost you want. One of them'll never do it on his own. They'll be searching the tea-leaves for that one.'

'It's not that hard, and you know it. Matt, I want your help.'

'Sorry. I'm too busy looking after myself.'

Mason was trying to close the door on the situation quite casually, but he was also waiting to see if Rayburn was forcing against it.

'That's what I mean, Matt. For your own sake, you'll have to help.'

Mason's quietness was deep enough to put a corpse in.

'It must be a bad line, this,' he said.

'No. You heard me right, Matt. You see, I told him things. A lot of things. The way you operate was one of them. He knows more about you than your mother. It wouldn't be handy for you for the police to get hold of him.'

Expletives geysered out of Mason's mind but not one of them reached his mouth. He didn't know if Rayburn was telling the truth but, essentially, it didn't matter. The desperation to make that up was just as dangerous as the desperation to admit it if it were true. Either way, it had to be defused.

'That would seem to be it, then,' he said. 'Why bother to ask when you can demand?'

'You taught me, Matt. Start nice, you always said. As long as you know the heavy stuff's in the post.'

It was a nice time to get nostalgic—thanks for the memory.

'You're a good learner,' Mason said. The tone was just about right, he thought—bitter but resigned. It should be enough to convince Harry that he couldn't pretend to like it but he would accept it. 'So you'd better tell me who he is and where he is. And I'll see what I can do.'

'No, Matt. I don't think I'd better do that.'

'Listen. You just said I've got a stake in the game. So give me a hand.'

'Later, Matt. Later.'

'I don't understand that.'

'There's complications.'

Mason felt the way the whole situation had turned till it rested in the palm of Rayburn's hand. He sensed Rayburn's awareness of his own power and decided at once that that was a very temporary state of affairs. He held his rage in check.

'The thing is I can't get him to move just now. He's terrified out his wits. I think there's only one thing real to him. And that's her pants. He has them with him all the time. He just won't move.'

It occurred to Mason that some folk were just too delicate to be murderers. But he said nothing. If Rayburn thought he had all the cards, let him play them.

'I'm going to try to get him to co-operate. But it won't be easy. And what's worrying me is, I maybe don't have too much time before the police connect me with him. And that's me not too useful. I mean, I'll have to stay away. That's where you come in. You're my insurance, Matt. And I'll be yours, of course. I just want you ready when I ask you. To get him out. I know he'll be safe with you. Because I'll be busy telling the police nothing. Won't I? Matt?'

Mason liked the nerve of Harry to try to maintain such a delicate web of pressures. But that was all he liked.

'Okay,' he said.

'Thanks, Matt. I'll be in touch.'

Mason stood, forgetting to put the phone down. He wondered if perhaps Rayburn had got a wrong number, had thought he was talking to Pickford Removals, Ltd. He put the phone back.

He looked round the room, seeing himself. Again he added up the sum of what he had achieved. This time he got a different answer. All of it equalled a dead man. It was as simple as that.

19

'POPPIES' WAS IN a court behind Buchanan Street, along with a couple of abstruse businesses and an anonymous second-hand bookshop. It was the most recent example in Glasgow of a pub with adjoining disco, recent enough for Harkness not to know it. He knew 'The Griffin' and 'Joanna's' in Bath Street, 'Waves' and 'Spankies' at Customs House Quay. The pub here, 'The Maverick', was closed just now but the door to 'Poppies' was open.

As they climbed the stone stairs to the landing, they heard a droning noise. The double doors closed behind them in green baize. The motif was gambling. There were cushioned dice along the walls for sitting on. Each wall light held a poker-hand in glass. The floor of the small stage for the go-go dancers was a mosaic of a roulette wheel. At the end of the room the bar-counter was an enormous up-ended domino, double six.

'Love would appear to be a lottery,' Laidlaw said.

The noise was coming from a Hoover. The woman who worked it had her back to them. Context gave her an uncon-scious poignancy. She was elderly and fat. Each bare leg was a complex of varicose veins from too many children. Just by being there she was commenting ironically on all this jumped-up sophistication.

Laidlaw crossed and touched her shoulder. She was halfway to the ceiling before she realised what was happening. The kicked Hoover gave out gradually like a mechanical heart-attack.

'Oh my God, son,' she said. 'Ye should tell ma next o' kin before ye do that.'

But behind the feminine flummox, she was smiling already, a face as welcoming as an open fire.

'I'm sorry,' Laidlaw said. 'We're looking for Mr. Rayburn.'

'Aye, he's in. He'll be up in his office, likely. Oh dear, that's the most excitin' thing that's happened tae me since Ah fell out the shawl.'

They went up the few carpeted stairs to the bar area. There was a corridor on the left. Behind the third door they knocked at, a voice shouted, 'Hullo therr.'

Laidlaw opened the door. The room was well carpeted, curtained, nicely furnished. Opposite them, behind a desk, a young man was sitting in a swivel-chair. He was sallow-faced and his lank hair had more grease than a chip-pan. A black leather jacket sat on his body like a suit of armour, His calf-length boots rested on top of the desk. He was cleaning his fingernails with an ornamental knife.

'Aye, whit's the gemme?'

'We'd like to see Mr. Rayburn,' Laidlaw said.

'Ye got an appointment?'

'What is he?' Laidlaw said. 'A dentist?'

The young man was concentrating on looking very tough.

'Put your sneer away,' Laidlaw said. 'It's getting faded. Keep it for a good thing.'

The young man swung his feet onto the floor, stood up without haste, letting what he imagined was the tension build. He came out from behind the desk, knife vaguely drooping. Laidlaw flashed his police-card.

'How's that for a counter-punch?' he said. 'Son. You are about to lose in two ways. If you don't stop playing at Jack the Rippers, I'll take that paper-knife off you and shove it up your rectum. Then I'll arrest you in an ambulance. Tell him to come out of his hidey-hole.'

The young man put the knife on the desk.

'Ah'm supposed to check on people for Harry.' He was like a boy complaining that the game isn't being played according to the rules. 'Ye can get some weirdies in here.'

81

'I see that,' Laidlaw said, and waited.

'Harry! It's the polis.'

The door across the room opened and Harry Rayburn emerged. He would be in his forties, big and tired-looking, the black curling hair long and decoratively streaked with grey. He wore a shirt like an action-painting, sleeves rolled up to show impressive hairy forearms. Melted down, the silver buckle of his belt could have saved the economy.

'Mr. Rayburn?' Laidlaw showed him the card. 'I'm Detective Inspector Laidlaw. Crime Squad. This is Detective Constable Harkness. We're investigating a murder.'

Rayburn nodded.

'What's the connection with us?'

'Well, it's a girl called Jennifer Lawson. From Drumchapel. She was murdered on Saturday night. We believe she came dancing here that night. If she did, it's odds on she met the man here.'

'It's their money we take, no' their photies. Eh, Harry?'

Laidlaw looked at the young man as if he was a headache. Harry Rayburn looked impressively annoyed.

'Can it, Lennie! A lassie's dead.' Then to Laidlaw, 'Is there any way you think we can help?'

'This is the girl.' Laidlaw passed him the photograph. 'It's a million-to-one chance but we have to take it.'

Harry Rayburn shook his head.

'I'm sorry. But these young girls all look as if they came off an assembly-line to me. See one, you've seen them all.'

Laidlaw passed the photograph to Lennie who glanced at it and laid it on the desk.

'How many evening staff do you employ in here?'

'It's a variable. In general? Say, three behind the bar.' He seemed to find it difficult to work it out. 'A couple of go-go dancers when we're having that. They spell each other. Two on the door. Maybe two other stewards.'

Lennie shook with voiceless laughter and whispered, 'Stewards', to himself, shaking his head.

'You can give me a list?'

That seemed to be a problem.

'Not off-hand. Some of the boys are just doing it for a bit extra. Casual, like. You know? It'll take me time. The bloke who handles all that isn't in.'

'You're not the manager? It's your own place?'

Harry Rayburn smiled.

'Every crack in the ceiling's paid for. I started with "The Maverick" years ago. And now this place.'

'All right. Thanks for your help. I'm afraid you'll be getting more visitors. They can collect the information.'

He picked up the photograph.

'You don't know her?' Harkness asked.

'Naw,' Lennie said. 'Fanciable. Too late now, though, intit?'

'And what about this vibrantly sensitive young man?' Laidlaw said. 'What does he do for you, Mr. Rayburn?'

'Lennie's only in in the mornings. Looking after food and drink that comes in. That kind of thing.'

Rayburn seemed to be only just managing to contain his anger. When Laidlaw and Harkness had closed the door on them, they heard the anger break over Lennie's head.

'I think that Harry Rayburn could be a hard man,' Harkness said.

'Come on, Brian. Hard man? Mary Poppins with hair on her chest.'

'How do you make that out?'

'I saw him putting on his tough face at the door. It was a bad fit, too. That's the kind you get out of a book. Fig. 1: Curling the Upper Lip. It's for hiding something.'

'So what's he hiding?'

'After we've looked for somebody I want to see, you can check in, Brian. See what's happening.'

'So what's he hiding?'

'So what's he hiding?' Laidlaw said. 'When found, make a note of.'

20

FOR HARKNESS LUNCH in the city-centre meant a pub. There were plenty to choose from. But 'Miranda's' was an old-fashioned unlicensed restaurant. He hadn't been in it before. He wasn't sorry. There were a lot of women with shopping-bags and a few businessmen who looked as if they weren't doing much business. The waitresses wore black with white collars and cuffs.

Harkness drank a glass of grapefruit juice that was oily enough to cook with, and said, 'So what's the idea?'

Laidlaw looked up from his soup. Harkness looked round the restaurant.

'The eating-house that time forgot. What've you got against yourself?'

'Some women,' Laidlaw said, 'take Sweetex in their coffee after a five-course meal. This is *my* pathetic token gesture. The best thing on the menu here's no drink. Any word?'

'There's nothing yet. I saw Bob Lilley. Says to tell you they nailed those blokes at Dumfries. Know how they were doing it? Very cute. Left their own car, stole two others. Drove into England, did the jobs. Met, transferred the stuff into one car, abandoned the other one. Brought the lot back to Dumfries, did the final transfer, abandoned the other stolen car.'

'Simple,' Laidlaw said. 'I wish we were up against something as straightforward as that.'

'We didn't get much this morning, did we?'

'How could we? Just now we're plumbing puddles.'

'Not a thing.'

'You don't know that. We've got to keep all the possibilities in the air just now. Don't let any of them fall out of mind. We just keep walking and talking.'

'Asking questions.'

'It's the questions you don't ask that count. People don't *give* answers. They betray them. When they think they're answering one thing, they're giving an honest answer to something else. Our problem is we don't know enough yet to work out what they're saying. So we have to try to remember everything till some kind of shape emerges. All we've got so far is that Harry Rayburn is too inefficient, too casual, too hard. That's maybe something, it's maybe nothing.'

Their waitress put down Laidlaw's roast beef, Harkness's fish.

'What is your secret, great man?' Harkness asked.

'Brains. Let's eat.' He looked at his roast beef. 'In a manner of speaking.'

After a couple of forkfuls, Laidlaw said, 'John Rhodes. That's who we'll go and see. He's an honourable thug. He won't like this kind of thing. He might lend us his eyes and his ears for a week.'

'I've heard of him.'

'I would hope so. Have you met him?'

'No.'

'You were talking about hard men. I'll show you hard. When he's in a bad mood, you phone the army.'

21

LENNIE SAID, 'THE heid bummer wis called Laidlaw. An' the ither wan wis some Harkness.'

Matt Mason sat very still at his desk. Only his right hand moved, exactly aligning the edges of the three desk diaries that contained no entries., re-positioning the pen-set that was never used. He hardly needed diaries when he had a memory like a telephone directory. He hadn't much use for pens when he could write a cheque with his mouth or serve notice with a nod. But they were furniture he liked, like the filing-cabinet nobody else had ever seen inside, the drinks-cupboard in the corner and the racing-prints on the walls.

Lennie looked out of the window. Because the office was a basement, all he could see of West Regent Street was a parade of legs. He passed the time by picking out the ones he wouldn't mind being between. Through the wall in the main office the tannoy was whispering its commentary on the two o'clock at Newmarket.

'That's some Laidlaw as well,' Mason said. 'You can take it from me. I don't specially want to mess about with him. He's bother. How big did Harry handle him?'

'Very quiet. Ah think maybe Harry wis feart. But no' me.'

Lennie was laughing. Mason wasn't.

'Very clever,' Mason said. 'What did you say?'

Lennie shrugged. He sensed the ambiguity of Mason's attitude but he couldn't resist the bravado.

'No skin off my arse if some scrubber's coughed it. Ah let 'im know that.'

'Clown!' Mason gave him the word as if it came out of a blow-pipe.

'Whit's wrang, boss?'

'You've got no brains, son, that's what. If you met Goliath, you'd put the head on his kneecap. What do you want to cause trouble for? People don't like trouble. Be nice to people. Then when you're not nice, it means that wee bit more.'

'Be nice tae the fuzz? Are you gettin' saft, boss?'

Lennie's laughter ran against a silence. He tried again, 'Eh-heh,' like someone knocking at the door of an empty room.

'You want to find out?' Mason's voice was so gentle it wouldn't have broken a cobweb.

'Whit's the gemme? Ah wis only—'

Mason held up his right forefinger.

'I could beat you with that.'

'But. Listen—'

The finger moved down to point at Lennie.

'No. You listen. Wee. Silly. Boy. Any more cheek out of you, and I'll stop your comic money. You better get brains, son. Even if you've got to steal them. I don't pay you to be stupid.'

Lennie said nothing, stayed perfectly still, knew himself hanging over the sheer drop of Mason's anger. Mason sat over his desk, staring at it.

'Surrounded with balloons,' he said, fogging the glass top. 'What am I?'

Lennie said nothing. He knew the way Mason sometimes used people like a mirror in which to examine himself. Mirrors shouldn't talk back.

'I'm a legitimate bookmaker. I've got my shops. I run the business. All right. But you know and I know that I've got other interests. And if we know, do you think the C.I.D. have no idea? I've got fingers in a lot of pies. If I get just one of them cut off, I lose the lot. Because the blood'll bring them to me. And that could be nasty. I've had to arrange some accident-insurance along the way. Some people live awful careless.

Never underestimate the polis, son. They're not daft. They're waiting for me. I'd like to keep them waiting.'

Lennie stayed silent.

'I don't want them encouraged, I want them turned away politely. I live in a big fancy house, son. But it's made of exploding bricks. Set one of them off and the whole thing'll come down on my head. Delicacy. That's what you need. That's why I don't go in for heavy breathing. That's why the carry-on about this lassie is such a mess. It could blow up.'

Mason took out a cigarette, threw one to Lennie. Leaning over for a light, Lennie supposed he had permission to speak. But he had no idea what to say because he couldn't begin to see what the problem was. To him Mason was worrying without cause.

'But whit's that lassie got to do wi' us?' he asked. 'Ah don't get it, boss.'

Mason smoked, looking at him.

'How long have you been with Rayburn, now? Months. Right? And what are you there for?'

'Tae keep an' eye on him. Without him knowin'.'

'Wee test, son,' Mason said. 'Just to see if you're keeping up with your work. This morning. Has Harry Rayburn done anything unusual?'

Lennie wondered.

'He seems kinna nervous.'

Mason was waiting. Lennie knew he had to think of something.

'There wis a wee thing. Nothin' much. He asked me to go out an' get some grub for 'im. An' then he changed 'is mind. Said no' tae bother. He's never asked me tae do anything like that before.'

Mason nodded.

'The food,' Mason said, 'was for the fella that killed that lassie from Drumchapel.'

Mason watched Lennie's eyes, seeing the implications jostle impossibly in Lennie's mind like a football crowd all trying to get through the Boys' Gate at one time. He sat and let it happen.

'But. Ye mean?'

Mason nodded again and thought he'd better relieve the congestion.

'It was Harry's boy-friend that killed her.'

'That means?'

'That means he's dangerous to me. So I want to know where he is. Rayburn's bound to go and see him again today. He won't be able to keep away. You follow him and tell me where the boy is.'

Suddenly realising he was a participant in a drama he hadn't known existed, Lennie struggled for a stance that would match events, wanted to rush the centre of the stage.

'Ah could duff Harry up a bit,' he said. 'Get it out him that way.'

'Grow up, son.' Mason was very angry. 'That's all you ever want to do. Lay into people with your wee jumping-jacks. Listen. Very carefully. The last thing you do is upset Big Harry Rayburn in *any* way. Because if you do, you've had it. If he even *suspects* you're interested, you better catch the next train to the moon. You've got today and that's all. You have to tell me the night where that boy is. See that you do.'

Lennie was still paralysed by the implications of it all.

'When ye find 'im,' he said. 'Are ye goin' to . . . ?'

His eyes were wide in enthralled anticipation of violence. It was what he had instead of an orgasm, Mason thought.

'Lennie!' Mason held up both hands. 'Don't think beyond what you have to do today. I don't want your head seizing up with two ideas. Just do what I've told you. And do it well. On your way out, tell Eddie to come in and see me.'

The betting-shop was busy. That was one reason why Lennie had difficulty locating Eddie in it. The other was Eddie. He was a natural member of any crowd, an identikit of middle age. He was one of those experience doesn't sharpen into facial idiosyncrasy, just erodes into anonymity. Lennie didn't find him. He found Lennie.

'Punters is mugs,' Eddie said at Lennie's ear. 'Aren't they?'

'The man wants you,' Lennie said.

Eddie turned and went. Lennie worked his way through the people in the shop and came up into West Regent Street very carefully, as if invisible cameras were tracking him. In the private office Eddie waited patiently while Mason sat staring at the glass-top of his desk. The room was chilly with silence. Eddie was glad Mason wasn't thinking about him.

'Eddie. A bad situation. It was Harry Rayburn's boy-friend that murdered the girl from Drumchapel.'

'That's oor pigeon?'

'No. But it could lead them to our loft.'

'Harry Rayburn's no' directly connected wi' us.'

'But he has been. All right, he was pensioned off. But he didn't hand his memory in at the pay-desk.'

'You think Big Harry wid shop you? Where wid he find the guts? His hert widny fill a contact lens.'

Mason didn't mind Eddie's questions. They were the measurements a good workman makes before he tackles a job. Eddie was a tradesman Mason respected, a competent fixer of things whose curiosity went no further than the necessary dimensions within which he would work. He brought no more tension to the job than a plumber would. He was a contented man, who did his work and took his wages, drank a bit and liked the television.

'I don't know. But his boy-friend might.'

'He knows about you?'

'I'm not sure. But there's pillow-talk. Who knows what the big man didn't say when that bastard was half-roads up his arse? His head could've unravelled like a ball of wool.'

'It's chancy,' Eddie said.'

'And I'm no punter. I'm a bookie. I want him taken out.'

Eddie raised his eyebrows and lowered them. The point was taken.

'Lennie's away to find out where the boy's hiding. I want somebody who can take advantage of the information.'

Eddie was thinking.

'The way I see it,' Mason said, 'it's hard to care about what's dead. Harry shouldn't give us any trouble once the boy's away. He'll remember to be terrified again. Everybody does sometime. The only thing we need to guarantee is that nobody can ever connect the thing with us. Not the C.I.D., not Harry Rayburn.'

Eddie waited for the clincher.

'I want you to come up with somebody that'll kill a man without asking questions. And without knowing too many answers. He's never to have been connected with us in any way before. And it's better still if he's never done this kind of thing before. And he works on his own.'

For the first time something other than bland acceptance flickered on Eddie's face.

'Apply care of God,' he said.

'The money'll be good. But don't talk prices till you've seen me.'

'It's a big order.'

'It's a big problem,' Mason said. 'Let me know what you think. You can draw up a list of possibles.'

'Have ye got a bit o' confetti?' Eddie asked.

Mason smiled. He liked Eddie.

22

'OVER HERE A minute,' Laidlaw said.

They were at Glasgow Cross. After waiting a little while, they managed to get across the street to the pedestrian area in front of Krazy House. Laidlaw stopped before the small grey building Harkness had always assumed was on the site of the old Tolbooth—a kind of midget tower with a small balustrade at the top and above that the figure of a unicorn.

'How about that?' Laidlaw said.

Harkness was puzzled.

'The inscription,' Laidlaw explained.

Harkness read the words carved on the stone: '*Nemo me impune lacessit.*' He knew it was Latin but didn't know what it meant.

'No one assails me with impunity,' Laidlaw said. 'Wha daur meddle wi me? Did you know that was there?'

Harkness shook his head.

'I like the civic honesty of that.' Laidlaw was smiling. 'That's the wee message carved on the heart of Glasgow. Visitors are advised not to be cheeky.'

The message gained force as they went beyond the Cross. At that point the Trongate divides into two streets running east, the Gallowgate on the north, London Road on the south. The sense of a choice is illusory. Both lead to the same waste of slum tenements hopefully punctuated with redevelopments, like ornamental fountains in a desert.

They walked along London Road and then into the area
between it and Gallowgate, called Calton. Harkness felt what
he always felt going east beyond the Cross, the sense of siege.
Small shops and cafés had wire netting on their windows. Some
pubs presented blank walls to the street with small, netted
windows about ten feet above the ground. Bleak tenements
mouldered among razed patches. And on the streets he saw too
many of the walking wounded.

Laidlaw had been checking on a few pubs as he went, looking
for somebody he called Wee Eck. As they walked, Laidlaw was
talking.

'Little Rhodesia,' he had said.

'What do you mean?'

'A lot of this is John Rhodes territory. A kind of separate
state. He did the U.D.I. before Ian Smith thought of it.'

'Come on.'

'All right. But I wouldn't go into any of these pubs and spit
on his name if I were you.'

The idea would have been much more bizarre to Harkness if
he hadn't been walking here when he heard it. It was the kind of
place where someone alone would be very careful how he looked
at people.

'The rule of fear, is it?' Harkness asked.

'Not entirely. Although that's a very intelligent response to
have to John. But he's more complicated than that. He does
have certain rules. He's not fair but he has a kind of justice. He
could've been a much bigger crook. Only he won't do certain
things. So he's settled for a level of crookery that still allows
him the luxury of a morality.'

'What kind of rules do you mean?'

'Oh, too complicated for me to fathom. Only John and God
know. And I think God's pretty puzzled most of the time. Just
trying to chat affably to John's like walking through a mine-
field. But I know the rules are there. I've caught the odd
glimpse. Like I heard of a silly man who gave John cheek. And
John took no steps.'

'Why was that?'

'He was a civilian. John knows how special he is in that

93

department. He knows a liberty when he sees one coming at him. And that's just about everybody else. Another thing is, he never claims people in their houses. The wife and weans are sacrosanct with him. Sex is another thing. He's about as permissive as John Knox.'

religious name?

'He sounds like quite a fella.'

'Let's hope you can find out for yourself. Crash helmets on.'

They were at a pub which from the outside looked as inviting as a public toilet. The small windows, well above eye level, seemed suspicious of the daylight. The walls were rough grey plaster, obviously quite recently applied, not so much redecoration as refortification. The name along the top was from before, written in old-fashioned script, 'The Gay Laddie'.

'Do yourself a favour,' Laidlaw said. 'Don't misinterpret the name.'

There was no danger. They went into more than a place. It was a precipitation of a way of life, the area they had walked in filtered through the old-fashioned swing doors and stylised in one room. Physically, it was a shrine to the Thirties, when the Depression had spawned the razor-slashers and brought King Billy of Bridgeton to prominence. The dominant fixture was wood, from the long, stained bar to the tables spread around the place. Here, Formica hadn't been invented.

Just about as tangible as the furnishings, and sharing their unadaptable solidity, was the atmosphere. Being new to the atmosphere, Harkness found himself trying to define it. The tension you felt had nothing to do with potential criminality, the fear of robbery or mugging. It was much more immediate than that. It came from knowing at once that you were in the presence of a lot of physical pride, a crowd of it, so that you sensed the need to move carefully, in case you bumped an ego. This room was the resort of men who hadn't much beyond a sense of themselves and weren't inclined to have that sense diminished.

Harkness recognised a feeling he had experienced in other East-End pubs, and understood precisely where the tension came from. It came from the realisation that just by coming in you had shucked the protection of your social status. In this place your only credentials were yourself.

Three young men at the bar were busy establishing theirs. Each had a tartan shirt, a battledress-style denim jacket, wide trousers worn high and rubber-soled boots. It seemed to be the uniform of their private army, which was at the moment occupying 'The Gay Laddie' with that youthful aggressiveness that spends a lot of its time advertising for trouble. They weren't talking, they were broadcasting, and their bodies seemed to take up more room than they needed.

They were the focal point of the pub for Harkness. But Laidlaw saw them as peripheral, a bit of accidental tourism. Their careless provocativeness suggested to him they might have dropped in from a housing scheme on Saturn. He saw the heart of the place in the comparative quietness surrounding them, in the few others sitting at the tables and the one other man at the bar. He was someone whose name Laidlaw had never found out but he recognised him from the scar that ran down his left cheek and under the chin.

Laidlaw went to the far end of the counter where it turned at an angle to the main stretch of the bar, beside the door to the snug. The barman had begun to polish a glass. He came slowly towards them, an ageing fat man with big forearms under the rolled-up sleeves.

'Has John Rhodes been in today?' Laidlaw asked quietly.

The barman kept on cleaning the glass, not looking up.

'Who's lookin' for 'im?' he asked.

'Don't piss me about, Charlie,' Laidlaw said. 'I didn't come in here to see a bad cowboy picture. You know who I am.'

'I know who ye are. But who's lookin' for 'im?'

Laidlaw kept his silence until the barman eventually looked up, as if to make sure that Laidlaw was still there.

'Maybe you should tell me the code,' Laidlaw said. 'Then we could talk ov that.'

'There's lookin' an' lookin',' the barman said, back at his glass. 'Are ye Laidlaw lookin' or are ye a polisman lookin'?'

'Oh, I'm Laidlaw looking. A friend looking for a friend.'

'Well, yer friend should be in the day. Whit'll ye have?'

Laidlaw bought Harkness the half-pint he wanted and took a whisky himself. The man with the scar went out. The barman nodded them through to the snug. It was empty. They sat down on the ribbed wooden seats. Laidlaw winked at Harkness and said in a voice hushed in mock reverence, 'I think we're getting an audience.'

A few minutes later the man with the scar came in with a pint. He nodded and sat down apart from them. Laidlaw made no attempt to speak to him. Then a new man came in. Harkness observed him.

Harkness reckoned him at five-ten-a-half, neither big nor small. He looked very firm but not very heavy. The suit wasn't noticeable but nicely cut. His face was almost completely unmarked—only a line across the right eyebrow where the hair didn't grow. He still had all his hair, black, in unfashionable waves. He would be about forty. Harkness added it all up and got the wrong answer.

'John'll be in in a minute,' the wavy-haired man said and sat down beside the man with the scar.

John Rhodes, when he came, was big and fair. His height surprised Harkness, in whose experience the hardest men tended to come in smaller sizes. He had wondered if it was because tall men already had an unearned status that made them not so keen on that instant hazarding of everything which finally defines the hardness of a man in the terms of the street. But John Rhodes refuted any theory. He was simply and categorically himself.

The kind of attention the three young men in the bar were desperately paging, he took as his right. The essence of him was containment—the measured nod to Laidlaw, the look at Harkness, the brief gesture to the other two men, an ability to move with nerveless exactitude. The face was slightly pockmarked. The eyes were pleasantly blue.

'Hullo, you,' he said to Laidlaw and sat down across the table from them. 'Ye'll hiv a drink.'

'A whisky for me,' Laidlaw said. 'With water.'

'I won't bother, thank you,' Harkness said.

The blue eyes turned on him like a blowtorch lit but not yet shooting flame.

'He'll have a pint,' Laidlaw said. 'He's such a fierce drinker.

When he says he won't bother, he means he'll just stick to the beer.'

'Is he age? John Rhodes asked.

Harkness began to wonder. As the wavy-haired man nodded through the door of the snug, Harkness realised that John Rhodes hadn't been making a suggestion, just stating a fact. They were visitors to his territory. He made the etiquette. Harkness became conscious that he and the other two men were just witnesses at a special kind of confrontation. The tension was that of a contest. Harkness didn't know the rules but he understood that he had already weakened Laidlaw's position by breaking one of them. He resolved not to be an embarrassment again.

The barman brought in the drinks and shut the sliding door as he went back out. Harkness felt surrounded. They drank in silence for a moment. John Rhodes was drinking port, Harkness thought.

'You'll be wondering why we're here,' Laidlaw said.

'Ah thought ye might tell me.'

'I think I will. You know there's been a girl murdered.'

'It wis in the papers.'

'It's about that then.'

'I'm not guilty, your honour.'

The other two men laughed and Harkness smiled. Laidlaw did nothing but wait.

'It's about that then.'

'Ye're repeating yerself.'

'No. I'm just keeping my train of thought in the face of facetious interruption.'

There was a silence. Harkness realised suddenly that the chilly core of it was 'facetious'. It was a word John Rhodes didn't know. That was why Laidlaw had chosen it.

'All right, college-boy. Go on wi' yer story.'

Laidlaw had brought out his cigarettes and offered them round to no takers. He lit up his own.

'When does the big picture stert?' John Rhodes asked.

The two men laughed.

'John,' Laidlaw said. 'I could do without this. Especially when you bring your studio audience.'

97

'The door's just behind ye,' John Rhodes said pleasantly.

'Oh aye.'

'If ye don't like the cabarett, don't come tae the pub.'

What puzzled Harkness most was that the impasse had no bitterness about it. Laidlaw and John Rhodes sat looking at each other, assessing. Two things occurred to Harkness: how big the gulf between them was, and that the bridge that made it possible for them to cross it was a kind of respect. Inhabiting opposed moralities, they could still appreciate each other. They were two different qualities of force, but evenly matched.

'Suit yourself,' Laidlaw said, and finished his drink. 'I won't make the same mistake twice.'

Before he could rise, John Rhodes had taken his glass from his hand and passed it to the wavy-haired man.

'Don't forget the watter,' he said. 'Touchy Jack Laidlaw. Come on. Ye had somethin' to ask me.'

'Like a favour,' Laidlaw said. 'But I *was* asking. Don't get the impression I'm begging. It's maybe the way I'm sitting.'

The man came back through with the whisky and put it in front of Laidlaw. John Rhodes was smiling at Laidlaw's remark.

'All right, Jack,' he said.

Laidlaw took the photograph and passed it across to John Rhodes, who looked at it carefully and nodded, smiling softly.

'Know who she's like,' he said. He gave the photograph to the other two men. 'D'ye know who she *is* like?' They were puzzling over it. 'Ye've seen oor Jeanie's lassie?'

'Oh aye. She is,' the wavy-haired man said.

'She's very like 'er,' John Rhodes said. 'Only Karen's fairer than that. She wis a nice-lookin' wee lassie.'

The man with the scar put the photograph on the table beside John Rhodes and Laidlaw let it lie there.

'Seventeen,' Laidlaw said. 'An only child. She was all her mother and father had. All she did wrong was go to the dancing. And you should've seen her when we found her. Used her like a lavatory and then killed her.'

Harkness saw John Rhodes looking back down at the photograph.

98

'The reason I'm here, is this. There are a lot of other daughters in this city.'

John Rhodes looked up slowly from the photograph.

'We've got to take this man out as fast as possible. I know the polis aren't your first love. But we're both on the same side in this one. You hear things that we don't. All I'm asking is if you hear anything that could help us, you let us know.'

John Rhodes lifted up the photograph again.

'The thing is,' he said, 'I don't mix a lot wi' folk like that.' He put the photograph back down. 'The other thing is. Ah've never grassed on anybody in ma life.'

'This isn't a rival team, John. This is a different kind of operation altogether. This isn't just another scuffler. There's another thing. The polis are going to be stepping on everybody's heels from now on. We won't get back to normal healthy villainy till this is over.'

'There's nothin' in it for me.'

'Nothing but honour.'

They were both smiling.

'Ah've always had that.'

'That's not something you get to keep. You've got to earn it every day.'

John Rhodes handed the photograph back to Laidlaw.

'Ah'll let ye know,' he said.

'I'm in the Burleigh Hotel this week,' Laidlaw said. 'Can I buy you all a drink?'

'Nah. Ah've got ma reputation tae think o'.'

The interview was over. Harkness gulped down the rest of his pint in case it wasn't etiquette to leave it. He had pulled open the door of the snug, noticing the three young men still harmonising toughness, when Laidlaw said, 'Brian.' They left by the outside door of the snug.

As they walked, Harkness said, 'That was some weird conversation.'

'One of John's pastimes. Like hand-wrestling without the hands. It's maybe that he's got so good at the violence, he's taken it on to a kind of mental plane. Like putting the head on somebody by Yoga.'

They were coming back towards the Cross along Gallowgate. 'The Happiness Chinese Restaurant' hadn't opened for the day yet. Harkness was still absorbing what had happened.

'Sorry about that at the beginning,' Harkness said. 'Refusing the drink. Maybe you should've given me a book of rules.'

'Forget it. He would've rewritten them anyway. I mean, I tried a bit of the hearts and flowers there. But how do you know what you're doing with John? You're liable to pluck a heart-string and find that's what operates his right hook.'

'The honour bit surprised me.'

'Aye. that was a bit heavy, wasn't it? I felt a bit like Baden-Powell with that. But he seemed tuned into it. Amazingly enough. Ah well. It's Sarah Stanley visiting-time, D.C. Harkness.'

'Wee Horrurs' seemed to be doing a good trade in children's clothes.

'Do you think he can help?' Harkness asked.

'He can if he will. Nobody better equipped to find things out. An ear in a lot of pubs. But you can't presume about which way *he* will jump.'

'Where's the car?' Harkness asked.

'What car?' Laidlaw said.

In the snug, John Rhodes said, 'No' bad, that Laidlaw. For a polisman.'

'It's that lassie's father Ah wis tellin' ye about,' the man with the scar said. 'Wi' that mug in the 'pub.'

'Ah know.'

'None o' our business, John,' the wavy-haired man said.

'Ye're right it isny,' the man with the scar said.

'Ah decide that.'

They sat quietly while he decided.

'Ah want yese to find out everythin' ye can aboot this.'

'John!' The man with the scar shook his head.

'Why?'

'Ah'll decide why efter. Ah want ye to find out. An' don't be hauf-herted aboot it. Ah want results. An' Ah want them the day afore the morra.'

They went out. John Rhodes finished his drink and went through to the bar. He gave the glass to the barman.

'An' see's the paper, Charlie.'

With the paper and a fresh drink, he went and sat at a table. It was closing time. The bar was empty except for the three young men. They were noisy with drink. It occurred to him they had done everything to get noticed except let off squibs. It was a neutral thought to him. That's what boys were like.

He read the article about Jennifer Lawson again. He hated that kind of thing. He hated the people who did it. He thought they should be put down, like rabid dogs. But that wouldn't happen if they caught him. He would get some years in prison or some other place. Steal enough money and they would put you away for thirty years. Kill a girl and they would try to understand. He hated the dishonesty of it. Money bought everything, even the luxury of being able to pretend that everybody really meant well and evil was an accident. He knew different. He had had to, to survive.

His rage came on him suddenly, as it always did, an instinctive reaction he relied on more than any other. Whenever the contradictions became too much for him, that terrible anger was waiting to resolve things into immediacy, confrontation. Its force came from his preparedness always to stand by what *he* was, at least. It also implied an invitation for everybody else to do the same. That at least, it seemed to him, would be a kind of honesty, for what he hated most were pretences, the lies that people get away with—the lie of being a hard man when you weren't, the lie of being honest when you weren't, the lie of believing in the goodness of other people when you didn't have to face them at their worst. Now he saw the way the courts would handle this case as another kind of pretence. It shouldn't be allowed. He would like to do something about that.

Charlie was having a problem clearing the bar. The three young men still had some beer in their glasses.

'Come on now, boys,' Charlie was saying. 'Ye'll have tae go. It's past time.'

'Piss off,' one of the young men said. 'Ye sold us the stuff. Give us fuckin' time tae drink it.'

'Lock us in if ye like,' another one said. 'We'll look after the place for ye.'

101

They all laughed.

'John?' Charlie referred it to him.

'Give the man a brek, boays,' he said, still looking at his paper. 'He's got his licence tae think o'. Drink up.'

'Oho,' the first one said. 'His master's voice. Ah don't see you drinkin' up.'

John Rhodes looked up at them. They were day-trippers, probably looking for a story they could take back to their mates like a holiday photo. They looked like three but they were really only one, the boy who had spoken first, the one in the green tartan shirt. The other two were running on his engine.

'Ah work here,' John Rhodes said. 'Now on ye go.'

He looked back at his paper.

'Away tae fuck!'

As soon as the one in the green shirt had said it, they all knew a terrible mistake had been made. There was complete silence for perhaps four seconds. Then John Rhodes' hands compressed the paper he had been holding into a ball. That crackling was as frightening as an explosion. When he dropped the paper onto the floor, the courage of everybody else in the room went with it.

He crossed very quickly to the doorway. The swing doors had been pinned back to let customers out. He went past them to the two leaves of the outside door, kicked them shut and pushed home the bolt. He turned back into the pub.

'Ye want it, ye've got it,' he said. 'Now ye don't *get* out.'

It was already too late for the young men to negotiate the saving of face. He left them no room for that. All they could do was admit their terror to themselves. The shock of it had left one of them struggling for breath.

'Charlie. Get a mop and a pail o' watter. For Ah'm gonny batter these bastards up and down this pub.'

'Now, John. Please, John,' Charlie said.

The incredible turn-around of the man they had insulted pleading for their safety finished them. One of them whispered, 'Naw, mister.' The one with the green shirt was trying not to admit it to himself. But he looked at John Rhodes and knew himself miserable with fear. With the dim light coming in from

102

the small, high windows fuzzing his fair hair, and the blue eyes flaring, he looked like a psychopathic angel.

'Please. Just let us go. An' we'll no' come back,' the one with the green shirt said.

There was a pause while John Rhodes wrestled with his own rage. The complete, honest admission of their fear was what finally calmed him.

'Apologise tae the man,' he said.

They said it in chorus, 'We're sorry', like a lesson in recitation.

'And we're sorr—' the one in the green shirt began.

'Don't apologise tae me,' John Rhodes said. 'As far as Ah'm concerned, ye're jist on probation.'

He nodded to Charlie. Charlie opened the door to let them out, although it seemed hardly necessary to him. They were so liquid with fear, Charlie felt he could have poured them out below the door.

23

As THEY SETTLED themselves upstairs in the bus, Harkness was still shaking his head and sighing quietly.

'Well, think of it this way,' Laidlaw said. 'There are tourists and travellers. Tourists spend their lives doing a Cook's Tour of their own reality. Ignoring their slums. Travellers make the journey more slowly, in greater detail. Mix with the natives. A lot of murderers are, among other things, travellers. They've become terrifyingly real for themselves. Their lives are no longer a hobby. Poor bastards. To come at them, you've got to become a traveller too. Think of this as a wee ritual exercise for opting out of tourism. A car is psychologically sterile, a mobile oxygen-tent. A bus is septic. You've got to subject yourself to other people's prejudices, run the risk of a mad conductor beating you to death with his ticket-punch. Two twenties, please.'

'Now have ye thought about this?' the conductor said. 'There's still time tae get aff. We stop for tea at the end o' this run. Ah usually like tae go berserk at least once before ma tea-break.'

Laidlaw and Harkness laughed.

'Ah'll pit yer name in for a Ministry of Transport Medal then,' the conductor said.

When he was gone, Laidlaw said, 'Of course, the Underground's worse. Then you're sealed off in a revolving tube with everybody else's hang-ups. Like laboratory specimens.'

Harkness shook his head.

'And here was me thinking you just liked the view from upstairs on a bus.'

'There is that,' Laidlaw said. 'I like sitting up at the front and playing at being the driver.'

Laidlaw lit a cigarette.

'Right. There are two basic assumptions you can make. Very basic. One is that it's a fruit-machine job. Sweet mystery of life and all that. That there was no connection between the villain and the victim. Except a time and a place. The lassie was the victim of a kind of sexual hit-and-run job. All right. If that's the case, *we've* got no chance anyway. It's up to Milligan and his soldier-ants to take the situation apart leaf by leaf. Except that, for me, putting your faith in Milligan is just a fancy term for despair.'

Harkness was niggled by the reference to Milligan but he let it go.

'So for you and me to be any use at all, we have to take the second assumption. That there *is* a connection. What happened in the park didn't just fall from out the sky one day. It's got roots. And we can find these roots. So we're going to make that assumption.'

'Right. We've made that assumption,' Harkness offered.

'All right. We don't know who the bloke is. He's no help. We know the lassie, but she's not saying much. But we know folk who knew her. And if she did have a connection with the bloke, there must be somebody around who knows about it. Must be. Who?'

'Her family,' Harkness said.

'You didn't see the father last night?' Laidlaw asked.

'No. Only the mother.'

'I saw her yesterday. What's left of her after Bud Lawson's been mincing her ego for years. He's an amazing monolith, that big man. The kind of father who eats his young to protect them from the world. If anything was going on with his daughter, he'd be the last to know. But if you could get the mother to talk, she might have something to tell. I'd like to try that. But first I'd like to know more, to have something to talk about. You'd have to know enough to be able to tease the rest out of her.'

'Maybe that's where Sarah Stanley comes in.'

'I hope so. I was going to say her friends are the other obvious area. Except that they don't seem to be there. One friend. Was that all you got last night, too?'

'Aye. She said she was a very quiet wee lassie. Kept herself by herself, she said.'

'One friend. Why aren't there more of them? Or are there? She must've been a funny wee lassie, right enough.'

'Well, if your theory's going to work, a lot depends on wee Sarah Stanley.'

'Aye. We'll have to be very thorough with Sarah, I doubt. No marks in this wee test for ambiguous answers.'

24

IT WAS LENNIE'S first bookshop. Coming to and going from 'Poppies', he had seen it often enough before but had never gone in. Inside, it felt strange. The mustiness oppressed him. That people came in to buy this junk was unbelievable. He felt the discomfort that comes from being surrounded by what you don't understand. His life was an attempt to play a single received rôle: Glaswegian hard man. Unfamiliar backgrounds made him forget his lines.

The other two people in the shop didn't help. There was a tall man with a soft hat and a briefcase at one of the shelves in the middle of the shop. He had his back to Lennie. The only other person was the old man at the desk, who looked up over his glasses as Lennie came in. They made Lennie feel like an actor who has wandered into the wrong play.

He stationed himself at the shelf beside the window and hid behind a book. He picked a big one, the kind that would have been handy for doing press-ups, opened it and held it up without glancing at it. He was concentrating on looking through the window across the court to 'Poppies'. It took a bit of concentration. It occurred to him that you could have planted tatties in the glass. He knew that Harry Rayburn was due to come out and he had left deliberately just ahead of him. Lennie shouldn't have long to wait. Now and again he flicked a page.

'They're easier to read if you hold them the right way up, son.'

Lennie turned to see a face like Walt Disney's idea of a grandfather. He would have done for the old man who made Pinocchio.

'Ah'm Chinese,' Lennie said. 'Okay?'

But he turned the book round. The old man smiled and went on taking out books and putting them back in exactly the same place. He started to whistle, very tunelessly. The sound didn't suit him. It was jauntily gallous.

'Through the back.'

Lennie couldn't be sure at first that he had heard it. The old man was back to whistling aimlessly. Lennie thought he must have imagined it. But it came again, very low and quick, hidden in among his whistling.

'They're through the back.'

Lennie looked at the old man. Now he was nodding while he whistled. Lennie looked round. The man in the soft hat was still standing in the same place, with his back to them. Lennie looked back at the old man.

The old man's mouth formed, 'Okay?' and he winked. Lennie shook his head. The old man wound himself up for more whistling and Lennie knew he was going to say something else. Lennie couldn't understand it. It seemed the only way he could talk was by whistling. It was like a very special impediment. Now he was in full whistle.

'The special stuff is through the back,' the old man hissed, and was whistling instantly.

Looking away from him, Lennie suddenly saw Harry Rayburn emerge from 'Poppies'. Lennie watched the direction he was taking and calculated that he had just time to put this mental old sod in his place. He chose his cruncher and put the book back roughly.

'Ye're aff yer heid,' Lennie snarled. 'Even yer books is a' secondhand. There's no' a new yin among them.'

As he reached the door, the old man called quietly, 'Away, ya ignorant get,' and then nodded smilingly to the man, who had turned round.

Rayburn was walking quickly. Lennie just managed to avoid getting knocked down as he crossed Argyle Street. Because the car blared its horn, Lennie dived into a shop doorway and counted five. When he looked back out, Rayburn was still walking. He had noticed nothing. Lennie smiled to himself and hurried until he was lying about twenty yards behind.

Rayburn crossed Argyle Street and went into Marks and Spencer's. Lennie panicked. He didn't want to chance going in and meeting Rayburn. But he didn't know how many doors the place had. He started sprinting round the building. There were three separate entrances. He spun like someone caught in a revolving door. He hesitated, and then ran back to the first door. Nothing there. He started running back to the second door, checked himself, and returned to the first. Still nothing there. He waited. A dread seized him that Rayburn was walking calmly out another door and out of sight. Lennie raced, his body arching like a bow. Nothing. He was beginning to run with sweat. What was he buying, the shop? He ran to the third door. There was still no sign of Rayburn. Lennie ran back. He was leaning against one wall of the shop quite close to collapse when Rayburn stepped out in front of him, carrying a plastic bag.

Lennie straightened up. The rest was easy, except that Lennie, intent on watching Rayburn, bumped into an old woman and was detained by her until he almost missed Rayburn turning a corner, but he didn't.

Rayburn took him on an elaborate detour that brought them eventually to Bridgegate. Lennie could hardly believe it had been so close all the time. One moment Rayburn was walking past a derelict building and the next he wasn't. It took Lennie a few seconds to realise he had gone in.

Quietly, Lennie approached the building, keeping close to the wall. He stopped before the entrance and bent as if tying a lace, although his boots didn't have laces. A young woman was looking in a second-hand furniture shop but she had her back to him. He eased the corrugated iron apart and slid in. The entry was damp and smelly. He listened. There was no sound from inside the building. He went all the way along the entry, listening, and there was nothing. He started up the stairs, very softly. He put his hand on the banister and it started to give. He pulled away as if it had burnt him. He waited again.

The stairs were very unsafe. He made the first floor and waited a minute. There was still nothing. The further you went, the worse the stairs were. He halted where the state of the stairs worried him. Then, just when he thought he had made a mistake, he heard the voices. Low, urgent voices, very eerie. In a building where no one should be.

Lennie buckled over to smother his giggle. Straightening, he looked up the well of the stairs. He barrelled his finger at the gloom and said softly, 'Bang!'

He was like a wee boy whose finger shoots real bullets.

25

'YOU MIGHT'VE RENTED a place with a more private entrance,' he said.

It was a bad joke but there were no good jokes here. The deadness of his own remark was like a tuning-fork for Harry. Here anything but silence would be discord.

Tommy was standing against the wall. He needed a shave and his clothes were grimy with the dust. His eyes, raw with sleeplessness, looked as if they had a horizon of two inches. Already he seemed as derelict as the building. He had been crouched at the wall as Harry came in and had risen when the door opened. Fear had given him focus for a second. But that dispersed instantly and left him looking eerily past Harry, having forgotten why he stood.

Harry thought he understood why Tommy had no reaction to him. What had entered wasn't Harry Rayburn. It was the non-appearance of whatever monster of fear Tommy was making in his head. And therefore it was irrelevant, because that obsession could admit nothing but itself.

'I brought some more stuff. Have you eaten anything?'

Tommy nodded vaguely. But the food Harry had brought for him yesterday seemed hardly to have diminished. A roll lay on the floor, one bite taken from it. It was unfilled, just dry dough.

'Tommy,' Harry said. 'Let me get you out of here tonight. Will you?'

Tommy wasn't looking at him.

111

'Please.'

He moved along the wall until he was in the corner at the back of the room. It was a kind of answer.

'The police have been to see me.'

Tommy's attention flickered towards him and moved away again. His stillness took the place of questions. He was waiting to hear what more there was.

'They don't know anything yet but they're looking. They'll find you if you stay. You'll have to get out of here, Tommy. Out of the city.'

Tommy stayed completely still. Watching him, Harry ran out of words. His eyes went out of focus and he saw only Tommy, distending hugely, relentlessly in front of him. He was aware of traffic noises, someone shouting, and Tommy, utterly alone in the middle of it all. He couldn't speak.

'There's nowhere to go from here.'

It was said quietly—by the way. It had the gentle sound of an absolute certainty, something that needed no force to maintain itself. For Harry, having been taught despair as the necessary result of what he was, it was a familiar sound, so familiar that it came to him not as an expression of what Tommy had done but of what he had been made to believe he was. The route didn't matter so much to Harry because he knew the destination was predetermined. Tommy was where so many people wanted homosexuals to be, trapped in a ghetto of self-loathing.

He had seen it happen often enough before to people he cared about. They opposed the presumption of others with the reality of themselves until the pressure became too much for them. They lost the necessary tension of their natures and became caricatures of themselves, capable of nothing except offering their arses to the world, like animals whose only recourse is placation.

He despised that. He had been taught despair but he had learned defiance. Out of its tension he had earned his own sense of himself. He wasn't a poof, taking his identity from a failure to be something else. He wasn't gay, publicly pretending to a uniformity that had no meaning in private. He was a homosexual, like everybody else one of a kind.

112

It was the hardest thing to be and, looking at Tommy, the difficulty of it hurt him again, enlarging his love for Tommy. He saw a nature that was driven by demands incompatible with the reality it inhabited. He remembered how good bed had been together, so good that it had frightened Tommy by offering him definition. Finding himself becoming one thing, he had rushed to try to prove himself another. Harry thought he understood the pressures that had made him make the attempt. They were a kind of absolution, as far as he was concerned. A lot of people had been present at that murder. Why should one person answer for it?

Tommy was speaking now—odd, unrelated statements. 'Thomasina. That's what they used to call me.' 'My uncle took me for a drink once.' 'But I embarrassed him. Just by being me.' 'I always felt I needed to prove people wrong.' 'I remember playing with a boy once and I got excited without knowing why. The way he looked at my face. It was like having a birthmark you hadn't noticed yourself.' 'They were right.' 'There's nowhere for me to go, Harry.'

The disconnection puzzled Harry until he noticed a couple of discarded sheets of paper on the floor and decided that Tommy was giving him some pieces of the past he had been trying to make sense of by writing them down. He had been looking for understanding of what had happened, and every moment of his own suffering he had unearthed had only added to his despair. Beside the enormity of what he had done, they were so trivial. They constituted no case for the defence. But then, it seemed to Harry, nobody's experience ever did until it was informed by the compassion of another person.

'Yes there is, Tommy,' Harry said. 'There are places you can go, all right. I'm making arrangements. All I want is that you let me get you out of here. I've been in touch with a friend. He's going to help. We'll get you out of here. You'll be all right.'

Tommy shook his head. But Harry had succeeded in reconvincing himself. The helplessness of Tommy intensified his love for him. It would happen. Whatever had been done, they had earned some right to be with each other.

The bleak, empty room they stood in was for Harry a kind of

113

natural precipitation of their experience. It was their portion of the noise and busyness that was going on around them. In this moment there hardened in him the admission of a knowledge he had been a long time acquiring. He knew the viciousness of public virtue, how it subsists through the invention of its opposite. He made a simple rule for himself: unjust suffering eventually writes a blank cheque for the sufferer. They would collect theirs.

'You're getting out, Tommy,' he said. 'You're going to get out. And later I'm going to join you. We'll live somewhere else. Together. You'll be all right. And that's the truth.'

He didn't feel it as a vague lover's promise. The nature of his experience precluded that. He knew the danger of the police getting hold of them. He knew the risk of trying to use Matt Mason. But he also knew precisely where his own strength was. It lay in his rejection of everybody else, in the loneliness they had taught him.

He wondered at his own ability to bury a dead girl in indifference, and every other scruple with her. But then he had been well taught.

'You'll be all right,' he said again.

Tommy waited.

114

26

HARKNESS WAS STILL fascinated by knocking at strange doors. As a teenager, he had sometimes gone for evening walks through wealthier neighbourhoods, imagining what dramas were being acted out behind the picture windows. The subsequent suspicion that they had probably been making instant coffee was something he didn't dwell on.

One of the bonuses his job provided was a licence to fulfil that adolescent curiosity. You pushed a bell, showed a card and were admitted to the exoticness of every other person. They covered up, of course. But in the vapour trails left by interrupted conversations and in the subtle realignments your presence caused, you glimpsed strange vistas. In this instance he had a special interest, because he remembered Mrs. Stanley.

'This is a terrific-looking woman,' he said at the door.

'Down, Fido, down,' Laidlaw said, and when the door opened thought maybe he was talking to himself.

Harkness was right. She was wearing a nylon overall, she had no make-up and her black hair was slightly mussed. Having none of the marketable props to beauty, she simply rendered them irrelevant. She would be about forty and thinner in the face than should have been acceptable. But they both accepted it. It was the intensity of the eyes that mattered most. They were still looking. Whatever it was she had come to do, she hadn't done it yet.

'Yes.'

'Mrs. Stanley?' Laidlaw said.

'That's right.'

'Police, Mrs. Stanley.' He showed his identification. 'I'm Detective Inspector Laidlaw. This is Detective Constable Harkness. It's about Jennifer Lawson's death.'

'Oh. Yese better come in.'

Before she closed the door, she glanced down the entry to see if anyone was watching. Harkness liked the living-room. It was attractive, tidy but lived in. It was a place where pride hadn't surrendered to circumstances.

'Ah saw you last night, did Ah no'?' she said to Harkness.

Harkness nodded, pleased she remembered. She had gestured them to sit down.

'It's actually Sarah we want to talk to,' Laidlaw said. 'Could we see her, please?'

'Oh. Sarah's at her work.'

'At her work?'

'Ma man an' me thought it wid be better,' she said, attacking the surprise in Laidlaw's voice. She crossed and pushed the living-room door to. 'Ma man's on the night-shift. No. Sarah wis jist gonny go tae bits. So we managed tae get her oot the hoose the day. My God, it's a terrible thing. It doesn't bear thinkin' aboot. Least of all by somebody o' Sarah's age.'

'She was Jennifer's best friend, I understand.'

'Well. For a while she wis. There wis a time Ah thought ye wid need an operation tae separate them. Like Siamese twins.'

'But not lately?'

'Well. Not so much.'

'Why was that?'

'People change. Ah suppose. Grow up. At different speeds.'

'And who was growing up faster? Jennifer or Sarah?'

Mrs. Stanley smiled. It was a beautiful smile, sad, preoccupied, unselfconscious. It hit Harkness like a ray-gun, and he felt his concentration atomise. He found himself imagining what she must have been like, say, fifteen years ago.

'Jennifer was a strange wee lassie. She used to like jist comin' here. An' sittin'. She listened an' she watched. Ah think she wis comparin'.'

116

'With her own home?'

Mrs. Stanley looked up at Laidlaw, impressed by the speed of his understanding.

'That's whit Ah think. But lately she wis changin'. It was as if she had made up her mind about something. Ah don't think she needed us any mair. No' even Sarah. But they still went out thegither sometimes. Sarah went to the disco with 'er on Saturday night.'

The living-room door swung open. The man knuckling his eyes in the doorway wore a vest and trousers. A belly like a vat overhung his unbuckled belt. His feet were bare. A rumple of receding hair and a chin like a hedgehog completed the ensemble. Beauty and the Beast, Harkness thought.

'Did we waken ye, Airchie?' Mrs. Stanley asked.

'Aye. Ah heard the talkin'.'

'It's the polis wantin' to see Sarah.'

'About Bud's lassie, is it?'

Airchie didn't acknowledge Laidlaw and Harkness. While one hand trekked across his stomach, he yawned enormously. He sat down by the fire.

'Sarah was with Jennifer on Saturday night,' Laidlaw said.

'Aye. But she lost her at the disco.'

'How do you mean?'

'Well. They don't go to meet ither lassies, do they? Jennifer got a click.'

'Did Sarah see him?'

'No. She says she lost touch wi' Jennifer early on.'

The silence wasn't accidental. A tension had come into the room with Airchie. He sat casually, resting his arms on his stomach, one forearm tattooed with an anchor, the other with a dagger. He was staring at his bare feet. He looked as if he was counting his toes.

The tension puzzled Harkness. He felt that Mrs. Stanley had said something which troubled Laidlaw, but he didn't know what it was. He sensed that Airchie's presence was a warning to his wife. He wondered how specific the warning was, if it was more than just the reflex 'Tell the polis nothin' ' that might have been the motto for a Drumchapel coat-of-arms.

117

'You talk about Jennifer making comparisons with her own family,' Laidlaw said. 'Was there something wrong at home?'

As soon as Laidlaw said it, Harkness recognised inspiration. It was asking exactly the right thing at exactly the right moment, because it evoked not an answer but an unrehearsed reaction.

'Whit's this ye've been sayin'?'

Airchie had wakened into anger. His wife ignored him carefully.

'Ah mean Ah don't think she wis happy at home.'

'Why not?'

'Her father wouldny give her room to breathe. He runs that house like a prison-camp.'

'That's enough!' Airchie shouted.

'Her mother hasny the life o' a scabby cat.'

'Ah said that's enough!'

'No. It's not enough.'

They stared across at each other. Laidlaw and Harkness sat silent. It wasn't the kind of look to interfere in. That stare was about twenty years of marriage and it was carrying more complicated traffic between them than the M1. It was no longer about a dead girl or policemen's questions. It was about other kinds of death. It was about how much a woman had never got out of a relationship and the decency she had maintained in spite of it, about how much a man had hidden from promises he perhaps didn't even know he had made. It was about pride kept and pride lost.

Across that long look they defined each other. Nothing he had ever been able to do had bullied out of her her hunger for whatever it was she wanted more than this. In her eyes there was still a light that he could neither feed nor douse. The only one his blusterings had intimidated was himself. He sat behind his enormous mound of Dutch courage and wilted. He did it gracefully. He had been practising for years.

'An' he did something to Jennifer once that she never forgot.' She spoke very clearly, very deliberately, carving her words carefully on her husband's silence. 'Ah think that was what changed her.'

'What was that?'

118

'Bud did whit anybody else would've done.'

They all looked at him. He was raking the ashes of his self-esteem, looking for an ember to blow on.

'She wis rinnin' about wi' a Pape. An' he put his foot down. Ah don't know whit youse boays are. But Ah'm tellin' ye this. Nae lassie o' mine'll ever mairry a Catholic. Nae offence.'

'Sarah'll marry whoever she picks,' Mrs. Stanley said. 'An' say Ah've said it.'

Before the frankness of her face and the intensity of her eyes. Airchie began to contemplate his belly.

'Ah'll no' be at her weddin' then,' he confided to it.

'The only wan that'll miss ye'll be the barman.'

The war was over. Among the dead Laidlaw and Harkness had found what they hadn't even known they were looking for. It was time to leave them waging peace on each other. Laidlaw stood up.

'Well,' he said. 'I'm sorry if we've caused any trouble.'

'Don't flatter yourself,' Mrs. Stanley said, and smiled. 'We can do this any time.'

'We'll see Sarah at her work.'

'She works wi' MacLaughlan the Printer.'

'Aye, we've got the address. Thanks very much for your help.'

The street was very wide after the tenseness of the house. There seemed to be a lot of sky.

'You think she'll be all right?' Harkness asked. 'In there with him after that?'

'Don't worry,' Laidlaw said. 'She's a lot bigger than him.'

'I wondered what it was that was bothering you. Till you asked that question about Jennifer's home life.'

'That's not what was bothering me.'

'What then?'

'Something else altogether. There's one thing she said that doesn't fit at all. Just a small thing. But then it usually is. It's the way lies are linked that give them away. There's a bum conjunction in Sarah Stanley's story.'

'So tell me, tell me.'

'Wait till we talk to Sarah.'

There was a man already at the bus-stop, sounding as if he

was in training for the world whistling championships. It was a performance of amazing intricacy, full of cunning chirrups and sustained flutings. He stopped suddenly to say, 'Aye, boays. It's no' buses they've got on this run, Ah think. Bloody stage-coaches.'

'Maybe the Indians've got them,' Laidlaw said.

It was sharp weather for standing.

'That Mrs. Stanley,' Harkness said, warming himself at the thought. 'Makes me wish I had a time-machine.'

'I can see we'll have to requisition you iron drawers,' Laidlaw said. 'April is the cruellest month.'

27

MacLaughlan's was a small family-owned firm in York Street. It was all blank walls and windows blind with dust. Upstairs there was a big communal room that served as canteen, locker-room and fly smoke area. That was where Laidlaw and Harkness found themselves, waiting among oily jackets, the smell of print and abandoned tea-cups brown with tannin.

While they were waiting, a small man in a boilersuit came in. 'Hullo therr, boays.'

It was a vaudevillean's greeting to his audience. Instant theatre. He looked the part. The boilersuit looked as if it had been made for somebody else and he was just standing in. It had been washed far away from its original colour and it was covered in oilstains of varying intensity, like a collage of his past. The bonnet hung miraculously on the back of his head. His face showed whisky-veins.

'Jist in fur a quick yin before we lowse. Ah only enjoy smokin' in the firm's time.'

He pulled up a leg of his boilersuit and fished in his ruler-pocket. A dowt black with oil emerged. He dusted some of the fluff off it and lit up.

'Like smoking T.N.T.,' Laidlaw muttered to Harkness.

'Travellers, eh? Listen—Ah've got a story fur youse. See that press there?'

He pointed to a big walk-in cupboard with the door ajar.

'This is gospel. No' last week but the week before. Big Aly

121

Simpson. Bloke in the work. He's fond o' his nookie an' that, ye know? Me. Ah'd rather hiv a fish-supper. Anyway, there's nane o' us perfect. Dinner-time. The horn goes. Back tae the galleys. Except Big Aly an' Jinty. Jinty's a big lassie that works wan o' the machines. Well, she's no' that big, but everybody's big tae me. Ah yince broke ma leg fa'ing aff the kerb. But she's gemme. So the two o' them wait in the canteen here an' lock the door. Jist gettin' doon tae it, when they hear somebody tryin' the door. Then there's the voices talkin' aboot gettin' the key. Panic stations. Big Aly's a mairrit man. Likes tae think that everybody else's heid buttons up the back. So he hides in the press there. Jinty sorts herself an' sterts yawnin' an' that. Goes tae the door an' opens it. "Ah must've fell asleep," she says, blinkin' like Snow White. Well, Wullie Anderson comes in. Whaur dae ye think is the first place he makes fur? The press there. Tae get a new brush-heid. Opens the door. There's Big Aly. Standin' like Count Dracula. Ye widny credit it. Know whit Big Aly says? Cool as ye like. "Is this where ye get the bus for Maryhill?" An' that's the truth.'

Through the small man's laughter, Laidlaw said to Harkness, 'That's what I love about Glasgow. It's not a city, it's a twenty-four-hour cabaret.'

As the foreman came in with Sarah, the small man stood on his cigarette and disappeared into the press in one movement. He emerged holding some rags and saying, 'Jist up tae get the machines cleaned before we lowse, Charlie.'

The foreman had a hand on Sarah's shoulder paternally.

'This is the second time the polis've seen this wee lassie the day,' he said. 'Ah hope it'll be the last fur a while.'

'I hope so,' said Laidlaw.

'The polis!' The small man stood holding his rags, staring at them. 'Ah thought yese were travellers. Nae wonder ye've got nae sense o' humour.'

Alone with them, Sarah sat down, looking at the floor. She was small and attractive in a way that was already hard. Her face was naturally bold but today a diffidence was detectable behind it, like someone moving beyond frosted glass.

She confirmed what her mother had told them. Yes, she had

122

gone with Jennifer to the disco. But they had separated early on. No, she hadn't seen who Jennifer left with. She had been very close to Jennifer at one time, but not so close lately. She told them what she knew about Jennifer. She remembered the time Mr. Lawson had forbidden Jennifer to go out with the Catholic. Jennifer seemed to have got over it. She talked until Harkness lost concentration. There was nothing for them here. Then Laidlaw said something the harshness of which tuned Harkness in again.

'The dancing seems to have changed a lot since my day, hen. "Poppies" isn't a big place, is it?'

'Naw. No' bad.'

'But you didn't see the fella she left with? I don't believe you, love.'

Sarah looked up aggressively but her eyes flickered. It was as if the slightest gap had appeared between her expression and her feeling. Into it Laidlaw drove a wedge of words, and prised.

'When I was there, lassies used to like letting their mates see that they had made a conquest. They kept tabs on one another. Jennifer would've let you see who was taking her home. You would've made sure that you saw him. She must have danced with him. You're lying, love. Now why would you tell a silly wee lie like that? No reason except to hide a bigger lie. What is it you're hiding, Sarah? What is it, love?'

It was like opening a shellfish. Inside, it was mush. Her face went pulpy with tears. Harkness could hardly bear to look at her.

'It's the truth,' she blubbered.

'No, it's not.'

'Lea'e me alane!'

'Like hell I will. With best friends like you, we could all be in terrible trouble. Jennifer's dead. In fact, she's as dead as I've ever seen anybody. Have you seen her, hen? Well, maybe I could arrange to show you.'

'Ma daddy'll murder me,' she said through the tears.

'No. That won't do, Sarah. They're all living that your father's killed. But somebody *did* murder Jennifer Lawson. So why don't you forget your own wee worries and tell the truth about her? The two of you were working some ploy together, weren't you? Weren't you? Weren't you?'

'She didny go tae Poppies.'

The admission really broke the dam. She started to cry hysterically. Laidlaw gave her a handkerchief and waited while she soaked it.

'All right. Tell us, love,' he said.

Jennifer had used Sarah as an alibi. She had a date with someone called Alan. Sarah couldn't remember the second name. But she thought it was MacIntosh or MacKinley. She had never met him. Since her father had stopped her going out with the Catholic, Jennifer had kept everything secret from her parents. Sarah didn't think Alan was a Catholic but she wasn't sure. Jennifer had told her that she met Alan in 'The Muscular Arms'. It was where he almost always drank, she had said. Sarah had been too frightened of what her father would do to tell the truth before this, and because she only knew Alan's first name she didn't think it was worth getting into trouble about. She thought that if it was him they would get him anyway. He worked at the airport, she was sure. She was still sobbing quietly.

'I'm sorry I had to do that, love,' Laidlaw said. She offered him his handkerchief. 'No. That's all right. But you'll have to learn the difference between domestic problems and the kind of thing we're dealing with.'

In the corridor the foreman passed them and nodded. When he saw Sarah, he doubled back and shouted.

'Hey! Jist a minute, you two. Whit've yese been daein' tae this wee lassie? She's greetin'.'

As the foreman was coming towards them, Harkness felt the wind of Laidlaw turning.

'Stay there!' Laidlaw was pointing at the foreman, who found himself stopping about three yards from them. 'Save yourself the fucking journey. She's greetin' because I made her greet. Because I made her tell me the truth about a girl that's dead. She *canny* greet. Now you go and oil your fucking machines or something. And don't interfere with my job. It bugs me enough without folk like you shoving your *Sunday Post* sentiments in.'

When they turned away, the foreman was doing a fair imitation of Lot's wife. Laidlaw's anger carried him into the street. They crossed the road and stopped.

'Listen,' Laidlaw said. 'You'd better report in now. See Milligan. Rather you than me. You better use a burnished shield. The way Perseus did with the Gorgon. And get yourself something to eat. Pick me up at the Burleigh. Tell them about Poppies and Alan MacThingwy. And see what else they've got. Ach! This job would depress the hide off you.' He looked across the street. 'Still, that helps a bit, doesn't it?'

'What?'

'That.'

The workers were coming out of MacLaughlan's. They were jostling and laughing. Somebody dropped a piece-tin and a neat inter-passing movement developed along the pavement before the tin was recovered. Harkness looked at Laidlaw, who was smiling.

28

'WHO NEEDS ROCKETS to go to the moon?' he thought. 'We can get there by motor.'

The man with the scar drove past 'The Seven Ways' and 'The Square Ring'. They weren't just pubs to him. They were part of his strange, personal horoscope, all those things that had helped to make him what he was. He didn't think of them as he drove past. It was a long time since he had been in either pub but that didn't matter. Six nights a week they went on manufacturing aggro and hangovers, churning people out into the streets just after ten, sustaining the confused climate that was his natural habitat.

He had never questioned that climate, just learned to live in it. It was who he was. His eyes registered nothing but preparedness as he swung through the streets. The dereliction around him meant not pity or anger or affection, only the way he was going. Just as his face was dominated by its wound, a scar with some features round it, so his nature was a reflex response to what it had undergone.

He didn't park the car on the waste-lot but in the street beside it under a lamp-post. It was an action expressing habit not purpose, because it wasn't dark. Some boys were hanging around. He flicked a ten-pence piece to the big one in the torn anorak.

'Nae problem, mister,' the boy said.

But there was. He was going towards it. On the outside the

tenement was scabby with age. But for him the inside was a series of familiar surprises. There was the neatly painted entry and stairs, the freshly varnished, flush-panelled door. Then it was the beautifully painted hall, the thick carpet, the bright paintings—like finding Ali Baba's cave.

'Hullo, Uncle.' It was Maureen, in purple flared trousers and matching woollen top. 'We're goin' tae the picturs.'

'Good for you, hen.'

She still called him uncle although she was thirteen now and knew he was only a courtesy relative. He liked that. He went on into the living-room to the final surprise the house contained—John Rhodes sitting at the fire, violence earthed in domesticity, insulated with a cardigan and slippers. John looked over his paper and winked by way of hullo.

The man with the scar sat down across from him. He knew the rules. When the family were around, it was strictly no business.

'How did the horses go for ye the day then, John?'

'Backwards. Bingers galore. Were ye puntin' yerself?'

'Nothing Ah fancied. Saw the card in Matt Mason's place.'

John Rhodes looked up once from his paper and back down. The message was received. He didn't want any references to what was on, even in code, while his family was still in the house.

That suited the man with the scar fine. He wouldn't have minded never getting round to business. This wasn't a caper he fancied. He just sat enjoying the bustle of the two girls and Annie, John's wife, getting ready for the pictures. He watched John sit bathing in the backwash of their busyness. Homeliness was no pretence with him. His family was the most important thing in his life. Everything else was just building fences round them.

Maureen and Sandra kissed John goodbye and Annie said they wouldn't be late and if he had to go out would he please make sure he put the guard on the fire. Maureen came across and kissed the man with the scar. She was a sweet girl who hated to see somebody left out of things.

When they were gone, John read the paper a little longer. It

127

was as if he was passing time until the lingering sense of his family's presence had evaporated. The man with the scar waited. There would be no drink, because John didn't keep it in the house.

'Well?'

'The word is that the man who did it is a friend o' Harry Rayburn's. A young fella.'

'But Harry Rayburn's a poof.'

'That's the word.'

'Ye mean a boy-friend.'

'It looks that way.'

'Whit's a poof doin' wi' a lassie?'

'Maybe he's ambisextrous.'

'Ah canny stick poofs.'

It was a chillingly simple remark. A vote had been cast. He was waiting. The man with the scar was hesitant. He knew the way he very much wanted the decision to go, but this was one election it wouldn't be healthy to rig. He looked at John Rhodes staring at the fire. his face almost prissy with disgust. That was a savage primness. He had an anger more vicious than the man had seen in any other person. He had seen the hands that were loose on the chair beat one man blind. There had been no regrets.

'Ah don't know his name. But. He's still in the city.'

'Where wid he be?'

'Ah don't know.'

'That's no' very clever.'

'Christ, Ah'm no' Old Moore's Almanac, John.'

'Ah know who you are. You remember who Ah am. You're paid tae find out, no' be a comedian. If Ah want a funny man, Ah'll hire one. An' don't you apply.'

'There's a way tae find out, Ah think, but.'

John Rhodes looked at him and smiled.

'So don't be shy.'

'It's Lennie Wilson'

'Who's Lennie Wilson?'

'He's jist a boay. A big, sully boay.'

'They're the best kind.'

'He works for Matt Mason. The funny thing is, he's workin'
for Harry Rayburn just now as well.'

John Rhodes was nodding.

'Uh-huh. So why should he be there? Except tae find things
out for Mr. Mason?'

'That's whit Ah'm sayin'.'

'Aye. That looks like it. Ye think he knows?'

'Ah think he should.'

'Well. Whit a boy like that knows, he gives out like an
information bureau. He's our man.'

'But.'

John Rhodes waited. There was nothing he needed to bypass
because there was nothing he couldn't deal with. The man with
the scar was being careful. Trying to get round John was as
easy as passing a bull in a close. The man had an infinite
respect for him. In a city where you could find a fight any time
you wanted, and often when you didn't, he had never seen
anybody harder, faster or less afraid. But in a sense that was its
own problem. John's violence had never found its limits. And
the man dreaded that, in looking for them, John would some
time destroy everything they had. This might be the time.

'We're cuttin' right across Matt Mason here, John. What for?'

'If Ah cut across somebody it means they must be in ma
road. Whose fault is that? Leave this Lennie Wilson till the
morra. The night, you and Tam get this Lawson man into 'The
Gay'. Then come an' collect me here. Ah want tae see whit he's
like.'

The man with the scar still wasn't sure what had been decided.
But there was nothing to say. John Rhodes rose and gathered a
pair of shoes that Maureen had discarded. He placed them
neatly under a chair. The man with the scar went out.

29

THE BURLEIGH HOTEL was at the West end of Sauchiehall Street. The architecture was Victorian and very dirty. It had been cunningly equipped with curlicues and excrescences, the chief effect of which was to make it an enormous gin for drifting soot and aerial muck. It stood now half-devoured by its catch, weighted with years of Glasgow, its upper reaches a memorial to the starlings that had once covered the middle of the city like an umbrella of demented harpies.

Braked by its draught-excluder, the big, glass-panelled door opened hesitantly, as if the place was coy about letting you in. The foyer was large, its sea-green carpet choking in a Sargasso of worn threads. It was hard for Harkness to imagine what might have done the wearing.

He trekked across the carpet to Reception. The keyboard held more metal than an arsenal. The pigeon-holes were crammed with emptiness. He couldn't see Laidlaw's name upside down on the register. He pressed the bell. It buzzed harshly, as if it was out of practice.

The woman who came out of the cubby-hole at the side was unexpected. A woman like her was always unexpected. She was mid-twenties, attractive, and she had that look of competence in being female that makes men count their hormones. She smiled once at Harkness and he wanted her to smile twice.

'I don't suppose you have a vacancy,' he said, nodding at the keyboard.

She had adjusted to the archness of his levity before he had finished speaking.

'This is our quiet year,' she said.

'Actually, I'm looking for a Mr. Laidlaw. Could you tell me his room number, please?'

The second smile didn't please him as much as he had expected, because he didn't understand it. He had the discomfort you feel when you find yourself in an expensive restaurant without having checked your wallet.

'You wouldn't be Mr. Harkness, would you?'

'That's right.'

'Your secret's safe with me,' she mouthed, flicking her eyebrows. 'The man's upstairs. In the Residents' Lounge.'

Harkness hesitated, reluctant to give the moment up, waiting for something witty to come into his mouth.

'Thanks,' he said.

'If your feet are sore, you can use the lift.'

Harkness saw the lift as he turned, gridded in black iron like an instrument of torture. He remembered a miserable hour stuck in a lift in San Sebastian. His feet felt good.

'You're not going to take him away from us already, are you?'

Harkness turned at the foot of the stairs.

'Why? Would you miss him?'

She laughed and concentrated on her desk. The gesture suggested to him that she was spoken for and left him with nothing to do but climb the lumpily carpeted stairs. The Residents' Lounge was on the left.

It was just a gigantic colour television with a room round it. The set was showing golf, Peter Oosterhuis shambling brilliantly round the course. Laidlaw sat with four others. A couple of them wore slippers. One had a glass of bottled beer from which he sipped as if it was medicine. The atmosphere was homely and genteel. They had brought their hearths with them. They were the travelling salesmen you never hear about in the jokes.

Harkness slipped into the wicker chair beside Laidlaw. The cushion was pap and within seconds Harkness felt the chair begin to impress itself on him. Laidlaw raised his eyebrows and nodded. He was drinking a whisky and he held up the

131

glass and looked a question at Harkness. Harkness shook his head.

The man with the beer uncrossed his legs, crossed them the other way. In the stillness of the room it felt like an event. He was one of those men who believe that baldness is a state of mind. He had parted his hair just slightly above his armpits and trained the strands to climb like clematis. 'Shot,' he said. 'Hm,' the others chorused. Harkness thought that ten minutes of this could make you geriatric.

He watched Oosterhuis drop a stroke to par and said to Laidlaw, 'You like golf?'

'Yes and no,' Laidlaw said.

Harkness said nothing. He wasn't in the mood for riddles.

'It's a good game,' Laidlaw said quietly. 'But I suspect all professional sportsmen. Grown men devoting their lives to a game. They're capitalism's temple prostitutes.'

Harkness said nothing. In their short acquaintance he recognised a trait in Laidlaw that was beginning to get him down. In certain moods, you could say hullo to Laidlaw and he'd have to analyse it before he gave you an answer. That could get wearing.

Harkness was glad when Laidlaw suggested they go to his room. They went upstairs, padded along dim corridors, Harkness aware how hard it was to walk steadily on the shifting levels of the aged floorboards, like being on the deck of a tilting ship. The ghosts of old smells drifted at them as they went, unexorcised by Lysol.

Room fifty-two was distinguished by nothing but a number. It looked as if it hadn't so much been taken over as broken into —electric razor, towel, shirt on the bed, uncapped toothpaste in the sink, a suitcase disembowelled on a chair. Laidlaw lit a cigarette and sat on the bed. Harkness handed him the list from Milligan.

'Rayburn's workers,' Laidlaw said. 'That's very neat. In alphabetical order, no less. Beginning at D and ending with T. It's nice. But at the moment it's about as handy as a telephone directory. Milligan'll see them.'

Laidlaw gave the sheet back to Harkness and concentrated on

smoking. His mood was mufti. He wasn't a policeman, just a tired man in a strange hotel room with somebody he'd only met that day. Harkness, with the expansiveness of spring still making him want to be other places, caught and shared the mood. It seemed that all they had in common was the futility of the day. At the Station Harkness had been struck by the busy purposefulness of what was going on. It had made him feel peripheral. To stop himself from blaming the feeling on Laidlaw, he tried to share it with him. He looked out of the window.

'He's out there somewhere,' he said. 'In the city. Maybe mixing with other people right now. Walking. Talking. But where?'

Laidlaw got up and filled himself another drink. He took water from the tap.

'Out of earshot of you, if he's lucky,' he said. 'Don't write your soap-operas in the firm's time.'

That was enough. Harkness was glad. His frustration had a focus. He was a fight just looking for a pretext. Laidlaw obliged.

'Maybe Milligan'll solve it,' he said, 'save us all the bother. And maybe power cranes can pick daisies.'

'Why don't you leave off Milligan?' Harkness said.

Laidlaw, sitting on the bed again, looked up at him.

'I didn't know you cared.'

'Oh, piss off!'

In the silence someone passed along the corridor.

'Maybe you'd like to translate,' Laidlaw said.

'Yes, I would. I'm cheesed listening to you put the boot in Milligan.'

'You're hypersensitive.'

'I don't think so. I worked with the man for a year. I quite like him.'

'Then you're a slow learner.'

'So teach me,' Harkness said. 'Maybe you could explain what it is you've got against Milligan.'

Laidlaw took a drink and nodded.

'Maybe I could,' he said. 'But for one reason only. To further your education. Not to justify myself to you. Your opinion of me at the moment worries me exactly as much as dandruff would a chopped-off head. I don't have to justify myself to you. I've got to justify myself to me. And that's a bloody sight harder. And the next time you feel a fit of self-righteous loyalty coming on, why don't you have it some place else?'

They looked at each other, about an eye-flicker away from fisticuffs.

'Fine,' Harkness said. 'But you still haven't said anything.'

'Milligan has no doubt.'

'How do you mean?'

'I mean if everybody could waken up tomorrow morning and have the courage of their doubts, not their convictions, the millennium would be here. I think false certainties are what destroy us. And Milligan's full of them. He's a walking absolute. What's murder but a willed absolute, an invented certainty? An existential failure of nerve. What we shouldn't do is compound the felony in our reaction to it. And that's what people keep doing. Faced with the enormity, they lose their nerve, and where they should see a man, they make a monster. It's a social industry. And Milligan's one of its entrepreneurs. There's plenty of them, but he's the one that keeps crossing my vision. Like a big, fat, fucking mote.'

'That's a bit heavy for me.'

'So that's your problem,' Laidlaw said. 'You asked the question.'

Harkness stood absorbing it. It was the same as had happened with the golf, he thought. You threw Laidlaw a question as casual as a snowball and he answered with an avalanche.

'It's an impressive charge,' Harkness said. 'But where's the evidence?'

'Here.' Laidlaw pointed to his head. 'You've known him a year. I've known him a lot longer. I've seen him splash through other people's grief like a child in the shallows at the shore. Just to make a pinch. I've seen him question a sixteen-year-old tearaway in a darkened street. Rib by rib.'

'That's sometimes the only way.'

'Maybe. But when you start to enjoy it, it's all over bar "Nearer my God to Thee".'

'He's not so bad.'

'He should be cordoned off. He's exhaling fallout.'

Harkness sat down on the only chair, shaking his head, feeling the complexity of Laidlaw's presence, He felt it was simpler than Laidlaw made it out to be, but he couldn't prove it. They sat letting their mutual depression bleed into the silence.

'Anyway,' Laidlaw said at last. 'Today's proved one thing to my satisfaction. Whoever we're looking for *was* known to Jennifer. And if she knew him, somebody else available to us *must* have known him. What did they say about Alan Whoever-he-is?'

Harkness had to bring himself back from a distance.

'They want us to get hold of him and bring him in for questioning.'

'That's fair enough. We'll start with 'The Muscular Arms'. I think you should do that on your own. That's a kind of kinder-garten place, isn't it? Pop music and pimples. If somebody my age goes in, they'll think it's a raid. But you'll be all right. Especially now you've changed your gear. See what you can find out. There's somebody else I want to try and see. I'll meet you at the Gordon Street side of Central Station. Say an hour. All right?'

Harkness nodded, wondering what Laidlaw would be like by then.

'How will I recognise you?' he said.

Laidlaw shook his head and smiled ruefully at the floor.

'I'll be the one stopping folk in the street and asking them if they could direct me to the nearest murderer.'

It wasn't till Harkness was walking along the corridor that he realised Laidlaw hadn't pulled rank throughout the argument. His anger began to turn again into liking for Laidlaw. He wasn't sure that he was glad.

In the room Laidlaw took another drink. He was thinking, not for the first time, how a given context precipitated definition. Arguments created an assurance you hadn't known you had. Left alone with himself, the doubts invaded him. Harkness wasn't too wrong. Milligan was more than Laidlaw allowed him. But his actions had to be opposed—a thing devised by the enemy.

He sipped his drink. He wanted to phone, to find out how the children were. He wanted to hear their voices. But he would do it later. He couldn't at the moment cope with the emotional traffic-jam involved in the simple act of phoning his wife. He was too sore.

Instead, he washed and dressed, a therapy designed to convince him that he was fit to handle whatever happened. It worked again. Cleaned and knowing how good he looked, he went downstairs. He crossed to the reception-desk and winked. The wink was an act of preposterous bravado.

'How long will you be?' she said.

'Jan,' he said. 'Who knows?'

'My God, you're corny.'

'The secret of my charm.'

'You do remember the room number?'

He laughed. She smiled at his receding back.

30

LENNIE WAS ENJOYING feeling deadly. He stood at the bar of the
'Burns Howff' measuring the remainder of a man's life with
sips from his pint. For he was sure Matt Mason must be
intending to get rid of the tenant of 17 Bridgegate. That meant
Lennie at this moment held the power of life or death over
another person.

He was careful not to smile, keeping his face innocently
straight, just another punter having a pint. He had been
putting off giving Matt Mason the information. He had walked
in the centre of the city, wondering how many of the people
going past could guess. For once, their indifference didn't
bother him. He carried a secret like a million-pound note.

The feeling made up for a lot. All the hard cases he had
grown up with in Blackhill would have to think twice about him
if they knew about this. The real tearaways had never taken him
seriously. He remembered Mickey Doolan saying to him once,
'Stick to yer granny's gas-meter, Lennie. That's your size.' So
look at him now.

He looked round the pub, giving a private performance. He
saw them all gesturing against the background of the plain brick
of the walls, trying to talk above the noise of the Pony Express
Disco. Some of them probably thought they knew about hardness. He had a marvellous sense of himself standing quietly at
the bar, a professional among amateurs.

But his time was up. He knew Matt would still be in the

office but not for much longer. Lennie came out of the pub as quietly as he had gone in. He left a little of his pint in the glass. Some people had other things to do besides drink.

Keeping to the same side, he went up West Regent Street. The shop was locked. When he knocked, it was Matt himself who let him in. They went through to the private office.

Lennie told him, and was disappointed that Eddie wasn't there to be impressed.

'You're sure?'

'Ah'm sure. At least that's where he wis the day. He could've moved, Ah suppose.'

'No chance. The way Big Harry explained it, he's nailed to the ground. Big Harry didn't see you? You're sure?'

'Not a clue,' Lennie said.

'That's very nice.' He took out a wad and peeled off two fivers. 'Here. Buy yourself some comics. In fact, buy yourself the *Beano Annual*. You did well.'

Lennie was glad of the money but the anti-climax of the event depressed him. It wasn't just the way Mason referred to him, although that felt as insulting as a secret agent being issued with a pop-gun. It was the inevitable way circumstances always seem to fall below the vividness of imagination.

Then Mason said, 'We've got the man for the job,' and Lennie's imagination was caught again. He could forgive events for making him just an extra because they were so exciting.

'Who is it?'

Mason let him wait for a moment. The pause was part of the circumspection by which Mason lived. For him walking was a simultaneous testing of the ground. All the corridors he constructed for himself had plenty of doors giving off them.

He had already made a decision about Lennie but there was still time to change it, if instinct suggested. The decision was to use Lennie further in this. That had its risks. His approach to things had all the subtlety of a mugging. Eddie would be a more obvious choice. But Lennie must know already what was going to happen. Even he could add up two and two. The best way to keep somebody quiet about something was to involve him more deeply in it. Mason knew that Lennie's lusting after fantasy violence was matched by his deep fear of it. To edge him just a little closer to the real thing might frighten him very effectively into silence about it. Besides, if that didn't work, there were other ways to frighten him, like to death.

'You know what the job is, Lennie, don't you?'

Lennie nodded, and realised from Mason's reaction that he had found exactly the right response. Professionals didn't need to spell things out.

'You're going to help. The man's coming here tonight. I want him to meet you. And you can show him where the job is.'

Mason watched Lennie feed his ego with importance. There was no point in telling him just now what the price might be. Let him enjoy it. Mason even decided generously to spice the experience for him with a little mystery.

'Who is he, boss?' Lennie asked.

'You couldn't guess.'

Lennie spread his hands.

'No. You could guess for a week and you wouldn't be near it. That's what makes it so good.'

'Who is it?'

'Minty McGregor.'

He was pleased to see Lennie go cautiously round the name, looking for the joke.

'But Minty wis never a hit man.' Lennie had seen a picture about the Mafia.

'It's perfect, isn't it? It puts it as far away from us as the moon. Who would ever think it was Minty McGregor? And if they get that far, who would ever connect him with us?'

The difficulty Lennie was finding in connecting Minty with them made Mason's point.

'But Minty's never done anything like this. He's a brek-in man. Always has been. Why would he change now?'

'He's got cancer,' Mason said, as if that explained everything. To Lennie it didn't.

'What's that got to do wi' it?'

'There's a point in everybody, Lennie, where if you reach it, you'll do anything. Minty's at his.'

'How d'ye mean?'

'He's worried about his family. Right? They don't have a great pension-scheme for house-breakers. We're his insurance policy. And he's ours. Because if they want to catch who did it, they'll have to hurry. And even if they catch him, what's he got to lose? No percentage for him in shopping us. Cast-iron investment. Think about it.'

Lennie did. The thought of it awed him—a man who had nothing to lose and so could do anything.

'That's terrific,' he whispered.

'It's not bad,' Mason admitted modestly.

There was a tapping at the outside door.

'That'll be him now,' Mason said. 'Eddie's bringing him to see me. Let them in.'

Lennie hurried through the shop. In his haste to see Minty as if for the first time, he fumbled with the lock. But when he got the door open, all that came in with Eddie was a wake of cold air.

'Where's Minty?'

'In ma inside pocket,' Eddie said.

Lennie followed him through to the office where Mason seemed to be counting them.

'What's the score?' he asked.

'Minty's no' comin' out tae play the night,' Eddie said.

'So what's the score?'

'He's got tae pace himself, he says. He's on drugs or somethin'. He'll be fine by the morra.'

'Are you sure he's fit for this?'

'He's got the badness. That's all ye need for a job like this. A long time since Ah spoke tae a meaner man. The way he is the now, the cancer must be the healthiest thing about 'im. But ye can judge for yerself. He wants tae see ye the morra. In the 'Ambassador'. He's no' known there. An' neither are you. He says if the wages is right, he'll do the job.'

'The money'll be right. You're sure he's on?'

'Ah'd say he's keen.'

Mason nodded.

'That's it then. The night would've been better. I don't like

140

leaving that Laidlaw any room. But Minty can do the job tomorrow. Lennie here's found the other half of the arrangement. That's us set.'

He took a bottle of Glenfiddich and two glasses out of the cupboard.

'You'll get a teacup through in the shop, Lennie.'

When Lennie came back, they stood having a drink. It was a wake at which the corpse was missing. Hearing traffic pass unaware of them in the street above, Lennie felt like a member of a secret society. Tonight he would be having a drink with a couple of mates. He would have to be careful not to give anything away.

31

JAMES CAGNEY AND Van Johnson were in drag. Fred Astaire and Ginger Rogers were, amazingly enough, dancing down a staircase. From the trunk of a tin tree, its sheets of metal nicely interleaved, there sprouted repetitious rainbows. On the ceiling the stars were permanently out. A girl was saying very quietly to her friend, 'Twice he did it. Twice. I nearly jumped out of my knickers. You couldn't believe it. In the middle of the British Home Stores. Twice.'

Although he knew and liked the Starlite Room of 'The Muscular Arms', Harkness felt disorientated in the place tonight. The cardboard cutouts of film stars depressed him like brochures of places he would never get to, especially Jane Russell in her spot above the Ladies. The snippet of conversation he had overheard seemed appropriately bizarre. The strangeness of things was assailing him.

It was the Laidlaw effect, he decided. One day of him was enough to baffle your preconceptions and make you unfamiliar with yourself. He was such a complicated bastard and in trying to adjust to his complications you rediscovered your own. Harkness remembered something he had read or heard somewhere: 'You never put your foot in the same river twice.' Tonight he believed it.

What it meant to him was that tonight he wasn't the same policeman he had been yesterday. The job was different and so was he. He remembered hearing Milligan call Laidlaw an

142

amateur. Harkness decided he knew now what Milligan meant though he didn't agree with it. Milligan was a professional. He took wages for doing a difficult job as well as he knew how. He discounted Laidlaw because Laidlaw abjured some of the most obvious techniques of professionalism that people like Milligan depended on.

But there are two basic kinds of professional, Harkness saw in a moment of self-congratulatory illumination. There's the professionalism that does something well enough to earn a living from it. And there's the professionalism that creates a commitment so intense that the earning of a living happens by the way. Its dynamic isn't wages but the determination to do something as well as it can be done.

Laidlaw was the second kind of professional. Harkness realised it was a very uncomfortable thing to be because, in their work, 'well' involved not just results but the morality by which you arrived at them. He thought of Laidlaw's capacity to bring constant doubt to what he was doing and still try to do it. The pressure must be severe.

Some of it was transferring itself to him, like a virus. As an antidote, he tried to concentrate on the immediate problem. He wondered if he should have stayed downstairs. Perhaps Laidlaw had meant him to approach the problem frontally, declare who he was and ask the relevant questions. But if he had wanted that, there would have been no objection to Laidlaw's coming himself.

Harkness ordered another drink and hesitated over it. The place was very quiet. He had a nightmare moment of seeing himself sitting here till he was stoned and finding out nothing. For the past ten minutes or so he had been listening to the girl behind the bar talking to one of the waitresses, pathetically hoping that they would accidentally reveal all. 'Alan?' 'You know. Alan that usually drinks in here. The one who goes with Jennifer Lawson.' 'Oh yes. That Alan.' 'Well. Tonight it seems he's going to be at 14 Bath Street all evening. That's where you'll find him, he says. He's not for moving. I met him in the street today and he was telling me.' It would have gone something like that, just a nugget of natural conversation.

143

As it was, Harkness had established strong eye-contact with the waitress. She was his best hope, he decided. But he would have to separate her from the barmaid. He smiled and the waitress smiled back. He finished his drink and very deliberately walked past the waitress and sat at an empty table.

It only took half-a-minute for him to notice the barmaid nodding towards him and the waitress turning round. She lifted her tray and came over. She was smiling.

'Oh, the wanderlust is on me,' she said.

'Well, some kind of lust,' Harkness rehearsed in his head, and then dismissed it. That wasn't the line. Something less chancy.

'I just wanted to get you away from your mate,' he said. 'And to watch you walking.'

He almost cringed himself but she was laughing. Harkness blessed again the strong practical streak in women that lets them forgive the corniness of the terms in which you declare your interest, just so long as you declare it.

'Now that you've seen it,' she said. 'Do you just want to watch me walking back? Or can I get you something to drink?'

'As long as I can get you something as well.'

'Can I have it later?'

'You can take it home with you if you want.'

Waiting for her to come back, his mood lifted. This was something he enjoyed, something he was good at. He liked that intimacy of strangers you could achieve in chatting up a girl. Everything was new, nothing was mundane. Last week, with his car in the garage, he had discovered a pretty, dark-haired conductress in the Glasgow–Kilmarnock bus. She had been born in South America and now lived in Patna. That was unusual enough for a start. Their chat had been enjoyable enough to make him want to catch the next bus back. Instead, he had left with an address and the name of a pub in Ayr. He achieved as many moments like that as he could, a kind of Platonic intercourse. It was his revenge on the fact that he would never be able to get round to every woman in the world.

While he was miming miserliness in getting out his money, he realised how much he liked looking at her, beyond the call of any duty. She was tall and slim. That had never been his favourite type but he decided he could change. Her eyes were a subtle colour. An interesting way to spend your life, he thought—fixing their colour exactly, like a Japanese artist painting the same flower till he died. Her mouth was neat in repose but beautifully wide when smiling. Her breasts were generous and firm. Her legs were strong and shapely. They could have been a dancer's legs. He wanted to ask her about her legs but remembered he should be asking her other things.

'Is there anything else you'd like to know? You don't want to count my teeth?'

The remark jolted him into laughter.

'Sorry,' he said. 'Well, I'm not sorry. I was just appreciating you. No crime in that. I think you're great.'

The confession opened a door, brought him where subterfuge couldn't.

'I've seen you in here before,' she said.

'When?'

'A couple of times. You spoke to me once.'

'You're sure it was me?'

'Definitely. I think you were a bit drunk. There were two other fellas with you.'

'If I don't remember you, I must've been drunk. What did I say?'

'Just that I was the only one who was to be allowed to serve you. And some other things.'

She smiled. Harkness had a vague memory of the occasion. Yesterday's embarrassment was today's gain.

'You've been working here for a while, have you?'

'About three months. I pack up at the end of this week.'

'Just my luck. Why?'

Harkness paused. The omens were propitious. The temptation to go on conversational walkabout with her was very great. He loved the bizarre lumber that you find in strangers' lives, uncles with wooden legs, a fear of butterflies, and bus-conductresses from South America. She promised to be interesting. He resented the job, how it made you use people, including yourself. Instead of exploring who she was, he had to try and pick her pocket.

'Actually,' he said, mentally hissing his own fakery. 'I was

145

hoping to see a bloke in here tonight. See, I'm a salesman. It's only sometimes I'm in Glasgow. And I meet him sometimes. He usually drinks in here.'

'Who would that be?'

'Alan,' Harkness said, and hoped for the best.

'Alan who?'

'Well, that's the thing,' he said, wondering what was. 'I'm murder with names. He gave me his name and address. And I've lost the thing. I promised to look him up too. The next time I was in. And this is it.'

She was waiting. He shrugged in a way he hoped was charming—little detective lost.

'Alan's not a lot,' she said. 'There's probably three of them in Glasgow. At least.'

He decided to take a chance on enlarging what Sarah had told them.

'He works at Abbotsinch. Ground Staff.'

She was concentrating hard for him.

'Oh. Yes. There is somebody like that. Alan. Wait a minute.'

She went over to the girl behind the bar. Harkness watched them talking. Her expression as she came back across made him hopeful.

'Alan McInnes?' she said.

'That's the man.'

'Aye. Alan quite often drinks in here.'

Harkness waited, not wanting to disturb the moment. But she said nothing else.

'But not tonight,' he said with careful melancholy.

'So it seems. Fiona says he said something about a party tonight. He was in on Saturday.'

'A party on a Monday?'

She laughed.

'That's what she said.'

'The thing is,' Harkness said, 'I've only got tonight. Tomorrow I'm away.'

She looked at him and understood. He knew by now that she wanted him to stay. She knew he was wanting to go. It was the test of her niceness.

146

'Pretty free, is it?' he said.

She smiled.

'Oh, I think they might let *you* in,' she said, watching his reaction. 'From what Fiona was saying. You want me to find out more?'

'It's just that I want to see him.'

She nodded knowingly. When she went back to the bar and talked, Fiona laughed a lot but she didn't. She came back and gave him a number in Byres Road.

'Fiona thinks that's the number. She's not sure. She's been there once for a party. But the name on the door is Lawrie. That's not their name. The folk who had it before left the nameplate. It's a student flat. More like a commune, I think. Alan said the party is an anti-Monday party.'

'Thanks. Can I get you another drink?'

'Not tonight.'

'When do you finish?'

'Tonight I'll be out about a quarter-to-eleven.'

He liked the way she said it without prevarication.

'Too early for you, I think,' she added.

'Don't underestimate me.'

He nodded and she smiled. Somebody called her over.

32

CITIES CAN TURN their backs on you, just like people. Standing in the opening to Central Station near the Boots Dispensary, Harkness was feeling that. It was that middle of the evening time by which if you haven't gone where you're going or met whoever it is you're supposed to meet, the city locks you out. Everybody seems installed in purposes. You're left with a vagrant mood.

Harkness was having his. His attention loitered about the quiet street, bumming animation from passing strangers. A young couple went past with their little girl between them. Every few steps they hoisted her off the ground by her hands. She cycled on air and giggled simultaneously, as if her legs were working her laughter. There were four taxis at the stance. Three of the men were out exchanging moods. The fourth had stayed in his cab, reading a paper and picking his nose.

A woman in a long green evening-dress and a man in a monkey suit came round the corner towards where Harkness was standing. The man was decanting a careful laugh—ha, ha, ha. The woman looked at Harkness in a way that annoyed him, a manner that was its own red carpet, a face like a Barclay card. She went along the grubby station porch as if it was the portico of her plantation-house and she was Scarlett O'Hara. They went into the Central Hotel. There must be a function on. If they were anything to go by, a convention of twats, Harkness decided.

It wasn't the usual paper-seller. He was a stand-in and he was having a bad night. The last copies of the *Evening Times* seemed glued to his arm. He was getting impatient, probably because he wanted a drink and something to eat before tomorrow's dailies came in nearer eleven.

Across the street the door of the Corn Exchange opened suddenly and a small man popped out onto the pavement, as if the pub had rifted. He foundered in a way that suggested fresh air wasn't his element and at once Harkness saw that he was beyond what his father called the pint of no return. His impetus carried him into the middle of the road, where a solitary car braked and honked. He waved with an air of preoccupied royalty and proceeded to negotiate the rest of the roadway with total concentration and in a zig-zag pattern of immense complication. The road, it seemed, was a river and he was the only one who knew the stepping-stones. The car drove on slowly, the three women in it looking out to watch the small man threading himself through the station entrance.

Harkness turned back from following the small man's lateral progression to see Laidlaw crossing the street. The difference between the slumped depression of the man he had left in the hotel room and the purposeful person coming towards him almost amounted to plastic surgery. Laidlaw stopped at the paper-seller. Being close enough, Harkness heard what he was saying.

'I've been trying to see Wee Eck. No joy. You tell him I want to see him. Tomorrow. Wee Mickey's, half-past one. Without fail. You've got the message?'

Laidlaw had his hand on the man's remaining papers.

'Yer line's on, sir. Ye've been clocked.'

Laidlaw handed him some money Harkness couldn't make out and took his papers from him. The man saluted and went away.

'Who is this Wee Eck anyway?' Harkness asked.

'Just another tout.'

'Not with the trouble you're going to.'

'He's causing the trouble. I think he's avoiding me. That makes me interested. He probably thinks it puts up the price. But it doesn't do that. So what's the word?'

'Alan McInnes,' Harkness said.

Laidlaw was impressed. Harkness savoured the rest, giving it staccato, dramatic as a teleprinter.

'He's at a party. Byres Road. I've got the address. We should catch him there.'

'Very impressive,' Laidlaw said. 'Oh yes. It is. I'll tell them about that. You're promising. In the meantime, all is forgiven. Come back at once.'

Harkness nodded.

'Let's go then,' he said.

'Okay. But give me a couple of minutes. I need some anti-biotics.'

Harkness followed him into the station. Laidlaw put the papers in a litter-bin as he passed. He went to where the phones were set in their row of hardboard shells. He tried three before he found one that was working. Harkness stood apart and watched Laidlaw dialling, putting in the money and talking.

On one of the benches along from Harkness the small man from the Corn Exchange was sitting. He had emptied stuff from his pockets onto the bench and he was chatting quietly to Glasgow. Harkness was catching most of it. 'Always pay yer way. That's the secret. The world doesny owe ye a livin'. Uh-huh. Here somewhere. Bound to be. Tickets, please. Uddingston, here we come. Make it in time for—'

And then something that sounded like 'The Deckman'. Harkness assumed that was the name of a pub and thought the man might be doing himself a favour if he lost his ticket till after ten. He turned back to watching Laidlaw. Laidlaw was bending down as if to get nearer the ear of the person he was talking to. Harkness understood that he was talking to children. He saw him wait while one went off and another came on. He watched his genuine laughter. It was the most vulnerable Harkness had ever seen Laidlaw. Depressed, he clenched. Happy like this, he looked defenceless.

But as he came off the phone, his face showed nothing.

'Byres Road it is then,' was all he said.

While they were travelling on the Underground to Hillhead, Harkness asked, 'How many children do you have?'

150

'Not enough.'

They both laughed but Laidlaw didn't refine it. Harkness remembered Laidlaw's reputation for being something of a mystery. Milligan had called his house 'The Shrine' because so few people on the force had been there. To his own surprise, Harkness found himself mentally defending Laidlaw against the resentment that had been in Milligan's voice. Harkness knew that if he repeated the question, Laidlaw would have to answer it. But Harkness chose not to, because he divined in Laidlaw's casual parry the apparently accidental tip of a deep and deliberate defensiveness. The reason interested him, but he decided this wasn't the time to try and discover it. With a concern for Laidlaw he hadn't known he had, Harkness directed the talk away from even so small a revelation.

'You think this could be it?'

'It could be,' Laidlaw said. 'But I don't think so.'

'Why not?'

'You ask yourself,' Laidlaw said. 'Is it likely? A fella as open to suspicion as he seems to be hasn't come forward to cover himself. What does that mean? I think it means he's frightened in the most natural way. He knew the girl. He was fixed up to see her that night. To himself, he's a suspect. So he hides. He admits nothing. But guilt's a different proposition. Guilty, you work out what everybody thinks of you. You go through the card. You start to place deliberate bets. Because you're working out the odds. This fella hasn't made a move yet. We could find him as easily as this and he hasn't moved. No. That won't do. I smell red herring. So we have to go where the smell leads us.'

'It could be him. He could be so petrified he can't think what to do.'

'I'll tell you what. If Alan McInnes is at this party tonight, it isn't him. That's the way I bet. But it's still important. He might tell us something.'

In that careful balance between pessimism, the assumed defeat of contrived expectations, and hope, the discovery of un-expected possibilities, Harkness recognised Laidlaw.

The number the waitress had given Harkness wasn't the number. But they tried a few others and the music brought them to it—Led Zeppelin, Harkness thought. The door said 'Lawrie'. They knocked several times before they got an answer.

Laidlaw showed who he was and said, 'We're police. May we come in?'

It was an amazing question. The girl who had opened the door stared at them, the glass tilting in her hand till the drink almost spilled. She was fairly fat, dressed in what looked like brocade curtains. Her broad, pale face was as innocent as a letter home to mother. But it was blotted slightly by her need to work out what she shouldn't say. While she was busy reacting, a boy with long hair and a headband manifested vaguely behind her and disappeared back into the room at the end of the hall, which sounded like the passengers on a liner that is sinking.

A moment later, a self-consciously brisk young man came along the hall to the door. The girl hadn't spoken, still hadn't come out of rehearsals. The best she had managed was not to spill her drink.

'Yes. Can I help you?'

Two things struck Harkness: the way so many people, taken socially by surprise, become receptionists; the silence that had occurred behind the young man's back, as if the Titanic had sunk. Where they were was the iceberg. Laidlaw showed his card again, repeated his question.

'What for?' the young man said.

He was wearing jeans that looked as if they had been dipped in a few paint-pots, and a cheesecloth shirt that had sweated itself to his nipples. He was shaky but determined. Harkness liked him.

'We want to speak to a boy called Alan McInnes,' Laidlaw said. 'Is he here?'

The girl had become a fascinated bystander. She was doing everything but take notes. The young man was out there in the middle of a crisis. It was his flat, his guest. He was trying to remember his rights. Harkness thought of his father. His father would have sympathised with this boy. So did Harkness.

'What if he is?' the young man said.

Laidlaw shrugged.

'Look, son,' he said. 'We just want to talk to him. If you don't want to let us in, that's up to you. This isn't a raid. But I can make it one, if that's what you want.'

Faced with no choice, the young man took his time to make it. He was all right, Harkness decided.

'I suppose you better come in,' he said at last.

They came in. The girl recovered enough aplomb to shut the door. A side room they passed smelled as if somebody had been burning joss-sticks. As they reached the main room, Harkness realised the music had only been turned down as far as it would go. In the stillness of the room you could hear it whispering. He heard the word 'police' muttered somewhere.

The party was the statue of a party. For Harkness, the city had turned its back on him all over again. There was no mistaking the meaning of this sculpture: nobody here likes the police. It was part of the folk art of the West of Scotland. Harkness should know. His father was one of its curators.

There seemed more people in the room than it could hold. To Harkness, the parts were somehow more than the sum. He took in fragments. A boy kept his arm round a girl. A big man with a beard stood very erect, auditioning for Moses. People sat or sprawled or stood motionless, looking at Laidlaw and Harkness. A stunning, black-haired girl leaned back against a wall, like the figurehead of one of Harkness's dreams. Smoke rose in a straight line from somebody's cigarette.

'This is the police,' the young man said, labouring the silence.

'I'm sorry to disturb your party,' Laidlaw said. 'But we're looking for Alan McInnes. Is he here?'

The reaction was a complicated event. It was relief and curiosity and resentment. When the figure stepped forward, he didn't simplify things.

'I'm Alan McInnes.'

He had left a girl, who stood conspicuously bereft, a poster of abandonment. Her innocent embarrassment made Laidlaw and Harkness look cruel. Alan McInnes was a good-looking boy, a bit pale, but perhaps that was temporary. Laidlaw nodded to him in a friendly way but it wasn't enough to ease the tension. The unease found a spokesman.

'Wait a minute! What's this about?'

It was the big man with the beard. His shirt was open to the navel. Carpeted with hair, his chest sported a medallion that could have anchored the *Queen Mary*. He stepped into the middle of the floor to make room for his sense of himself. He made his focus Laidlaw.

'What's this about?'

Laidlaw was patient.

'We just want Alan to come with us and answer a few questions. We think he can help us. Alan knows what it's about. Don't you, son?'

'I think I do.'

'Son!' The big man waited till the reverberations of his voice had subsided. 'Son? Paternalism is the silk glove of repression.'

Harkness saw Laidlaw relax and read the sign correctly. The big man had sold the jerseys. He was an ego-tripper, not concerned about Alan McInnes, only about how good he could make himself look in relation to him. Laidlaw ignored him.

'You don't mind coming with us. Do you, son?'

'No, I'll come.'

'No, wait!' The big man was still trying. 'If you've got to have hostages to conformity, take me. I'm against everything you stand for. I'm a dropout. A hippie. A mystic. An anarchist.'

'I'm a Partick Thistle supporter,' Laidlaw said. 'We've all got problems.'

Some people laughed. Laidlaw had Glasgowfied what was happening. Alan McInnes came over to them. The man with the beard appealed to an emptying theatre.

'Capitalism at work,' he said.

They were looking at Laidlaw. He let the silence build itself into a rostrum.

'I would say Alan'll be back before the night's out,' he said. 'While you're waiting,' he nodded towards the man with the beard, 'why not put out some of your empties? It would give you room to have a real party.'

They left. The young man in the cheesecloth shirt saw them

out. The girl dressed in curtains had drifted back to the door, still balancing her drink. She was getting good enough to make a career of it.

It was quiet in the tube. They sat in an empty coach like three friends on a night out. Perhaps it was the lack of threat Laidlaw presented, but Alan McInnes began of his own accord to talk to him about Jennifer Lawson.

'You had a date with her on Saturday night,' Laidlaw said.

'She didn't turn up.'

'Why didn't you tell us?'

'I got frightened. I thought maybe she hadn't mentioned it to anybody. She was like that. So I kept quiet.'

'How long have you known her?'

'Six, seven weeks.'

'Can you get people to be witnesses to where you were on Saturday night?'

'I can. It was supposed to be a foursome.'

He went on talking, building up a lot of evidence against the way he thought things looked. Only one other thing he said seemed to interest Laidlaw particularly.

'What did you say?'

'There was somebody else she was going out with. Just the past couple of weeks. She explained to me about it. Wanted to be fair to me. So that I could pack it up if I wanted. But I said we'd wait and see. I liked her a lot.'

'What was his name?'

'She wouldn't say. She was very close about some things.'

'You know anything about him at all?'

'It was somebody she had been out with before. But her father didn't approve. The bloke was a Catholic.'

'Any idea where he came from, what he did?'

'No, that's everything she told me. Except she seemed to think he needed her. Wasn't sure of himself.'

'How did she mean?'

'I don't know. That's just what she said.'

They walked him from St. Enoch's Square to Central Division. Outside the door of the station, Laidlaw took Harkness aside.

155

'You take him in,' he said. 'You did the work, you get the kudos. But I think he's all right. I'm off on a wee tout-hunt.' To Alan McInnes he called, 'Take it easy, Alan. Just tell them the truth.' And then to Harkness again, 'Let me know what the word is. I'll be in the Burleigh.'

Harkness felt the evening go off again. Gratified at having brought in Alan McInnes, he was dismayed at Laidlaw's casualness about it. Looking after him, he reflected that he was the kind of policeman his father might like.

33

'THE GAY LADDIE' was busy. John Rhodes had to accept a lot of
hullos and touches on the back before he reached the closed door
of the snug. Tam opened the door and closed it again behind
him, just happening to stay standing outside it, drinking a pint.

In the snug a man sat alone at the table. In front of him was an
unbroken bottle of White Horse two empty glasses and a jug of
water. John Rhodes looked at him, judging him against the instincts that were the most refined equipment John had. The man
looked big and strong but so did a lot of people. What impressed
about him was the stillness. He didn't fidget under the stare,
just gave it back like a bouncing cheque.

'Bud Lawson? Ah'm John Rhodes.'

Bud Lawson nodded and reached out his hand to shake.
John Rhodes ignored it and sat down opposite. He poured out
the drinks. Bud Lawson took water.

'Mr. Lawson. Understand. You came intae this snug by the
side door there. Ye'll go out the same way. Nobody'll see ye.
That's the first thing. The conversation we're gonny have never
happened. Ye understand?'

'Ah understand.'

John Rhodes took a drink.

'Ah wis sorry tae hear about yer daughter.'

'Aye.'

'Say ye could get yer hands on who did it. Surmisin', like.
Whit wid ye do?'

'Ah'd kill 'im.'

It was a simple statement of fact.

'They might catch ye.'

157

'So who's worried?'

'But if they did?'

'It wid be worth it.'

'Whit wid ye tell them?'

'Nothin'.'

John Rhodes was convinced. But he waited a moment. He topped up both glasses.

'Ye've got the knackers tae do it all right, Ah wid think. But have ye got the knackers tae keep yer mooth shut for the rest o' yer life? That's the hard bit.'

'Ah widny give the polis the time o' day. Anytime.'

'It's no' jist the polis. Whit about yer friend?'

'Whit friend?'

'The fella ye were with in the Lorne.'

'Nae chance. If Ah just get a go at this yin, Ah widny even mention it tae maself.'

'Ah think by the morra Ah can take ye where he is.'

They sat in stillness, looking at each other.

'If Ah do that, Ah want your word that if anythin' happens, ye're on yer own. We can cover ourselves anway. But Ah want your word.'

'You've got ma word.'

John Rhodes watched him closely and then nodded.

'That's it then. You've got mine. By the morra night ye'll get yer chance. We'll work out the story ye tell if anythin' happens. An' Mr. Lawson. Ye better stick tae it.'

He stood up.

'Ye're ma friend for life,' Bud Lawson said.

'Naw. Ah'm a stranger tae you. Ah don't want tae see you efter the night. Don't you forget that. Ah'm doin' whit Ah think is right. Ah've got daughters as well. We're strangers talkin'. You finish yer drink. Then go out that side door. The man there'll tell ye arrangements. Don't ever come back in here. Even if ye're passin' an' it's on fire. Don't try tae save anybody. Jist let them burn.'

He went out. As Bud Lawson drank, he knew that in the eyes of John Rhodes he had passed a test—in his own eyes too. He was capable of doing it, he knew. He had never killed anyone before but he had never had so strong a reason before.

34

WHAT TIME IT was didn't bother Harkness, only what time it wasn't. It wasn't quarter-to-eleven, and it wouldn't be again tonight. The waste of a night weighed on him. He had passed up something in order to arrive at nothing. The aimless scuffling that composed the whole day made him feel like a bit-player in his own life.

The Burleigh didn't help, locked and dark, a storehouse for sleep. He had to get the night-porter to let him in. The old man obviously knew the plot of Harkness's day. He wasn't about to change the ending.

When Harkness rang, the small figure appeared out of the dimness beyond the glass door with infinite patience, like a genie materialising atom by atom out of a bottle. You knew he was getting nearer because he wasn't getting any further away. Once there, he cupped both hands against the glass, giving himself a letterbox of shadow he could keek through. It took him a day or two to focus. He was a slow mover, Harkness decided, the kind who could miss a world war by glancing away.

While the old man was plotting his position, Harkness had a strong desire to put on his Frankenstein face, shoot out his arms and stiff-leg it up and down the porch. He contented himself with trying not to look like a letter-bomb.

Then it was the ritual of the keys. He brailled his way through them, made his selection and dropped the lot. The whole process began again, taking him so long that Harkness was hoping he wouldn't take a tea-break in the middle. Inside, Harkness tapped him on the sleeve of his brown dustcoat.

'Thanks,' he said with relief.

But the receptionist was waiting to continue the art of walking backwards to meet you. She wasn't the one from earlier. She was younger and harder and looked as if she wanted the world to go away and bother somebody else. In the time it took Harkness to safari to her desk, she didn't look up once. When he got there, she still didn't look up.

She was making entries in a ledger, presumably working out when the world would end. She didn't glance at him. While the point of the pen in her right hand bounced like a bagatelle-ball among complicated figures, her left hand spun the register round for him.

'Will you be a single-room?' she said.

She was the perfect end to a crappy day, brusque, supercilious and precisely as pleasant as a boil on the sphincter. Harkness stared at the crown of her head, deciding where the axe should go.

'Only if you'll be a bungalow,' he said.

The pen-point jabbed purposefully a couple of times more and then staggered to a halt in mid air. She looked at him as if she didn't want her pince-nez to fall off.

'I beg your pardon?'

'Of course you do. I'm going upstairs to see a Mr. Laidlaw. I'm just letting you know. He's in, I take it.'

She had checked the register and the key-board and said, 'Yes', before she caught up with herself. Harkness waited patiently for discomfiture to give way to annoyance and for annoyance to exercise itself into indignation before he showed her his card.

'He's a policeman, too,' he said.

She wasn't pleased.

'I suppose it's all right. But keep it quiet, please. The residents are sleeping.'

'And here was me hoping to have a dorm feast,' Harkness said.

The old man offered him the lift but Harkness said, 'No.

160

Thanks all the same.' He was in a hurry. He went upstairs and walked the tilting decks again. At Laidlaw's door he knocked gently several times and nothing happened. He tried the handle and it opened. He switched on the light. The room was empty.

Leaving the door open, he went to the Residents' Lounge and put on the light. There was nobody there, just a beer-glass ringed with white and a newspaper lying open at the television programmes. He put off the light and went back to Laidlaw's room. The note he left said 'Alan McInnes seems to be in the clear.'

Even Laidlaw was avoiding him. He went back downstairs and was heading for the door, where the old man was waiting, when he turned and crossed towards the desk. He needed one last squeeze at the boil to get the frustration out.

'That's me leaving now,' he said.

She nodded curtly. He must have cost her another calculation.

'You don't have a lounge-bar open just now, do you?'

She looked a reprimand at him.

'No, it's closed. And even if it was open, it would only be for residents.'

He let her misunderstanding go.

'Where's the other woman? Who was on the desk earlier?'

'She's upstairs in bed,' she said, and then wondered how he knew her. 'You mean Jan?'

'I don't know her name. But you can't miss her. She's the one who treats people as if they were human.'

'How can she tell?'

'It takes one to know one,' Harkness said.

The old man opened the door with all the ease of the Venus de Milo cracking a safe. The street cooled Harkness down. He thought maybe he had over-reacted. Laidlaw must be catching. He remembered he was supposed to have phoned Mary and wished it was quarter-to-eleven. He wondered about Laidlaw.

161

35

THEY HAD MADE love twice. The first time was hurried and desperate, less a love-letter than a note for the milkman. It was a quick inventory of basic equipment and a fitting of the essential component parts together, followed by about a minute-and-a-half of grunting mayhem.

After it, they lay in the darkness, trying to remember how to breathe. It was several minutes before she managed to speak.

'Would you mind arresting yourself for assault and battery?' she said.

'I'm sorry,' he said.

He started to laugh.

'By the way,' he said. 'Here's your left tit back. It just came away in my hand.'

They were both laughing. She tapered hers off into an operatic groan.

'My God,' she said. 'I feel so *sore*. I wish you'd taken your boots off.'

'It's so long since I've seen you. I had a wee bit bother finding my way around.'

He put his arm round her and thought about it.

'When you can't pick the lock,' he said, 'you've got to batter the door down.'

'Yes. But I left it open.'

'I'm so virile, I didn't notice.'

She waited patiently for his head to come back from a walk

around his guilt. His complexity didn't annoy her. She accepted that the situation was more fraught for him. The only trammel to her love was the fear of causing hurt to him through disrupting his life irrevocably. Her right hand stroked his stomach, an insistent but gentle presence.

The second time was a slow discovery. They had lain face to face, saying what came into their heads and breathing on each other. He lipped her ear. Her hand defined the inside of his thigh. Gradually they became mouths that went out on each other, blindly exploring. They were two roundabout journeys looking for a meeting-point. Their mouths took bearings from a lot of places as they went. Beneath the lips of each the other distended, mysterious as a continent, until he was coming at her, manic as a conquistador with a new world to colonise. It was as if he was fighting an ebbing tide to come ashore, where she reached for him. His mouth was talking, making wild threats that she was welcoming. When they finally rolled over, separate but having merged, they didn't know how long it had been. They just knew it felt exactly long enough.

The fierceness he had felt towards her cleansed his sense of her. He saw her as beautiful. They lay as if they had fallen very far—luxuriously fractured. It was enough.

'All better now,' she said, and giggled. 'You may have been rough before. But you've got good ointment.'

Laidlaw stirred, reached across and switched on the bedside light. He took his cigarettes and matches.

'Can I have one of those, please?' Jan asked.

Then it had been at-home time, a delicious parody of domesticity—pillows improvised lengthwise into armchairs, Laidlaw padding about like a naked butler getting whiskies, the two of them ensconced smoking, her breasts appearing coyly over the bedclothes.

Now it was that unpolluted feeling that Laidlaw appreciated, when your head is free of fog and thoughts come out of your mouth natural and fully formed. He was lying on top of the covers with the ashtray balanced on his stomach.

'Be careful where you put your ash, love,' he said. 'We don't want to start a forest fire.'

'Delusions of grandeur. Has your guilt arrived yet, by the way?'

'Who said it ever left?'

'You're amazing. It's a sport, love.'

'Aye. But it's a blood sport.'

'Come on.'

'True. Kisses are wee assaults. Just turning towards someone is turning away from somebody else. There's always hurt.'

'Oh God. I see John Knox is back. Goodbye, Don Juan.'

'You're just immoral.' He blew smoke in her face. 'Amoral, maybe. You don't see the implications. That a man of my deep sensitivity has to cope with.'

But his face did look sad.

'It's a service industry, darling. For a lot of people.'

'For you?'

'I've shown you enough to make that question an insult. Say "Let's live together," and I'll do it. It's all right. That's not a proposition, just a fact. There's nobody I want but you. There may be later. Meantime I'll take what I can get from you.'

'Your Laidlaw period.'

'What are you trying to do? Justify yourself by cheapening me?'

'No. But why?'

'Because there's not a lot like you about. So far you're the only one of you I've met. You're an improbable person.'

'Everybody is.'

'Not true. I know a lot of people who're imitating one another.'

'They must be kidding. The results may look the same. But in every case the contortions it took to get there are unique.'

He had put out his cigarette and lit another. Jan reached for a fresh one and lit it from the stub, which she dropped into the ashtray. Laidlaw had to put it out. Watching his tenseness, Jan wanted to encourage him to talk if only to release the congestion in his head.

'What do you mean?'

'Well, I suppose we try to make ourselves parodies of everybody else,' he said. 'Because it's safer. Owning up's a terrible

164

chance to take. That way you don't know who you are until you happen. And then you're lumbered with it.'

'How *do* you mean?'

He wasn't sure.

'Like whoever killed that lassie. Maybe that's what happened to him.'

They both were silent for a time, just smoking and drinking.

'I mean, who knows what went wrong?' he said. 'Love is such a violent thing. For me it is, anyway. It's a murderous skill to practise at any time. In a bed, especially. Like trying to conduct a thunderstorm. With your wee baton of flesh.'

'A thunderstorm? I hadn't noticed.'

'No. I'm not presuming. It may hit you like a zephyr. But it comes out of me a bit differently. Anyway, I did say a *wee* baton.'

He was silent. He was admitting to himself how much he cared for her, experiencing that lonely part of loving, the bit that you can't say. It came to her as just brooding, not something particularly to be encouraged, especially in him. He could do that anytime.

'Don't sulk. I admit that when you're on form I feel slightly surrounded. Like a city you were trying to sack.'

'I knew I was getting through to you.' He sighed.

'You have your faith. I'll have my instincts. When I touch you, I know the difference. When I hear you, it's a private station. Nobody else I know is sending out those signals.'

'It's mainly static.'

'That's what makes me listen hard. Your lovely complications. They rivet me.'

'Nice lady.'

'How are the children?'

'They're all right.'

They lay letting the children come between them. Jan wondered what they were like. She had an image of each but had never been able to check it against the reality. She wondered if she ever would.

'How *is* the case going?' she asked.

Her drink was finished. She put her empty glass beside the bed.

'It isn't yet. Sexual murder's so different. Everything you do stays somehow irrelevant, just a process you're involved in. Even if we solve the case, I'll feel worse than I did before. Lumbered with information I can't ignore. And I can't understand. As if I've been reading God's mail.'

He started to laugh. It struck him again how easy it was to laugh after making love.

'It's ludicrous. Just about the entire corpus of Glasgow police in frenetic pursuit of its own ignorance. Because even if we get him, what is it we'll have found? We haven't a clue. And the thing is I don't believe there's *anybody* can tell us what it means. It's just that we have to do something. And then the courts'll have to do something. Still. Who thinks the law has anything to do with justice? It's what we have because we can't have justice.'

'Good night, Aristotle.'

You had to shut the door eventually on that stuff, Jan decided, and give yourself some room just to be. She gave him her cigarette. He stubbed it out and then his own. He finished his drink and put the glass and the ashtray on the bedside cabinet. She blew ash from his stomach and he came under the covers. But he still sat upright, feeling the headboard bite into his back through the propped pillow and watching the lighter square of wall where the mirror had been before it was moved.

'Maybe the only answer to a crime like this isn't arrest and conviction. Maybe it's for the rest of us to try and love well. Not amputate that part. Just try to heal the world in other places.'

She had lain down again. Her hand had happened casually to come to rest between his legs.

'Do you fancy trying to heal the world some more?' she asked. 'I'm not randy. Just full of self-sacrifice.'

Laidlaw put out the light.

'No chance,' he said. 'But you can watch me sleeping if you like. I'm a very sexy sleeper.'

36

To HARKNESS IT sometimes seemed that every day was a separate evolution. He got out of bed speechless and breakfast was a thing of empty-eyed chompings and guttural grunts between him and his father, a kind of chimpanzees' tea party. He progressed slowly, usually developing a brain about midday, and by evening he had re-evolved to polysyllables. Sometimes after midnight he was superman. That was why meeting Laidlaw at half-past eight in the morning was a bizarre conjunction, like a Neanderthal getting run down by a tractor.

'We have to see Mrs. Lawson. If it wasn't Alan McInnes she saw, who was it? She uses Sarah Stanley as an alibi for her parents. She uses Alan McInnes as an alibi for Sarah Stanley. She was a complicated wee lassie. She probably went to the lavatory via Paisley. That big man has a lot to answer for. Imagine creating that depth of duplicity in your wean. So that she wouldn't tell you the time of day in case you use it against her. Whatever game she was playing, it's more involved than ludo. As far as our information takes us, there's only one person, except for the man we're looking for, who could possibly know about it. We have to see Mrs. Lawson. In Mr. Lawson's absence. If that's possible. I think he's transistorised himself and crawled inside her head.'

Harkness nodded. He consoled himself with the thought that Laidlaw looked terrible, with a right eye like a road-map. It was maybe the result of the time-warp caused by trying to rush to humanity this early in the morning.

But Harkness had to admit it had an effect on him. Before they reached Drumchapel, he was having ideas.

'See that place last night. In Byres Road. I'm just thinking about the big fella with the beard. I think you could catch them with pot if you went.'

'Come on,' Laidlaw said. 'Every city's got cancer. Who's got time to clean their fingernails?'

They were lucky because while they were waiting at a bus-stop near the Lawsons', hoping a bus wouldn't come and deciding how they would go about separating Sadie Lawson from her husband, they saw Bud come out of the house and go in the opposite direction from them. The house still had its curtains drawn. It was the woman from across the entry who answered the door. When she heard what they wanted, she said she had things to do in her own house.

Sadie Lawson wasn't so bad as when either of them had last seen her. The skin of both cheeks was abraded by her tears, but the tears had dried. She sat in a chair by the fire, which was cleaned and freshly set with coal but still unlit. The three of them sipped at the cups of tea the other woman had made before she went out. Mrs. Lawson sighed a lot, waiting for them to approach her isolated grief.

'I'm sorry,' Laidlaw said. 'But I need to talk about Jennifer. Not for very long. I know it's sore.'

'It's a' right, son,' she said.

What she called Laidlaw was a status bestowed on herself by what she had been through. It gave her a kind of authority she had never had before and, exercising it, she simply started to talk without waiting for any questions. The way she spoke seemed at first to have the eerie irrelevance of a seance. But all the pieces cohered in a strange, hidden deliberateness. What she was all the time saying came to the one conclusion: how sorry she was to have sometimes supported Jennifer against Bud, to have sometimes gone behind his back, because this had been the result. She was to blame for some of it.

Harkness found her calmness more harrowingly moving than

168

her tears had been, because he thought it meant something more terrible. That people should suffer such grief as she had had was difficult to endure, but that their suffering should only teach them how to lie to themselves, that was unbearable. And, watching her, he couldn't hide from the conviction that she was burying her daughter in a lie, that, even dead, Jennifer was not to be allowed herself. Mrs. Lawson's confession was a subtle deception. She was like somebody who claims to be throwing down bricks without thought and is building a wall.

Her grief had developed a style and, genuine though it had to be, it had already acquired utility. Harkness realised that people often choose the guilts that they can handle. It's a way of hiding from the truth.

'Mrs. Lawson,' Laidlaw said quietly. She had paused. Harkness watched Laidlaw watching her and letting silence come like a cushion between what she had said and what he would have to say. 'Jennifer didn't go to "Poppies" on Saturday night.'

The silence ran between them like a fuse. Harkness saw her head come up and the eyes widen in disbelief.

'Oh yes. She said she wis goin'.'

'Was it only her father she told lies to, Mrs. Lawson? She never told you any?'

'Whit d'ye mean?'

'Jennifer told you she was going to "Poppies" with Sarah Stanley. She told Sarah she was going on a date with a certain boy. She did neither. That's two lies already, Mrs. Lawson.'

'Ah canny believe it.'

'It's true.'

'She even lied to me at the end. Wait till oor Bud hears this next.'

She had started to cry.

'I'm sorry, Mrs. Lawson,' Laidlaw said. 'But Jennifer's dead. And there's not too much her father can do to her now.' He paused. She rocked slightly, shaking her head. 'And we both know that Jennifer had good reason to be the way she was. We both know that.'

She looked up at him. Her grief had become defenceless again and she looked frightened.

'How d'ye mean?'

'I'm talking about the Catholic boy she went with, Mrs. Lawson. I'm talking about that.'

'Whit Catholic boay?'

'The one her father wouldn't let her see any more. Did you know him?'

She stopped on the question. It seemed to be asking her much more than Laidlaw had meant. She hesitated, looked away, then was suddenly refusing to turn back.

'Ah don't blame her!' Her eyes took in both of them as she said it, the most direct look Harkness had seen her give. 'Ah don't blame her at all. God bless ma lassie. Ah don't blame her at all. Ah blame maself for no' standin' up for her mair. Why should she trust us? We didny deserve 'er trust. Aye, Ah knew about that boay. The wan boay she wanted tae go wi'. And he widny let her. She trusted me up tae that time. But Ah couldny stand up for her. Ah never could. An' she never forgave me, God love 'er, she never forgave me.'

'Did the boy ever come to the house?'

'Are ye wise enough? Bud widny have that. Airchie Stanley telt him it wis a Catholic. Sarah let it slip. And that was it. We never got tae see the boay. It's a funny thing, intit? It wis at that "Poppies" place that she'd met the boay.'

'Mrs. Lawson,' Laidlaw said. 'What was his name?'

She shook her head. 'Ah don't know. Ah never knew.' She looked at Laidlaw steadily. 'But Ah know who should know.' Harkness watched her small crisis of daring with sympathy. It was her Martin Luther moment: here I stand. She wasn't practised in courage but she found it. 'Maggie Grierson! Bud's sister could likely tell ye. Jennifer loved tae go there. Ah think it wis more her home than this was. Lives in Duke Street.'

She gave them the number, and Harkness saw why it had been hard for her to tell them. The rest had been only attitudes and so could be renegued on. This was a fact which they would follow up and Bud Lawson could hear of it. She had said something that she would have to stand by against her husband. It must have been a long time since she had done that.

The woman across the entry had asked them to fetch her

before they left. While Harkness went for her, Laidlaw was still talking to Mrs. Lawson, applying words like bandages. As they left, the woman was making her another cup of tea.

On the bus back into the city, Harkness thought Laidlaw was looking worse. His nose had started to run.

'What's up?' Harkness said.

'I think it's what I hope it's not,' Laidlaw said. 'Migraine. If we ignore it, it might go away. Mrs. Lawson did a brave thing for her, didn't she?'

'She's probably regretting it just now.'

'I hope not. It looks as if that boy could be the one. We've got to get his name. A Catholic who used to go to "Poppies". That won't stand up in court. Funny how "Poppies" keeps coming back in. But that was where she *didn't* go.'

Laidlaw put his hand up to his head.

'Oh no,' he said. 'That's the early warning system. Like somebody playing croquet with my right eyeball. In ten minutes I'll have a head like a Borough Band.'

'Nothing you can do?'

'I'm sorry. You'll have to go to Duke Street on your own. If you get the name, check it off with Milligan. I'll have to go back to the hotel. And get my pills. If I catch it fast enough, I can contain it. If I don't, it can take me a day to recover. Dear oh dear.'

Laidlaw spent the rest of the journey pressing his head as if he was trying to keep it from bursting. So much for rushing evolution, Harkness thought, but sympathetically.

37

As THE MAN came into the lounge, the barman looked up from the racing pages of the *Daily Record*. The interruption was a relief. The card was full of three-legged horses.

'Yes, sir?'

He was big, padded with good living, a businessman in a lightweight suit. 'The Ambassador' was on the South Side, commercial gentility. The big man was genteelly desperate.

'Well, let me see. I'll have a Bell's. Oh, make it a double. Might as well. Hair of the dog, eh?'

He took it over his throat in one piece, like an oyster. That must have been some dog, say a Borzoi. He closed his eyes and stood, listening to his nerve-ends harmonise.

'Same again.'

While he took that one and then another one, he talked excuses. The excuses weren't for the barman, they were for himself. The barman hadn't seen him before but he recognised him. He was trying to convince himself that what he was doing was still just a masculine convention, not yet a lonely compulsion. The way he took the drinks was too fast, as if he didn't want to catch himself at it. He was caching them. By the time he left, the barman would have been feeling sorry for him except that his departure revealed again to the barman the small man who had been sitting beyond him.

That was somebody the barman was really sorry for. There was always somebody worse. Minty had asked for water while he was waiting for friends. By the look of him, they could have been pall-bearers. Where he sat, he was surrounded by the box-plants that seemed to have tropical ambitions. The flowers spilled tendrils, encroached on the plastic seating that ran around the alcove.

He was a small man, slight, his head already well on the way to becoming a skull. He looked cold and still as an icicle, thawing occasionally into the soft tapping of his forefinger on the table. The three men who came in went in single file, a little cortège, to the alcove.

The barman followed them. Two of them ordered beer, the other one Glenfiddich. Minty stayed with water. They waited till the barman had brought them and gone back to his paper. Mason sipped his Glenfiddich, enjoying the feeling he got at such times that everybody was on the market and he knew their prices. He was in no hurry to bid. Waiting was good for them. He sneezed, looked at the flowers.

'You seem to be partial to the flowers, Minty.'

'No' really. Ah'm just practisin'.'

'How are you, anyway?'

'Dyin'. Apart fae that, Ah'm fine.'

'It's cancer, I hear.'

'That's whit Ah hear, too.'

'What kind of cancer is it?'

'The kind that kills ye.'

'They give you no hope?'

'It's fower-nothin' wi' two minutes to go.'

'Well, it comes to us all. Our turn's coming.'

'Ye can have ma turn if ye want. Ah don't mind waitin'.'

Mason nodded as if Minty was doing well in his interview.

'Well,' he said. 'Eddie would put you in the picture.'

'Ah want tae hear it fae you,' Minty said. 'Matt Mason himself.'

Mason looked round.

'What's he got that fan on for?'

He made to signal to the barman.

'Ah asked for it,' Minty said. 'Ah fever up a lot. Ye know?'

Mason nodded.

173

'Well,' he said. 'I've got a wee problem. A two-legged problem. You know that lassie that was found on Sunday. I know who did it. And I'd like him taken out before the polis get there. That's it.'

'Ye know where he is, then?'

'Oh, yes.'

'An' ye want me tae kill him.'

'That's the idea.'

'Is he hard?'

Eddie and Lennie laughed. Mason looked towards Lennie.

'Yer only danger,' Lennie said, 'is he might hit ye wi' his handbag. Or strangle ye wi' that lassie's knickers.'

Minty stared at him. Mason explained what Lennie meant.

'How much?' Minty said to Mason.

'Five hundred quid,' Mason said.

Minty shook his head.

'It's no' much for that kinna work.'

'How else are you going to make that kind of money, Minty? Take out life insurance?'

'Two thousand's nearer the mark for a job like that.'

'What is it you've got, Minty? Cancer of the brain?'

Minty took a sip of water, sat. He looked past the three of them. He seemed completely alone. They just happened to be there.

'Anyway,' Mason said. 'How do I know you can do it? You must be weak.'

Minty looked at Lennie.

'Put your elba on the table,' he said.

Lennie glanced at Mason. Mason nodded. Lennie obliged and Minty took his hand and started to press it back towards the table. Lennie resisted but Minty's stick of a wrist projecting from his jacket seemed charged with electricity. Lennie's knuckles touched Formica. Mason looked at Lennie and shook his head.

'Ah wisny ready,' Lennie said. 'Hiv anither go.'

'Nae chance,' Minty said. 'Ah canny do it twice. Ah've got tae save those up. Ah don't know how many Ah've got left. But Ah only need one mair.'

Mason nodded.

'A thousand,' he said. 'That's your lot.'

'Ye must want rid o' somebody badly if ye'll pay a thousand tae have him put down.'

'Badly enough. Are you on?'

'Ah'm on. But five hundred now. Five hundred efter.'

Mason took out a roll of money with an elastic band around it. 'That's five hundred,' he said.

Minty smiled as he put it in his pocket.

'Ye've been playin' wi' me, Mr. Mason. Ye knew yer price all along.'

'Business, Minty, business. It has to be done by the night at the latest. Lennie'll be back in for you in five minutes. Go easy on that water. I want you sober.'

Mason finished his drink. Eddie and Lennie took what was left of theirs in a oner. They all stood up.

'You're not hoping to hide, now, are you, Minty? I mean, you'll meet your obligations.'

'Ask around, Mr. Mason. Ah've never been known to welsh.'

'No. For if you did, cancer would be the least of your bothers. Your family would be joining you. One headstone would do the lot.'

They left Minty sipping his water, like a temperance meeting of one. In the street, Mason breathed deeply.

'That wee man makes any room a sick-room,' he said. 'You show him the place, Lennie. Tell him I'll see him before eight o'clock in St. Enoch's car park. With the thing done. No later than. And he gets the rest.'

They left him. Crossing to his car, Mason was stopped by an old man.

'Ye hivny the price o' a cuppa tea, sur. Ah hivny had a bite fur two days, son.'

Mason gave him a fifty-pence piece. Going back into the lounge, Lennie saw Minty sitting quiet and still. And deadly, Lennie thought. He remembered the name he'd thought up for Minty last night. The cancer man. The name excited Lennie. Minty went out with him and the barman went across to the alcove to collect what had been left.

175

38

HARKNESS CHECKED THE time. It was just on half-past eleven. The room was a part of memory for Harkness but the memory wasn't of another place. It was of a feeling, an ambience of vulnerability that reminded him of his mother. She had died of pneumonia in a mental hospital. But what stayed with Harkness was the time at home, before she went in, when he and his father had watched hopelessly as she unseamed in front of their eyes. Watching her had taught Harkness how much casual pain there was and undermined seriously for the first time his arrogant sense of himself.

Now he felt recurring that awareness of the presence of someone in such a sensitised state that a snowflake might crack their skull. Laidlaw was lying on the bed facing towards the door. The curtains had been drawn. Harkness had closed the door very gently and Laidlaw's eyes had opened. Harkness waited.

'Hullo,' Laidlaw said to the wall.

'Hullo.'

Harkness watched the body on the bed reassemble itself with difficulty. The effect was grotesquely clownish, accentuated by the pallor of the face, the inappropriately jazzy underpants and the fact that he still had one sock on. The rest of his clothes were scattered around, as if a drunk man had decided to go for a swim. He worked himself round until he was sitting on the edge of the bed. He picked delicately at the corners of his eyes.

'How do you feel?'

Laidlaw seemed to be deciding. He yawned and massaged his left armpit. Looking up, his eyes were wide and clear again. He nodded.

'Thank God for the cavalry. The wee magic pills seem to have made it in time. I'm all right. Considering my head's just been a few rounds with Ali.'

Talk seemed to animate him. He got up and wandered about until his jacket found him. He found what he was looking for. His mouth milked the cigarette of an enormous drag. He came back and sat on the bed.

'First the good news,' Harkness said.

Laidlaw laughed.

'They're still making that stuff out there, are they?'

'The boy-friend's name is Tommy.'

'No second name?'

'Not yet. The name means nothing to anybody else on the case.'

'That's the *good* news? What's the bad stuff? I've been con-demned to death?'

'Not quite. The Commander wants to see you. A complaint went in about you from MacLaughlan's. It must've been the gaffer you spoke to.'

'When?'

'Right now.'

'Come on.'

'That's what he said. It won't take long.'

'Long's comparative. Two minutes of that stuff is a long time. I don't need it.'

He left his cigarette burning in the ashtray and went across to the sink to brush his teeth.

'There's more,' Harkness said.

Laidlaw turned his head towards him, frothing at the mouth. Harkness began to laugh. Laidlaw stared at him, then, turning towards the basin, caught his own face in the mirror—curled lip, dripping fangs. He snittered at himself and rinsed out his mouth.

'You don't liaise.'

'I don't what?'

'You don't liaise. That's what he said. "He puts everybody's back up." That's actually what he said.'

'What does he think we're dealing with? A traffic offence?'

Laidlaw washed very thoroughly, soaping his torso as well. The body still looked youthful except that the stomach muscles had started to surrender. While he was shaving briefly, he said, 'I should've been a lawyer, the way I wanted.'

It was the first unsolicited statement about his past Harkness had heard him make. The self-containment of the man occurred to Harkness again. The more he talked, the bigger the silence at the centre of him seemed. He was a very private man, surrounded by fences and 'Keep Out' signs. Perhaps that was why so many rumours circulated about him. Harkness remembered another one.

'Is it true that you failed university?' he asked.

Laidlaw had taken off his sock and was putting on a fresh pair.

'No,' he said. 'University failed me.'

'How?'

'I took acres of fertile ignorance up to that place. And they started to pour preconceptions all over it. Like forty tons of cement. No thanks. I got out before it hardened. I did a year, passed my exams—just to tell myself that I wasn't leaving because I had to. And I left.'

'And joined the police.'

'Not right away. I finished up here after a while.'

'Why?'

'I don't know why.'

'You're very good at answering questions.'

'I don't like questions. They invent the answers. The real answers are discovered, before you even know what the question is.'

'Aye, okay. But I mean even with simple things. Like I asked you last night how many children you have. You didn't answer.'

Laidlaw pulled on his trousers. He studied the buckle of his belt as if it was the problem.

'No,' he said. 'But I couldn't tell you without giving you what you didn't ask for.'

'What does that mean?'

Laidlaw breathed deeply.

'It means,' he said, 'that I've got three children by my marriage. It also means that I got a girl pregnant when I was twenty and I wouldn't marry her. But I wanted to be a father to the child. I even offered to take it from her. She wouldn't wear it. She had it adopted out. She wouldn't tell me where. I understand her, but I don't forgive her. What you feel is your own affair. But what you do with what you feel admits of judgment. I judge her hard for that. If she was dying in the street, I'd be hard pushed to put a pillow below her head. I have four children. But only three of them have me. That's a hard thing to admit to somebody passing the time on the Underground.'

Harkness was silenced. He had been watching Laidlaw draw protection from his clothes, socks, trousers, shirt and jacket, until the rawness of himself had grown a shell. Laidlaw shaped the big knot on his tie. He jutted his chin out and ran his hand along its edges, checking for bristles. He put his tongue across his teeth and showed them to himself in the mirror. He was no longer at home to visitors. What he said showed it.

'There had been a funny phone-call for me when I got back to the hotel.'

'Information?'

'I don't know. Just checking that I could still be reached here. We better keep in touch with the desk today.'

Harkness nodded. Laidlaw smiled at him.

'Well,' he said. 'Time to face the bloody bureaucracy. While I'm doing that, I think you should check with Sarah Stanley. About Tommy. I'll meet you in the 'Top Spot'.'

They went out, Laidlaw leaving the room like a litter-bin.

39

COMING ROUND FROM Stewart Street, Laidlaw negotiated the
traffic with an absent-mindedness that was almost suicidal. In
his head he was still talking to Commander Robert Frederick.

They had had these confrontations several times and always
Frederick was at least as understanding as you could expect him
to be, and always Laidlaw finished up depressed. The pair of
them had the art of conjuring hopelessness together. They had
managed it again. But at least Laidlaw had the melancholy
satisfaction of feeling that he understood why, a little more
clearly. Listening to Frederick's advice, he had thought again
of how much he disliked that room, the deodorised furnishings,
the uncluttered desk, the smiling photograph, the ashtray that
was never used. It was like a shrine to a God he didn't believe in.
It was the God of categories.

The way Frederick spoke was the key. His speech had a
rhythm that had often puzzled Laidlaw. Now he understood. It
was dictation. Everything was for the files. What didn't fit on
paper was just a nuisance. He went by statistics and reports. He
believed in categories. Laidlaw had never been able to do that.
There wasn't one category that he could accept as being
significantly self-contained, from 'Christian' to 'murderer'.

It was a heavy thought, the kind that needed the help of everybody else to carry. He wondered if the depression he felt at times
like these came from a seemingly irrefutable indication that there
were those who would never share it. There were those for whom
the divisive categories were cast iron. They would always be there.

In the heart of such realisations was the seed of an enormous
tiredness. It was almost enough to make him accept the categories. He could almost envy Frederick his neat divisions.
Certainly, he could understand Frederick's doubts about his

180

validity as a policeman, even agree with them. Most of all, he could appreciate the Commander's determination to have his neat divisions adhered to. If you went beyond them, it was simply harder to go on living.

'You mentioned earlier about our different terms of reference. Well, I'm afraid in this job it's my terms of reference that are going to apply. Even to you. They are as follows. You have until to-morrow. Everything you find out between now and then gets fed back to us immediately. Through Harkness. After today, you'll get your assignments from me. A day at a time. Any questions?'

'D'you mind if I go now?'

'Please.'

As Laidlaw was leaving, Frederick had said, 'You know. It's only when you actually appear in front of me that my hackles rise. At other times I can think of you quite calmly. Why is that?'

Laidlaw had looked ruefully at him, taking in the reprehensible sterility of the room, had thought about it sadly.

'I've got such a charming absence,' he had said.

At the top of Hope Street, the 'Top Spot' presented a clutch of entrances. If you went left, as Laidlaw did, you came into a public bar. This was much used by policemen. It was a narrow bar and near the door a wooden partition came out from the counter, isolating a few feet from the rest, like the hint of a snug. That was where Laidlaw went, not being in the mood for fraternising. He needed some pain-killer.

'An Antiquary and a half-pint of heavy, please.'

He didn't know the girl. He didn't want to.

'What's up with you, Greta Garbage? You want to be alone?'

He knew the voice. He had to smile. He turned into Bob Lilley's big rosy face, a farmer in plain clothes. He took a mock punch at Bob's stomach.

'Aye, Bob,' he said. 'And how's the man who gets the easy jobs? All right?'

'Until you started insulting me again,' Bob said. 'I'd forgotten how much you did that. I must be missing you. So how was it?'

'Like being beaten to death with medals,' Laidlaw said. 'What do you do when they accuse you of your virtues?'

'Jack! You're hallucinating again.'

'Aye, maybe that. But don't take bets.'

The girl came with his drink and Bob took a White Horse. He toasted Laidlaw with it.

'I leave you for a day,' Bob said. 'And you land yourself in it again. Will you not take a telling?'

Harkness arrived, carrying a half-empty pint of lager.

'How did it go?' he asked.

Laidlaw clenched his teeth and shook his head. He became aware for the first time that there were other policeman further down the bar. He could hear them laughing.

'Take it easy, Jack,' Bob said. 'It's natural.'

'So is shite. But I don't have to eat it,' Laidlaw said.

'Behave yourself, Jack.'

'I'm telling you, Bob. I'm pretty near to packing it in.'

'Is that all?' Bob Lilley said. 'I thought it was serious. You've been going to do that every week since I knew you.'

Laidlaw laughed. Harkness realised how close Laidlaw and Bob Lilley were and was surprised. Laidlaw was less of a loner than he had thought he was. Milligan came up.

'Well,' he said. 'Did you shove a book down your trousers?'

'Spare us,' Laidlaw said.

'Don't take it so hard. Everybody's been on the carpet. We've all had that experience.'

'Milligan. You're still waiting for your first experience. Send a cabbage round the world, it comes back a cabbage. What are you doing in the polis, Milligan?'

'Come to that, what are you doing in it?'

'Trying to counteract people like you.'

'My God, Laidlaw. It must be wonderful to be you.'

'I don't know. I have to use the lavatory every day. And sometimes I get sore heads.'

'No. I don't believe it.'

'Straight up. Especially after talking to you.'

Harkness was concentrating on the bottles arranged behind the bar. He could hear the murmur of pleasant conversations all around him and Milligan breathing heavy in the middle of it. He remembered visiting the flat where Milligan lived alone,

182

and the emptiness of the place, the sense that nobody lived there, made him angry at Laidlaw's antagonism. He thought how Laidlaw improvised every situation into a crisis. It was an exhausting trait, if not for Laidlaw, then for him. Who wanted to be a batman to a mobile disaster area?

'Does it never cross your mind,' Milligan was saying, 'that a bunch of us could give you a kicking you'd never forget?'

'Fine. Then all you'd have to do is travel roped together for the rest of your lives. Because you're right. I wouldn't forget.'

'Your time's coming,' Milligan said darkly as he went away.

'Read any good gantries lately?' Laidlaw said to Harkness.

Harkness looked at him, none too friendly, and shook his head in disagreement with what Laidlaw had done.

'I don't know how much crime you solve,' Bob Lilley said. 'But you must cause plenty. You're what they call extreme provocation. I'll go down and pour oil on troubled Milligans. Do yourself a favour, Jack. Buy a muzzle.'

He went away. Harkness felt like joining him.

'For somebody who doesn't believe in monsters,' he said, 'you do your best to try to make Milligan into one.'

'I don't think so. I think he's trying to do that to himself. I'm just disagreeing with his efforts.'

'Listen! Have you any idea of the kind of life that big man's trying to cope with? He lives like Robinson Crusoe in that house of his. Nobody comes, nobody goes. His marriage is finished. His only relatives are in the cemetery. Give him a break!'

'Which arm? No, fair enough. But just because you've got a wooden leg doesn't mean you've got to go about battering all the two-legged folk over the head with it. His problems I can sympathise with. But not his reaction to them.'

They drank, considering each other from opposite sides of an attitude.

'What about Sarah Stanley?' Laidlaw asked.

'She says she's never heard of Tommy. I managed to miss the gaffer. But she had nothing.'

The group of policemen were laughing.

'Policemen,' Laidlaw said, looking into the last of his beer, 'have proprietary laughter.'

40

WEE MICKEY'S WAS new to Harkness but obviously not to itself. It had that atmosphere of helpless entrenchment in its own nature which people often call 'character'. It was neither West End nor City Centre, a small bridge of sighs between two firm convictions. He saw an old place, not so much a pub as a transit-camp to dereliction. The bar was small but there was a large, badly lit room beyond it, partitioned down both sides into narrow wooden booths, each with a wooden table. Laidlaw chose a free one, giving himself a clear view of the door.

After they'd waited a couple of minutes, a small man in an apron brought in a tray with a bottle of wine and a couple of glasses.

'Here we are then,' he said. 'The pick o' yer Vatican cellars.'

Laidlaw turned the bottle round.

'Aye, you're buying in some good labels these days, Mickey,' he said.

'Nice tae know it's appreciated.'

'But you're supposed to buy the labels attached to the bottles. Would you bring another glass, please?'

When the glass was brought, Laidlaw turned it down on the table and poured out two drinks.

'Try to drink it without tasting it,' he said.

Harkness sipped and put down the glass.

'I'll just keep it as a prop,' he said.

He looked round. The predominant impression the room gave was of stains and scrapes and scuffs, a haunting history of past moments, not deliberate memorials, just the accidental graffiti of a lot of passing lives. He felt like a tourist in the sense that Laidlaw used the word. The quiet preoccupation of these people somehow excluded him, made him feel his life was still on holiday. Looking from booth to booth, he saw this room like a street of artisans in some Eastern market. Here each had come to practise his own obsessive craft, beating a life into a bizarre shape, fashioning a slow, deliberate death.

'How about this?' Harkness said. 'Breughel meets Hieronymus Bosch.'

Laidlaw knew what he meant. Across from them were four round a bottle, three women and a man, as if it was the tit of the universe. Each face was a ruin. Further along an old man and woman performed a parody of courting. In one booth a young man sat alone.

'I once saw a painting in the Prado called *Un Alma En Pena*,' Harkness said. 'It was a holiday picture compared with that fella.'

'What was that painting called?'

'*Un Alma En Pena.*'

Harkness waited, knowing the question would have to come. He wondered if there was a Latin quotation for 'revenge is sweet'.

'All right, college boy,' Laidlaw said. 'Interpreter, please.'

'A soul in pain.'

'I could've got it if I'd seen it written down,' Laidlaw said.

Harkness smiled. Their vision was blocked by a bulky man who stood in front of their table. He must have been about sixty but the relaxed physicality of his presence reminded you that he hadn't always been. He wore a black suit. Out of the open neck of his grubby white shirt, black hair sprouted. He had a face like a war museum.

'They telt me ye were in,' he said.

'Hullo, Sam.'

'Ye need any favours? Ah still owe ye some. Anybody ye want seeing to?'

'No. Thanks, Sam. Things are quiet.'

'Well, we could always have a go oorselves. Just tae pass the time.'

'I'm too young to die.'

The man winked, which—given the slowness of his reflexes—was as casual as lowering and raising a flag. His speech had come out like ink in the rain. You had to strain to make out the shape of the words in the blur. He went away.

'I thought you were a hard man,' Harkness said.

'So does Sam. He's as simple as you.'

'You always talk as if you were very handy.'

'I've been known to lose on points shadow-boxing.'

'So who's the man?'

'Sam Bell. He was a good middleweight before he became two middleweights. But he was never as good as they told him he was. That's why his brains are omelette. But he's a good man. A sight better than the bastards that managed him.'

They waited. Harkness looked at the downturned glass.

'Who *is* Eck?'

'Eck Adamson? A wee man with a gullet down to his ankles.'

'What's his business?'

'Same as any tout's. Other people's.'

'So why are we meeting him here? That must be a bit chancy for him.'

'Not really. The first thing is. If you took Eck into a reasonable place, he'd stick out like a nudist at a winter sports resort. I mean, they'd think it was Hallowe'en. Then again. Where he's known, he's known to be scrubber, even as a tout. Who's going to claim Eck? He'll only die when he graduates to turpentine. He knows the value of nothing. He's like a corporation coup of information. He's as likely to tell you who won the Cup Final in 1923 as anything. That's how you'll know him when you see him. He even dresses like a coup.'

'I don't see why we're waiting for him then.'

'Because of my hangups, I suppose. I can't stop believing that there are always connections. The idea that the bad things can happen somehow of their own accord, in isolation. Without having roots in the rest of us. I think that's just hypocrisy. I think we're all accessories. It's just that in specific cases some are more directly involved than others. Now, given that. There are people in the city who know about it, even if they don't know they know. So take Eck. He's my personal walking refuse-dump. Now that I've got a half idea of what I'm looking for, maybe it's time to wade through the baldy tyres and the empty aerosols.'

Harkness knew him when he saw him. He wore an overcoat

baggy enough to take in lodgers. His head seemed to move on ball-bearings. He passed their table, having noticed them. Laidlaw didn't look up. Eck drifted back, pretended to notice them for the first time.

'Hullo therr, friend.'

'Good afternoon, Eck,' Laidlaw said.

'Uh-huh. A stranger in the comp'ny.'

Eck was still glancing around.

'Siddown, Eck,' Laidlaw said. 'You're so discreet, people are getting suspicious. You look as if you're trying to tail yourself.'

'Ye never know the day or the minute, eh?' Eck sat down. 'Night has a thousand eyes, eh?'

'It's broad daylight,' Harkness said.

'Anyway,' Laidlaw said. 'It could find something better to look at.'

He did the introductions.

'He's sharp, ye know,' Eck said to Harkness. His own eyes were sharp and astonishingly mobile, reminiscent less of a hawk than a flock of starlings. 'He's sharp, eh? They don't call 'im Gillette for nothin'. In fac', they don't call 'im Gillette. Still. Ye never know. Night and the city, eh? It's a rough town we live in, boays. Ye've got to look out for yourself. Ah'm no' as big as youse boays. So Ah've got tae keep on ma toes. Ah'm a bobber an' a weaver. Ah bob an' Ah weave, eh? Ah can look after maself. Ah know the big city.'

Eck was a romantic.

Laidlaw talked to him for a time, patiently mentioning names like a teacher who wants the student to do well in his oral and is concerned to find anything he knows about—Bud Lawson, Jennifer Lawson, Airchie Stanley, a Catholic called Tommy. Eck showed no signs of passing the test. All that happened was that his lips parched and his eyes returned again and again to the wine. Harkness was smiling.

'Eck,' Laidlaw said. He lifted the empty glass and started to pour. Eck's eyes lost some of their defensiveness. 'Harry Rayburn. Think about it.'

'Who is he for a Rayburn?'

'Poppies Disco.'

187

'Aw. Down near the pedesterian bit an' that. Big Harry! The second name threw me therr. Ah jist know 'im as Big Harry, eh? Oh yes. Big Harry. Definately. Ah know the same Big Harry.'

Laidlaw slid the glass towards him gently. Eck held it in both hands.

'Yes. He's a hard item, Big Harry. "Poppies" is his place. No messin' about in therr. "Poppies Disco", eh? Uh-huh. Okay?'

Eck raised his glass to his mouth. Before he could drink, Laidlaw put his hand over the glass, took it from him, poured the wine very carefully back into the bottle, waved the glass up and down to shake out any dregs, put the glass upside down on the table again, wiped his palm—where some of the wine had spilled—thoroughly on Eck's sleeve, and said, 'Fuck off.'

'Whit's this about? Ye give a civil answer to a question an' that's the thanks ye get? Come on. Whit's it about then?'

'Fuck off,' Laidlaw said. 'Do your comic turn somewhere else. You're not appreciated. If I want an echo, I know where I can get one that doesn't drink. You've told me nothing I didn't tell you. What do you think we are? Banana-skin trippers? You'll be selling me a drink out my own bottle next.'

Laidlaw sipped his wine, letting Eck watch.

'All right. Keys, eh? Ah just thought maybe there'd be more tae get that way. But Ah do know 'im. Ah know somethin' about that big man some people don't. But give us a drink first, eh?'

Laidlaw turned the glass up, poured out the drink again and placed it in front of him. As he took it, Laidlaw kept his hand on it for a moment.

'You tell any wee fibs. And I'll put my fingers down your throat and take it back.'

Eck drank so eagerly his teeth hit the glass. Laidlaw gave him a refill.

'Well. First thing ye might not know. He's as queer as a three-pound note.'

'He's a poof? That big man?' Harkness sat back dismissing him. 'Come on. It's great what some folk'll say for drink.'

'So you might know better nor me.'

'That's straight, Eck?' Laidlaw asked.

'He's been screwed that often his bum's got a thread on it.'

'On you go,' Laidlaw said.

'Well. Ah don't live in his inside pocket, do Ah? But if ye're like that, ye meet a lower classa people, don't ye. Eh? He's got connections. Bound tae have, eh? He's got connections.'

'What exactly?' Laidlaw asked.

'How would Ah know?'

Laidlaw shoved the bottle across to Eck.

'Have a good lunch.'

Harkness was disappointed. Once he had got over the initial surprise of hearing about Harry Rayburn, he remembered Laidlaw saying, 'Mary Poppins with hair on her chest.' He had begun to believe in the inter-relationships Laidlaw preached. Several things began to seem like echoes of each other—the recurrence of 'Poppies', the homosexuality of Harry Rayburn, the fact that the main assault on Jennifer was anal. He had felt that out of Laidlaw's 'refuse-dump' they were about to pick the very thing they needed. Now when one sign was all it would have taken to complete his conversion nothing was forthcoming. Laidlaw was making to stand up.

'That'll no' go far,' Eck said to the bottle.

'Your information won't go far either. Eh?'

'Listen. Ah can do ye a wee turn here.' He had Laidlaw waiting. 'Ah could give ye a name.'

'Eck,' Laidlaw said. 'With you I'm probably buying air. And I can get it fresh for free.'

'Ah can give ye two names. Wan big. Wan no' sa big.'

'A quid a time.'

'Gi'es a brek.'

'So sell them somewhere else.'

'Matt Mason. He's —'

'I know who he is. What's his connection with Rayburn?'

'They've worked thegither.'

Laidlaw gave him a pound under the table. Eck's hand crumpled it to a ball.

'Harry Rayburn. There wis talk about a boy an' him. Some boay Bryson. Ah think it was. Aye, it was.'

'What was his first name?'

'Ah don't know.'

'Does "Tommy" mean anything to you?'

'There wis a pictur called that. Wis there no'?'

'Thank you, Eck.' He gave Eck the other pound. 'But it's something.'

Eck secreted his money. Laidlaw was nodding Harkness out when Eck said something else.

'He's a braw boay, it seems. Works at "Poppies".'

There was a pause while the moment waited for them all to catch up with it. Laidlaw and Harkness had frozen before they knew why they were doing it. Something seemingly ordinary had glinted in among the rubbish and they sat staring at it, wondering why it was so valuable. Watching Laidlaw's eyes, Harkness saw him get there first. Laidlaw smiled at him.

'You know what it is?' Laidlaw said.

Harkness couldn't track it down. He shook his head.

'Beginning with D and ending with T,' Laidlaw said.

Harkness remembered and understood.

'No Bryson on Milligan's list,' he said.

'Ser—en—dip—it—ee.' Laidlaw said it like a cheer-leader.

'What?'

'Serendipity. The art of making lucky finds. The art is in knowing they're finds. I think we've got him. Eck. Where does this boy live?'

'Ah've nae idea.'

Laidlaw slipped him another pound.

'That's all right. I know somebody who has. Buy yourself a barrel, Eck. And I'm sorry about the sleeve. That was meant for somebody else.'

Laidlaw winked at Harkness and lifted his glass. Harkness did the same.

'To Sherlock Adamson, public benefactor,' Laidlaw said.

They drank sincerely but not deep. On the way out, Laidlaw said, 'We're almost there.'

They left Eck mesmerised by the third pound note. Like most success, his was modified by the fact that he had no idea how to repeat it. But his bewilderment didn't last for long. He put the money away and gathered their two glasses to him. It was Christmas already. To a romantic, the incomprehensible is natural.

41

Run run as fast as you can
you cant run away from the cancer man

IT MIGHT HAVE been Michelangelo at the Sistine Chapel.
Working, Lennie was total concentration. The wall of the
lavatory was rough white plaster and it was hard getting it to
take the biro. If you leaned too heavily, the point of the pen went
and the flow of the ink was stopped. You had to use a lot of
light strokes, one on top of the other, to lay the ink on the
surface of the plaster. He would have to get a felt pen.

While he was working, he was contrasting what he was doing
contemptuously with his well-stocked memory of other things
he'd seen, the shaky drawings, the invitations, the same old
jokes ('It's no use standing on the seat, the crabs in here can
jump 10 ft.'). They were all daft, the sort of thing he used to
write himself, but not now.

He remembered the feeling of walking in the street with
Minty McGregor. The coldness of the thought was exciting—
the idea of a man who could kill for no more reason than wages,
who walked about the streets like a disease that would settle
where it chose, who had nothing to lose and therefore wasn't
afraid. It was a dream of himself so overpowering that he
would have to be careful. He had gone too far already.

Last night in the pub it had been. He had been drinking with
a couple of the boys he used to knock about with and he

couldn't resist making unexplained references to 'the cancer man'. The three of them had finished up saying in chorus, 'Oh, the cancer man'll get you if you don't watch out.' Lennie remembered a man with a scar looking bitterly along the bar at them. He hoped Matt Mason didn't get to hear about it.

But at the moment nothing could interfere with his pleasure. It was a feeling of two things simultaneously, wildness and safety. His imagination ran amok and yet faced him with nothing more difficult to deal with than some words on a wall.

Morgan the Mighty and Desperate Dan
take off their hats to the cancer man

He was satisfied. He flushed the lavatory and opened the door. He didn't know for a second whether he was seeing or still imagining. Looking at him was the man with the scar. While Lennie's stomach came up and went back down, he could hear the noise of music in the bar. It sounded very far away. The man nodded as if confirming Lennie's fear.

Lennie's first instinct was to shut the door again. He was starting to do that when the man's foot hit the door, slamming it against the wall with Lennie's arm between them. Lennie screamed.

'Whit hiv you been doin' in here?' the man asked.

He was leaning with his back against the door-jamb so that he could exert the maximum amount of pressure with his foot. What was he, a lavatory inspector?

'Whit's the gemme?' Lennie managed.

'Ah think you've been wankin',' the man said. 'That's no' nice in public places.'

'Who are you?' Lennie asked.

'Ah'm the man that's got your arm jammed in the door. There's a fella wants tae see you. When Ah take ma foot aff this door, you're gonny come wi' me. If ye cause the least wee bit bother, it's your heid Ah'll use as a door stopper. Fair enough?'

Lennie's head nodded for him. As they came out into the small area where the washhand-basin was, another man was waiting.

192

'Take it easy!' he said to the man with the scar. 'Ye'd think the boy had done somethin' wrang. Ye're all right, son. It's just that a friend of ours wants a word wi' ye. An' that's all. It's as simple as that. But he's got to have that word. That's the kinna fella he is. Now if ye'll just come to the car quietly with us, we'll take ye there. If ye cause us any bother. Like goin' through the pub here. We'll leave ye for dead. No question. It's your choice son. D'ye understand? Okay?'

From his tone, he might have been explaining to a child why he had to wash behind his ears. He had a nice suit on and careful, wavy hair. Both approaches, the instant, vicious malice and the fatherly promise of massacre, were for Lennie just different notches on the same thumbscrew. He was stiff with fear of the next turning, a dread so acute that they got him through the 'Howff' and into the car without a murmur.

The man with the scar drove. The other man was in the back with Lennie. He got Lennie to crouch down on the floor.

'No keekin' now, son. It's for yer own good. What ye don't know, ye can't tell. An' what ye can't tell, nobody's gonny kick yer head in for. All right?'

One of them thought he saw a Rangers player on the street and they started talking about football. On the floor, Lennie realised he had left most of himself behind, like luggage. He had nothing that fitted this. But eventually there caught up with him a response he should have had a while ago. He tried it.

'Whit man is this?' he asked.

The wavy-haired man looked down at him, his face showing pleasant surprise, as if he hadn't realised Lennie could talk.

'No' Santa Claus, son.'

But Lennie had at least found a reaction. Listening to their ordinary chat with each other, he tried to rehabilitate himself on it. Maybe it wasn't so bad. *They* didn't seem to be taking it all that seriously. Perhaps he could brass it out.

By the time the car stopped, he was wearing an attitude he hoped would get him through. He unwound himself and stepped steadily out of the car, even flexing his right leg, which had gone stiff. They were in what looked like a warehouse with an arched, corrugated roof. It was a long place, so that the car didn't take up much room in it. It reminded Lennie of the kind of place he'd seen in Molendinar Street.

'Talk nice an' ye'll be all right, son,' the wavy-haired man said.

The big double doors had been closed before they got out of the car and the two men went out of the inset door. Lennie was alone. The place was empty except for a couple of boxes. There were oil-stains on the stone floor. He could hear traffic.

Given some time to himself, he began to use it. The very drama of his position raised him to meet it. He was in a tight spot. This was the time for turning up. They would know they were dealing with somebody. No surrender.

The inset door opened and the impression was that the man coming in had to feed himself through it. He closed the door, straightening up. He was big and fair and his eyes were that light blue colour that can look quietly mad. But the ticker-tape in Lennie's head was still unravelling its mechanical responses, urgent abstractions, stored up from years of fantasy. Fair enough. A one-to-one situation. Call your play. Come and get it.

'Hullo, son,' the man said nicely. 'Lennie, intit?'

Lennie nodded, one quick jab of the head, just one. So you've heard of me.

'D'ye know who Ah am?'

Lennie shook his head. Should I? He didn't take his eyes from the big man's. No surrender.

'Ah want ye tae tell me a few things, son. All right?'

Lennie smiled, hardly a smile, just a quiver in the corner of his mouth.

'Uh-huh. An' whit if Ah don't choose tae?'

The man looked away from Lennie. That was one-up for Lennie. The man's eyes moved vaguely round the warehouse as if he was thinking about the problem Lennie was presenting. Lennie was waiting to see how he would handle that.

'Aye, well,' the man said and took Lennie by the collar.

It was like being caught in the slipstream of a jet. Lennie was sucked off his feet and the man's knee had mashed his groin and as he hung there writhing and jerking with the pain, he felt his cheek being blasted by the man's right hand and simultaneously

194

the man released him and he was pitched onto the concrete floor. He ricocheted off it and the other side of his face came down flat and hard against the stone. It was like being hit on the jaw with the back of a shovel. For Lennie, nurtured on the legends of Glaswegian violence, it was as if his city had fallen on his head.

He seemed drowning in nausea and the nausea was mixed with the fumes of oil and pain was banging in his head. The first thing he knew was that his face was lying in an oil-stain. He tried to raise his head but the warehouse was turning cartwheels.

'Jist gettin' acquainted, son,' the man's voice said.

The warehouse slowly subsided.

'Now, son. Whit's your connection wi' Minty McGregor?'

Lennie had the feeling that if he didn't hold onto the floor he would slide off it. He couldn't get his head up and as he spoke the floor seemed to be grinding against his jawbone.

'Nae connection wi' him.'

The floor scraped along his face and it was only when it stopped that he knew his body had jerked and then that it had jerked because the man had kicked him in the ribs.

'Ah work fur Matt Mason. Minty. A job tae do fur Matt.'

'Very good, son. Very good.'

Lennie felt himself being lifted off the floor, just a bag of pains, and being dumped on one of the boxes, He was slumping off it when the man's foot propped him up.

'Sit on yer wee box, son. That's yer reward for tellin' the truth. We give prizes here.'

Fear deputised in Lennie for a backbone, somehow gave him the capacity to stay more or less upright on his box while his body cringed and sagged.

'Ye went a wee walk the day wi' Minty. Whit's special aboot the Bridgegate?'

'Bridgegate?'

The box was kicked from under him. As he sprawled on the floor, the man had stepped on his throat. Lennie was retching for breath, bucking on the end of his foot like a gaffed fish.

'End of fuckin' interview,' the man said. 'Ah can see Ah'll have

195

tae get rough. Ah'm gonny kull you, son. Unless ye tell me everythin.' Right now. Ma name isny Simon. It's John Rhodes.'

He said it like a battle-cry and it unravelled what was left of Lennie. He became pure terror, a desperation to talk. But John Rhodes didn't make it easy. The pressure on Lennie's throat stayed unrelaxed and he found that everything he wanted to say had to fight its way out.

'That lassie in the papers. Fella that killed her. In the tenement. Up at the top. Minty gonny get rid o' 'im the night. Minty's got cancer.'

John Rhodes pressed on Lennie's Adam's apple as if toying with the button of his private hydrogen bomb, then he released him. Air battered Lennie's lungs. He lay gasping and boking and coming to terms with the fact that he was still here.

'When?'

Lennie didn't look up. Even as the lie formed in him, it frightened him. But terrified of John Rhodes, afraid of Matt Mason, he made his own small compromise between them, clung to it like a spar.

'Jist before ten o'clock. He says there's a quiet time then.'

'Stand up!'

That was an agonising activity for Lennie. By a series of deliberate acts of will, he put himself together like a meccano-set. It felt as if some of the parts must be missing and he couldn't get fully upright, settled for a lopsided sway. Separate pains were beginning to isolate themselves, clamour for his attention. His head felt crushed, one eye was closed, a cheek swollen. At least one rib must have gone. His hip ached and he must have bruises everywhere. His breathing came voiced, a repetitive moan.

With his one good eye, he stayed focussed on the man, a legend who had become real for him. Lennie hadn't a fantasy to his name. He just knew utter fear and a desire to get away from all of it.

John Rhodes stood containing himself, like somebody reining in a runaway horse. Lennie waited, still dripping blood.

'You!' John Rhodes said. 'Mention this tae anybody, even yer mirror, an' you're dead. Understand?'

'Ah understand,' Lennie managed to say.

'All right.' Then he said, 'Ah, wid ye look at this! That wis you, boay.'

He extended his right arm and on the cuff of the jacket was a fleck of blood.

'For that. An' as a wee last warnin'.'

Lennie saw it as if it was through a telescope. The hand at the end of the outstretched arm clenched and swung. Lennie's head bounced off the wall and he slumped at the foot of it, like thrown refuse. He was unconscious. John Rhodes wetted his thumb and rubbed it on the cuff of his jacket, Crossing to the car, he leaned in the window and pressed the horn.

The inset door opened and the other two came in. Rhodes pointed to Lennie, then to the car. The wavy-haired man dragged Lennie across and put him in the car. He opened the doors and backed out. The man with the scar closed them.

'Minty's been set up tae kill the poof,' John Rhodes said. 'Can ye imagine it? Wee Minty. If he wanted tae crack an egg, he'd need tae form a gang.'

'It saves us the trouble, anyway.'

'Ah gave ma word.'

'John. As long as it's done.'

'Ah'll decide the wey it's done. Ah'll decide!'

The man with the scar looked at him and then looked away. It was like staring into a furnace.

The wavy-haired man pulled up in a quiet cul-de-sac. Lennie had come to, with his head on a newspaper to protect the seat. He was glad they had stopped because he thought he was going to be sick and was frightened of what would happen if he vomited in the car. The man checked that the street was empty and opened the door.

'Right, son,' he said briskly.

Lennie crawled out and teetered on the pavement.

'Now away an' play with yer plastic sojers or somethin', son.'

He took out the paper, smeared with Lennie's blood, and dropped it in the gutter. He drove off, leaving Lennie like a pre-packaged street accident. Leaning blindly against the railings, he could think of nowhere to go but away.

197

42

THEY WEREN'T NEARLY there, Harkness discovered. The rest of the day was like cycling on rollers. No matter how much energy they expended, they were still in the same place. They expended plenty.

Harry Rayburn wasn't at 'Poppies', wasn't at home, wasn't anywhere they could find. The general hunt for a Tommy Bryson was yielding nothing. They knew now where they were going and they knew that they would get there. But what worried Laidlaw was when. During the afternoon something happened which made Laidlaw say, 'Maybe we've got a grip of a one-way hour glass here.'

It was when he phoned to check with the Burleigh. A small boy had come in off the street with a sealed envelope he handed in at the desk. Laidlaw's name was on it. He said a man in the street had given him ten pence to bring it in. Laidlaw asked Jan to read it to him. The message, printed in pencil, said, 'Minty McGregor has cancer. He wants to take somebody you are looking for along with him before he goes.'

But Minty wasn't home either. Laidlaw and Harkness saw Minty's house in Yoker, the worn wife, the five children, even the hen-run at the back door. But they didn't see Minty, and they didn't see Minty's fourteen-year-old son leave the house after them and go to another house a few streets away.

There the boy found his father and the man he called Uncle James sitting alone in the house. They put a grown-up silence between him and them as soon as he came in. His news that the police had been to the house didn't seem to bother his father at all. He nodded and smiled at Uncle James. All he said was, 'Tell yer mither Ah'll no' be hame till late on the night.'

It was fairly late on and beginning to get dark before two policemen at Poppies reported that Harry Rayburn was there. The news was especially heartening for Harkness because it inspired Laidlaw to use a car.

43

HAVING DONE WHAT was necessary, Minty was slow climbing the steps of the Underground and as he came out into St. Enoch's Square, he rested a minute before tackling the curving hill that led to the pedestrians' entrance to the car park.

The morality of what he had done wasn't his concern. All it meant to him was something troublesome and tiring, but worth it.

St. Enoch's Station had been a part of the Glasgow he knew. Now the high, arched, glass roof that had fascinated him as a boy was patched with sky. What had seemed before unimaginably far away now only served to give perspective to the vastness of the distance beyond it. Those squares of starlit sky were a bottomlessness he was falling into. There were acres of macadam where the rails had been—nowhere for him to go from here.

Walking among the pillars, he could see no light or movement among the cars. Then far out beyond the roof, he saw the lights of a car flash on and off. As he walked towards it, the front passenger door swung open.

It was Matt Mason in the driver's seat. Behind Minty was somebody else but he didn't bother turning round to find out who it was. He stared at the windscreen in front of him. The car was fogged with breathing. There was a smell of drink that made Minty feel like retching.

'Well?'

'The job's done,' Minty said.

Minty heard a soft sound which he knew was a smile taking place behind him.

'How did it go?'

'Nae problem. Like droonin' cats. He wis a pathetic boay, that yin.'

'How did you get to him without him getting the wind up?'

'Ah knocked at the door.'

There was quiet laughter from the back seat. Mason wasn't amused.

'Come on,' he said.

'Ah'm tellin' ye. Ah knocked at the door.'

'Who did he think it was? Avon calling?'

'Lennie telt me aboot Harry Rayburn. Ah said Ah wis fae him. Wi' a message. He couldny get away an' it was urgent, Ah said. Ah took him up a fish-supper as well. Dae Ah get that aff expenses?'

Mason was staring at him.

'How did you do it?'

'Wi' a bit o' rope. That way ye don't need too much pressure. Ah let him eat maist o' his supper. There wis only a few chips left when Ah gave him it. Ah hope he wisny the kind that keeps the best chips tae the last.'

The other two were impressed in spite of themselves. Their breathing seemed self-consciously loud, as if they were deliberately indulging it.

'He wis an awfu' quick eater that boay. Ah saved him fae a terrible case o' indigestion.'

Mason was the first to recover.

'How do I know you've done it?'

'Ye want a receipt?' Minty asked.

He put his hand in the pocket of his coat and dropped something on Mason's lap. Mason switched on the interior light. He was holding up a pair of yellow lace panties, only slightly torn and hard with dried blood in places. He switched off the light and made to hand them back.

'They're yours,' Minty said. 'Ah don't want them. Ah want paid for them. That's a five-hundred-quid paira knickers ye've got there. The dearest drawers on the market.'

Mason thought for a moment and said, 'If they're not genuine, they'll be helluva dear to you.'

He gave Minty the money.

'Thanks, Mr. Mason,' Minty said. 'Ah'll pit in a word for ye wi' the heid man when Ah get there.'

He got out of the car and walked slowly out of St. Enoch's. Watching him go, Lennie stayed in the shadow of the pillar he was hiding behind. He waited till he saw Matt Mason's car ease itself out of its berth and check out of the car park. Then he headed for the left-luggage office in Central Station, where his travelling-bag was.

In Argyle Street Minty asked a man at a bus-stop for a light and gave him five hundred pounds for it. Then he made his way towards the nearest police station, which was in St. Andrew's Street.

44

HARRY RAYBURN WAS angry. In early afternoon he had managed
to get Tommy to stop saying no to being taken from the tenement. He hadn't agreed to go but his passivity was all Harry felt
he needed. Tommy had stilled to the point of being just another
part of that ugly room. Furniture you could move—it didn't
struggle.

Since then Harry had been trying to make contact with Matt
Mason. He had phoned all the places he could think of, he had
gone to his bookie shops, he had even in desperation gone to
Bearsden, to be turned away by an elderly caricature of gentility
calling herself the 'housekaypah' and playing at the Lady of the
Manor. Working-class parvenus were the worst. Her voice was
East End garrotted by Kelvinside. 'Eh'm afrayd they're both
aht. Perhaps yew could call again. No, Eh've no ideah when
Mr. Mason wull be beck. Perhaps yew'd care to leave a
massage?' 'Yes,' Harry said. 'Fuck 'im!'

Perspiring and panicky, he came back to 'Poppies' to begin
phoning again and found it had closed on him like a trap. The
policemen were very polite but he would have to wait in his
office until he could be seen. He was raging but he soon gave up
trying to vent it on them. You might as well try to get a reaction
out of garden gnomes. 'We've got our instructions, sir.'

He walked up and down the office, burning Mason in effigy
and suing the police into abject apology. The threat to himself
represented by their presence was made trivial by the danger

to Tommy the delay was causing. It was hours now since he had seen Tommy, a lot of hours. Anything could be happening. Tommy would have expected some fulfilment of Harry's promises by this time. He might panic. He might get out of the tenement himself, and that would be it. The state he was in, he wouldn't last an hour in the street without doing something crazy. He might come walking in here.

The frustration of it was fierce, and the sense of persecution he felt reactivated all his past frustrations. There were plenty of those. They made up most of his life. The injustice of this moment connected up with all the other injustices, the sneers, the dismissive looks, the time three men had followed him into the toilet of a pub and left him unconscious there, for doing nothing more than being himself.

The effect of this latest insult was out of all proportion to its cause. It was like one glass of whisky to an alcoholic. It found its way so far into him that by the time they knocked at the door he was almost hysterical with rage. The two who had been here yesterday morning came in.

'Not you again! What the hell is going on here? If you've got a lawyer, get him! I'm going to mince you for this.'

'Oh daddy-mammy,' Laidlaw said.

'I'm telling you. You've got no official sanction for being here. You've encroached on my rights already. Now get out. You're trespassing. Get out! Before I throw you out.'

'If you don't stop frightening me, Mr. Rayburn,' Laidlaw said very quietly, 'I won't hit you—I'll make love to you.'

It was like stopping a runaway horse with your pinkie. Harkness could see Rayburn's presence go soft, filleted with one remark. The anger that had etched his face lost definition, and his features became blurred. The whole bias of the place had shifted. It was Laidlaw's room. As Laidlaw walked into it, Rayburn moved backwards clumsily. Laidlaw gestured backwards at Harkness, who came in and closed the door.

'Take off your hairy chest, Mr. Rayburn, and sit down.'

Rayburn disintegrated into the chair that Laidlaw offered him. Laidlaw leaned into him, almost whispering.

'I've watched your act long enough, Mr. Rayburn. It's a bad

204

act. And now I want my money back. I could knock you out with my eyelashes. But that's not what we're here to talk about. We're here to talk about Tommy, Mr. Rayburn.'

Rayburn looked up, looked away.

'I don't know any Tommy.'

'Mr. Rayburn. I don't think you understand. If you don't answer the questions I'm going to ask, I'm going to jail you. Right now. Because if you don't answer them, I'm going to assume you're implicated in a murder.'

Rayburn's face attempted incredulity but Laidlaw's face gave him nothing back.

'You're a homosexual, Mr. Rayburn. For some time you've had a homosexual relationship with a boy called Tommy Bryson. Is that correct?'

The silence was the time it took for Harry Rayburn to realise that the last thing he had left to hope for was never going to happen.

'Yes.'

It was the smallest word Harkness had ever heard.

'His name doesn't appear on the list of staff you gave us. But he works for you. Is *that* correct?'

'No. No, it's not.'

'Mr. Rayburn—'

'He *did* work for me. But not any more.'

'Since when?'

'Two or three weeks ago. He packed in. We broke up.'

'Why?'

'None of your business.'

'Mr. Rayburn, I don't want the details of your private life. Believe me, I don't. You bowdlerise it any way you want. But give me the shape of what happened.'

Rayburn shut his eyes, talked into his own despair.

'He couldn't come all the way out. A lot of people can't. He still wanted to be straight. Heterosexual.' He hated the word. 'He wanted to try to make it with girls.'

'And you haven't seen him since then?'

Rayburn opened his eyes. They looked like bruises.

'No.'

205

'Mr. Rayburn. That's not easy to believe.'

Harry Rayburn looked up at Laidlaw evenly. His eyes had the calmness of complete despair.

'Not much that's happened to me is,' he said. 'At least not for me.'

Laidlaw looked at him and accepted. There was no choice.

'What's his address?'

'I'm not sure.'

'You better develop a memory quickly, Mr. Rayburn.'

'It's Manley Gardens. But I'm not sure of the number. Fifty-something I think. It's an old building.'

'I know where that is.'

'But he won't be there.'

'How do you know?'

'He was going to England, he said. To try and sort himself out there. There'll only be his mother in the house. His father shot the crow years ago.'

'Thanks, Mr. Rayburn,' Laidlaw said. 'You're sure that's all you know?'

Rayburn nodded.

'I hope so,' Laidlaw said. 'We'll be back. In the meantime, I'll try not to offend against your sense of civic liberty by taking the policemen out.'

Turning to close the door, Harkness saw Harry Rayburn with his head in his hands, huddled as if he was in the middle of a private air-raid.

Before they left, Laidlaw posted the other two policemen outside 'Poppies.'

'It's worth a try,' Laidlaw said in the car.

'No,' Harkness said. 'He's never going to buy that. He *knows* you've just moved them outside. Waiting to follow him.'

'Knowing isn't accepting,' Laidlaw said. 'A panicked elephant'll try to thread itself through a needle.'

45

THE BELL HAD a sugary chime, a fingerful of schmaltz. It was an appropriately sentimental password to that land which defies geography, where domesticity has enchanted all things into stasis. The inside of the house was a carefully distilled negation of its exterior. Harkness had seen a few houses like this before, but only a few. It was, he suspected, what Mary's parents were in search of. But they were novitiates.

Crossing the doorway here, you passed a frontier into a defiant immutability. The sense of a shrine wasn't due merely to the crucifix in the hall. It related to the muted atmosphere, as if a shout would be a sacrilege, to the almost uninhabited exactitude with which each object had its placement. You felt as if the ornaments had been fixed upon foundations. Rudeness, anger, disorder didn't happen here. The nearest thing to turmoil would be when the tea was stirred.

The keeper of the grotto was older than they had expected—greying hair neatly done, glasses, a navy-blue twinset, imitation pearls. She had agreed she was Mrs. Bryson, had listened to Laidlaw explain it was about Tommy, and had asked them in, glancing at their feet as if they might be muddy. In the living-room Harkness sat on the edge of his cushion, not wanting to crush its flowers.

'Nothing's happened, has it?'

The gentleness of her voice was like a charm against the possibility of anything happening.

'We don't know yet, Mrs. Bryson,' Laidlaw said. 'We just wanted to talk to Tommy. He isn't in?'

'But Tommy's in London.'

'Are you sure?'

Her look chastised him gently for the insult to her motherhood.

'Well, he's somewhere down there. He hasn't written since he left. You know what the young people are like nowadays. He said he was going to London.'

'When did he leave?'

'Oh. Let me see. Two or three weeks ago. But what's *happened?* Is he in some kind of trouble?'

'Maybe nothing's happened. Very possibly nothing. What about Tommy's father?'

'What about him?'

'Where is he, Mrs. Bryson?'

It was over in a moment. Her concentration flickered and when her eyes went bland again, Harkness was left wondering if what he had seen in them could really have been that depth of hate. Perhaps more had been cooking here than the wholesome meals a growing boy would need.

'I haven't known where he is for about twenty years.'

'He left you?'

'He left *us.*'

'Then Tommy knew him.'

'Tommy was five months old when his father left. He couldn't stand Tommy's crying. So he went where he couldn't hear it.'

'And you don't know where he is? And Tommy wouldn't know?'

'I know where he's going. If he isn't already there. R.I.P. Roast in peace.'

It was a kept joke, a bitter fermentation with a phrase for phial. The venom of it in her gentle mouth was a shock, as if Santa Claus should come on like Lenny Bruce.

'Mrs. Bryson. Do you know Harry Rayburn?'

'Rayburn, Rayburn. Oh. The gentleman Tommy used to work for.'

'That's right.'

208

'I know *of* him. But that's all.'

Laidlaw stared at her, looked away.

'Well. Do you mind if we look at Tommy's room.'

She hesitated.

'Why? Look. I think you'd better tell me what all of this is about. Is Tommy supposed to have done something? What has happened?'

'I don't know what's happened, Mrs. Bryson. But I want to try and trace Tommy. For questioning about something. Anything I know about him might help. But I'm *asking*, you understand. I've no authority to oblige you to show me his room. It's up to you. I want you to understand that.'

After a moment she got up and they followed her. It was a small room. The walls were white and there was nothing on them, no mirror, no posters, no pictures. It seemed to Harkness like a monk's cell, the room of someone very ascetic. It was what wasn't there that defined it. It was just walls and furniture. There was no trace of a hobby or an interest. Nobody knew who lived here.

Laidlaw bent down suddenly, opened a couple of drawers and closed them again at once.

'What are you doing? Those are Tommy's private possessions.'

'All right, Mrs. Bryson. All right. I'm sorry. Thank you for helping us. There's nothing more you can tell us?'

'Just what I've told you.'

Laidlaw and Harkness looked at her. Her face told them that nothing more was going to come. Its prim sweetness was made of iron. Whatever you wanted to say, it had made its choices.

'Thank you,' Laidlaw said.

They were in the car going back before either of them spoke.

'What's more sinister than respectability?' Laidlaw said.

'You think she knows where he is?'

'What difference does it make? Torquemada couldn't get it out of her.'

'So what does all that tell us?'

'Everything. Weren't you listening?'

Harkness changed up.

'All right,' he said. 'I'm listening now.'

'Bud Lawson is a monolithic Prod. Tommy is a Catholic. Jennifer's in the cross-fire. Made to choose. She seems to choose but the lies she tells to everybody would suggest she renegued on her first choice. If Harry Rayburn's telling the truth about Tommy trying to straighten out his deviations, well. Who else would he practise on but the girl he left behind. So he teams up with Jennifer again.'

'It's a wee bit speculative,' Harkness said.

'A wee bit. The second thing. Mrs. Bryson has no curiosity. Some folk faint when they see the polis at their door. Mrs. Bryson didn't show much of anything. Because she was expecting us. She'd been rehearsing. Every time she asked what it was all about, I gave her nothing back. She didn't get more frantic, she got more mechanical. Because once she knew we didn't have him, she didn't really have to ask. Either she knows what's happened. Or she doesn't care.'

'God. Yet she would cover up for a sex murderer. Some sons do have them.'

'I would hope so. I would expect my mother to do the same for me. Home is where they'll hide you from the polis.'

'Anything else?' Harkness asked.

'She says he left two or three weeks ago. "Let me see"? You take the mother of an only child, she knows to the hour when he left. Mrs. Bryson doesn't know because Tommy didn't leave. His gear was still in the drawers. Who sets out on the great English adventure without a change of socks?'

'So?'

'Tommy Bryson killed Jennifer Lawson. He's still in Glasgow. Harry Rayburn knows where he is. So we'll have to go back and be unpleasant to Mr. Rayburn.'

Harkness drove in silence for a moment.

'Did you notice the pictures in his office?' he said. 'It just struck me. They're pin-ups of men. Does it not make you sick?'

'That's evidence for the defence. When you think of the crappy attitudes like yours he's had to cope with, he's made not a bad job of surviving. You can almost admire him.'

'I can't help it. I just hate their guts.'

'So that'll worry us. Marlowe was a poof. And his farts were more articulate than most mouths.'

They had to stop at lights. Across their windscreen some people passed outside a cinema—a boy and a girl clowning with each other, two men in conversation, a foursome involved only with themselves.

'Maybe that's why he killed her,' Laidlaw said. 'Maybe he was just trying to catch his daddy's attention.'

46

WHAT HAPPENED THEN took Harkness by surprise, not just by
its speed but by the suddenness with which there was revealed
to him the true nature of what they were involved in. When he
thought of the case afterwards, the reel of sensations he ran
most often in his mind began at the point when he and Laidlaw
stepped out of the car at 'Poppies.'

He had thought they were just coming back from Mrs.
Bryson's. It felt not greatly different from all the other things
they'd done. But suddenly that simple action, coming at the end
of the distance they had walked, the people questioned, the
places gone to, the thoughtful talk, was like the last act of a
conjuration. Using all the skill they had, they had demanded
access to a secret. What Harkness was to realise was that the
catch-clause in such a demand is that you have to give the
secret access to you.

The court was dark by now except for the lights of 'The
Maverick'. In that glow of other people's pleasure they met one
of the policemen they had left. It was the taller one. He walked
out of shadow towards them and, behind the preoccupied
voices coming from the pub, they talked like conspirators.

'Harry Rayburn left, sir. But he's back. Just a minute ago.'

'Where did he go?'

'To the Bridgegate. A condemned building. Number Seventeen.
Don's watching it now.'

'We'll be faster on foot. You stay with Rayburn. Phone the

Division. But give us some time to ourselves first. I don't want him frightened.'

He said the last words on the run. Harkness caught up. An old woman ahead of them turned round in alarm and cowered into a doorway. Laidlaw was just managing to talk.

'Knew we were coming . . . Tip-off to get away . . . Keep us talking.'

Concentrating on breathing, Harkness thought that the last part of Laidlaw to die would be his mouth. People were pausing to look at them inquisitively, with that special Glasgow assumption of communal rights, as if they should stop and explain what it was about. They went along Argyle Street, down Stockwell Street and then cut off to the Bridgegate.

The running changed Harkness's sense of himself, put him outside his own preconceptions in the way that physical exertion does. The stance of forensic enquiry he had adopted towards the case was effectively penetrated. He wasn't just a mobile head any longer. He was a confused bundle of tensions and stresses, aware of the problem of breathing, of the changes of surface under his feet, of tiredness tautening his legs, His perceptions weren't a progression. They were fired fragments, coming at him like flak. A car making a U-turn at the end of the Bridgegate. The other policeman starting to run towards them. Somebody stepping out of the doorway of a derelict tenement. Somebody walking towards the tenement from the end of the Bridgegate. Laidlaw shouting, 'Hey, you! Bud Lawson!' The figure at the doorway disappearing back into the tenement. Bud Lawson running and reaching the tenement before them. Laidlaw shouting to the other policeman, 'Watch the door!'

The entry snuffed out the city. For Harkness, already dizzy with exertion, it was like falling down a shaft. The suddenness was overwhelming—a foetid smell and four men running in the dark.

He was moaning for breath, Laidlaw in front. The stairs were blows that jarred him to the thighs. His lungs seemed hedged with thorns. A piece of railing clattered away from his hand. The four of them seemed labouring up a descending spiral stair, a murderous aspiration. That ended suddenly, grotesquely, in accident.

213

The stairs gave way. The boy and Bud Lawson had reached the upper landing. Behind them the stairs collapsed. The noise battered their ears, halted Laidlaw and Harkness cringing like an act of God. The bouncing debris defined how far they could have fallen. The dust settled on them like a benediction, choking them. Between them and the landing a pit of black, about eight feet across. The landing itself was in blackness. But they knew what was going to happen there. A whimper like a trapped hare came to them.

'Too late, polisman,' Bud Lawson said. 'He's mine.'

The voice terrified Harkness. It came brutally out of darkness, never to be denied. The gulf between them and it seemed impassable. The exhaustion Harkness felt was more than physical. It reached remorselessly into who he was and taught him futility. He had thought that what they were trying to do was a difficult thing, to locate and isolate whoever it was who carried about with him the savage force that had murdered Jennifer Lawson. Now it came to him as impossible, because that force wasn't isolated. It had already multiplied on itself to create a twin, this moment of ravening viciousness whose spores were in each of them.

'Bud Lawson!' Laidlaw threw his voice across the space, grappling what was on the other side. 'You don't touch that boy!'

The voice was an atavism, like Lawson's. The ferocity in Laidlaw's voice was a part of Harkness, just as he shared Bud Lawson's rage. In the stillness he felt himself enclosed in their animal breathings, and the pathetic whimpering of the boy was like a plea against what Harkness himself was.

'Ah'm gonny kill 'im.'

'You dae. An' Ah kill you. No question.'

The voices were the same terrible force talking to itself.

'Because o' a rat like this?'

It was a question, Harkness realised, the sound of something human. If Lawson had the certainty he claimed, the boy would be already dead. All he had to do was drop him over the edge like waste, if he was waste. Uncertainty had happened, and with it hope. Harkness listened to Laidlaw try to enlarge it into doubt.

'What gives ye the right?'

'Ah'm her feyther!'

'You didn't even know 'er.'

'Shut up, polisman.'

'No chance. You didn't even know 'er. She hated you!'

The following silence frightened Harkness because it meant that maybe Laidlaw had misjudged. And if he had, the boy was dead. But what came was Bud Lawson's voice, humanised with pain.

'How wid you know?'

'I've had to ask a lot of questions. Not all the answers tell against that boy. Don't kid yerself! She hated you. And she was right. Feyther? Feyther's more than bairnin' yer wife. Feyther's more than you ever were.'

'Ah loved ma lassie!'

'That's not what I hear. She lied to you, she hid from you. She didn't trust you because you gave her none. You wouldn't let her be herself. You helped to make what happened to her happen.'

'No!'

'You helped! That's all I'm saying. What rights have you? What right has any of us to touch that boy?'

'Shut up!'

'Never shut up. If you can't stand the words, don't listen. That's what you've been doing all your life, isn't it? Hiding! You're a hider. You couldn't face who your girl was. She was another person, a separate body. She would've been a woman. She would've wanted *men*. Catholics? It wasn't Catholics you were against. Hate Catholics, hate people! You couldn't stand for her to have somebody else. That's what it was. What was it, did you fancy her yourself?'

'Shut up, shut up!'

'It's just a question. I don't know the answer. Do you? Well if you do, then kill him! He's there, he's helpless. You're such a hard man, aren't you? Except that you *know* you're hiding. Kill him! So that you don't have to face up to what's really happened. Kill him! If you can't take the risk of leaving him alive.'

215

There was silence. The silence built gradually into a terrible scream and the splatter of an enormous blow, the sound of bones fragmenting. Laidlaw jumped. The railing he caught came away but held long enough for his body to moor to the landing.

Harkness heard the metal rebound down the well of the stairs, measuring the depth of his awe. Then a surprised voice said, 'Jesus Christ.' It was a visitor from ordinariness, a beautiful sound from a place that to Harkness seemed miles away. The other policemen had arrived.

As they came up the stairs, Harkness demanded a torch. He shone it above him. It made an arbitrary patch of light in total darkness. Its centre was Laidlaw. On his left was Tommy Bryson, a handsome, pale-skinned boy cowering away, the front of his light blue trousers dark where he had wet himself. On Laidlaw's right Bud Lawson was slumped, his right hand cradled in front of him, a mess of blood and protuberant bone. The obscenely scabrous wall beside him, that served as a frame for all three, was blotched with red where his hand had smashed it. Laidlaw was buffer between them, blinking against the manufactured light, the mouth that had saved a man's life curled in annoyance at the intrusion.

After some consultation, a door was broken off downstairs and used as a bridge to get them from the landing. As the small group came back out the entry into Glasgow, the torch that pointed their way flicked across some graffiti that nobody noticed. One legend in ballpoint read:

> Arrest Hampden Park
> put them all in the van
> hell still be lose
> hes the cancer man

47

JUST AS A defused bomb can be recycled into household ornaments, the aftermath became routine, as it always does. Tommy
Bryson gave a confused statement, the clearest part of which
was 'I loved her, I loved her, I loved her.' He was given a change
of clothes from somewhere and put in a cell. Bud Lawson
denied that the car they had seen in the Bridgegate had any
connection with him. He said he had gone to 'Poppies' and
followed Harry Rayburn from there. Once he found where
Tommy Bryson was, he had decided to wait till night and then
go back and kill him. He was taken to hospital. Minty McGregor
was released, saying, 'This is some bloody way tae treat a dyin'
man.' When the police went into 'Poppies' for Harry Rayburn,
they were left with a corpse to collect. He had gone to get his
jacket and had cut his throat.

'You're the healthy one,' Laidlaw said to Harkness. 'How
many people have you ever loved like that?'

They were sitting in an office at Central Division. Harkness was
working at their report, Laidlaw was working at coffee, smoking
and staring at the wall. Harkness had thought the end of it
would feel different. He felt cheated of the euphoria he should
be experiencing. It was like knowing there was a party on but
not being able to find the address. It certainly wasn't here.

'That must've been a hard thing for Bud Lawson to do,' he said.

'Aye. It's welcome to evolution for the big man. He'll have to
think instead of hitting for a while.'

217

'It's a good thing you managed to convince him he was wrong.'

'I don't know that I did that. I don't even know that he *was* wrong.'

Harkness was surprised again to discover that the most certain thing about Laidlaw was his doubt. Everything came back to that, even his decisiveness.

'So what was all that about?' Harkness asked.

Laidlaw took some coffee.

'What I've got against folk like Lawson isn't that they're wrong. It's just that they *assume* they're right. Bigotry's just unearned certainty, isn't it?'

Harkness went back to typing. The phone rang and Laidlaw took it. He listened for a time, making faces at Harkness.

'Thank you,' he said, 'I'll tell him,' and put the phone down.

Harkness knew but wanted to hear it.

'The head man sends all congratulations. He's impressed with you. He'll be seeing you himself.'

'Thanks. What about you?'

'Aye. He was very nice there. The rest of my life'll be an anti-climax.'

Laidlaw went back to wall-staring. He was wondering how much more energy he had to go on inhabiting the fierceness of the contradictions in his life. He would go back home tomorrow —he looked at his watch—today. The forebodings in that thought of some kind of imminent disaster oppressed him.

'John Rhodes,' he said.

Harkness stopped and looked up.

'Who set the boy up, you mean?'

'Must have been.'

'I've been thinking that. And tipped us off about Minty McGregor. To lead us away.'

'It fits him. He believes in the man to man thing. An eye for an eye and a son for a daughter. Jehovah Rhodes. Well, there'll be other times with him.'

'You feel up to them?'

'I wasn't thinking in those terms. But if it came to that, all right.'

218

'I thought you didn't fancy yourself as a hard man?'

'I don't. But I don't really fancy anyone else as one either. I hate violence so much I don't intend to let anybody practise it on me with impunity. If it came to the bit, he'd win the first time all right. But I'd win the second time, if there was enough of me left to have one. No question about that. I'd arrange it that way. I don't have fights. I have wars.'

To Harkness it seemed unnecessarily gloomy to be talking about next times before they had even savoured this one.

'It's a good feeling, though,' he said. 'A crime solved.'

Laidlaw lit another cigarette.

'You don't solve crimes,' he said. 'You inter them in facts, don't you?'

'How do you mean?'

'A crime you're trying to solve is a temporary mystery. Solved, it's permanent. What can the courts do with this then? Who knows what it is? It's maybe just another love story.'

'What? I'd like to hear somebody trying to tell you that if you were the girl's father.'

'No way, I agree. I'm sure I'd be in the Bud Lawson stakes if it happened to one of my girls. But that wouldn't make it right. I'm never very clear exactly what the law's for. But that's one thing it can do—it can protect the relatives of the victim from atavism. It can pull the knot on all those primitive impulses by taking over responsibility for them. Until we get them into balance again.'

'It's still a long way from a love story.'

'I don't know. It's maybe *Romeo and Juliet* upside down. I mean she really fancied him. And he loved her. He said it himself. And I suppose her father tried to love her the way he could. And poor old Harry Rayburn loved him. And his mother.'

'You really believe that?'

'I don't know. But what I do know is that more folk than two were present at that murder. And what charges do you bring against the others? Against Bud Lawson. He's made a clenched fist of his head all his life. Sadie Lawson's more submissive than the world can afford anybody to be. John Rhodes. Because he's very handy, he's going to play at Nero with a boy's life. Who the

219

hell does he think he is? I don't care that he could beat every-body eight days a week. Then there's you with your deodorised attitudes. And me. Hiding in suburbia. What's so clever about any of us that we can afford to be flip about other people? We only get our lives on tick for so long. Every so often it's got to be divvied up. Jennifer Lawson and Tommy Bryson were the ones that had to foot most of the bill. I mean— what *happened* in that park?'

Harkness exhaled slowly.

'But,' he said. 'Take it far enough and it's all just an act of God.'

'So maybe we should find out where He is and book Him.'

Laidlaw stood up.

'I think I'll go up and see that boy,' he said. 'Maybe he needs to talk to somebody. You get the headstone typed out in holy triplicate.'

Harkness sat staring ahead after Laidlaw had gone out. In the bleakness he felt, one thought sustained him like a raft. He would be in 'The Muscular Arms' tonight.

He lifted the sheet of paper they had taken from Tommy Bryson's pocket. It was a page of writing which had been almost entirely scored out with great care. Holding it against the light, he tried to make out some of it. It was virtually impossible but, speculating on the fragments of letters he could see, he thought he deciphered 'I think she thought she knew who I was.' But you couldn't be sure. All that was clearly left of whatever he had written was one small statement near the bottom: 'I tried to love her'.

48

MATT MASON TOOK his drink with him when the phone rang. It had been a good meal. He was feeling pleasant. He didn't recognise the voice that said, 'Mr. Mason?'

'Who is this speaking?'

'It's Minty. Minty McGregor.'

'Yes?'

Mason was wary. He could hardly believe that Minty would have the cheek to put the squeeze on, but the thought occurred to him.

'Ah want tae thank ye for contributin' tae ma pension fund.'

'What?'

'Ah feel that after a life o' crime it's only right that the business should gi'e me somethin' back.'

'What's this supposed to mean?'

'It means they arrested that boy Bryson half-an-hour ago. An' you're sole owner of a paira knickers outa C&A. Handy wee shop that. If ye want the use o' them, Ah can recommend a good detergent. Takes oot hen's blood without a trace.'

There was a pause while Mason let his apoplexy gather.

'You bastard!' he hissed. Then he nodded and smiled as his guest made his way to the toilet. 'You're dead.'

'No' quite. Ye're a week or two early.'

'Time enough to get you.'

'What are ye goin' to do, Mr. Mason? Give ma cancer cancer?'

Mason experienced powerlessness. It was a strange feeling. The voice coming through the phone seemed already to be speaking out of a grave. It expressed nothing—not fear, not satisfaction—just a chilly deadness that frosted his ear.

'You've got a family,' Mason managed.

'Aye. Ah've also got a friend. He's straight as a die. Great bloke, this. Ye couldny imagine whit he's like. An' he's got a tape o' that wee recordin' session we did in the pub. Names and numbers. An' he's got a statement fae me. He's wean daft an' a'. If ma wee lassie as much as cuts 'er leg, he gets all annoyed. But he'll never use them, of coorse. Sure he'll no'?'

Mason was busy learning how to breathe again.

'All a best furra future.'

Mason stood holding the phone while it purred like a cat.

Sweating southwards, as if the compartment was a Turkish bath, Lennie didn't yet know that he had made another mistake.

49

WHEN LAIDLAW REACHED the cell, the door was slightly open. He paused with the cup of tea he was carrying and listened. He could hear Milligan's voice.

'Come on, son,' he was saying. 'Do yourself a favour. You're for the high jump, anyway. Your fancy-man must have been into something. So tell us. You can't hurt him. Didn't you know? They found him with a throat like Joe E. Brown's mouth. He'd cut it. Made a helluva mess of the carpet.'

Laidlaw put his cup down carefully at the edge of the corridor not to spill the sugar-lumps. He pushed open the door.

'Excuse me,' he said. 'Detective Inspector Milligan. Could I see you for a minute, please?'

'Think about it, son,' Milligan said. 'You think about it.'

As Milligan came out into the corridor, Laidlaw pulled the door to.

'Aye?' Milligan said. 'I hear you got there too early.'

Laidlaw took him by the lapels and flung him across the corridor. Milligan jarred against the wall and was coming back off it when he halted himself. He made as if to come on for Laidlaw.

'Please,' Laidlaw said.

They stared at each other. Milligan realised that Laidlaw had chosen his moment carefully. The corridor was empty. Milligan would either do something now or forget it, because to report it would be an admission about himself.

'You shouldn't have opened the door to come out,' Laidlaw
~~id~~. 'You should've walked under it.'

Milligan decided to be cool. His expression fell somewhere
between a sneer and a wince.

'Oh, Laidlaw,' he said. 'You're really insane. You know that?
Something bad's going to happen to you.'

'So volunteer.'

'I can wait.'

'What you mean is you can't do anything else.'

'No. I mean I can wait. You want to see your boyfriend, go
ahead. I'll be back. I've got plenty of time.'

Laidlaw nodded bitterly. The look between them was like a
promise. He lifted the cup of tea and went into the cell.

The boy didn't move, didn't look up. He sat huddled into
himself, trembling slightly, like a rabbit caught in the glare of a
lamp. The trousers they had given him were beltless and too big
for him. If he stood up, they would fall to his feet. The shoes
had no laces.

Laidlaw crossed and sat on the bed beside him.

'Here, son,' he said.

The boy looked blindly at him.

'I brought you a cup of tea, son.'

The boy looked at the cup and looked at Laidlaw, as if the
two formed a connection he could never understand.

'For me?' he said. He was watching Laidlaw solemnly. 'Why?'

Laidlaw saw the countless flecks that swam in the boy's eyes,
a galaxy of undiscovered stars.

'You've got a mouth, haven't you?' Laidlaw said.